PENGUIN BOOKS

THE SUGAR MOTHER

Born in the industrial Midlands of England in 1923, Elizabeth Jolley was brought up in a German-speaking household – her father having met her mother, the daughter of an Austrian general, when engaged on famine relief in Vienna in 1919. She was educated at home and at a Quaker boarding school. She later trained as an SRN and nursed during the Second World War.

In 1959 she moved to Western Australia with her husband and three children. She worked in a variety of jobs, as a nurse, a door-to-door salesperson and a flying domestic among other things, and now cultivates a small orchard and a goose farm. She conducts writing workshops in prisons and community centres and is a part-time lecturer at Fremantle Arts Centre and the Curtin University of Technology in Perth.

Elizabeth Jolley is the author of three collections of short stories, *Five Acre Virgin* and *The Travelling Entertainer*, which have also been published together in one volume entitled *Stories* (1984), and *Woman in a Lampshade* (Penguin 1986). Her other novels include *Palomino, Mr Scobie's Riddle, The Newspaper of Claremont Street, Miss Peabody's Inheritance, Foxybaby, The Well, Milk and Honey* and *My Father's Moon*, all published by Penguin. Her work has been acclaimed in America as well as in Australia and the United Kingdom; the *Washington Post* called her style 'effortlessly comic' and her characters 'battily original'. The *Daily Telegraph* described her novels as containing 'more of Australia than is to be found in many of those that simply echo its size', while *The Times Literary Supplement* wrote: 'Elizabeth Jolley's fiction is notable for the sharpness with which its incidents are envisaged and assembled . . . She knows how to make things hum.'

THE · SUGAR · MOTHER

ELIZABETH JOLLEY

PENGUIN BOOKS

PENGUIN BOOKS

Published by the Penguin Group
27 Wrights Lane, London W8 5TZ, England
Viking Penguin Inc., 40 West 23rd Street, New York, New York 10010, USA
Penguin Books Australia Ltd, Ringwood, Victoria, Australia
Penguin Books Canada Ltd, 2801 John Street, Markham, Ontario, Canada L3R 1B4
Penguin Books (NZ) Ltd, 182–190 Wairau Road, Auckland 10, New Zealand

Penguin Books Ltd, Registered Offices: Harmondsworth, Middlesex, England

First published in the USA by Harper & Row, Publishers, Inc., New York 1988
Published simultaneously in Canada by Fitzhenry & Whiteside, Toronto
Published in Penguin Books 1990
1 3 5 7 9 10 8 6 4 2

Made and printed in Great Britain by
Richard Clay Ltd, Bungay, Suffolk

For Leonard Jolley

I would like to express my thanks to the Curtin University of Technology (formerly the Western Australian Institute of Technology) for the continuing privilege of being with students and colleagues in the School of Communication and Cultural Studies and for the provision of a room in which to write. I would like, in particular, to thank Don Watts, Peter Reeves, Brian Dibble and Don Grant.

A special thanks is offered to Nancy McKenzie who, for a great many years, has typed my manuscripts. Her patience is endless.

Elizabeth Jolley

THE · SUGAR · MOTHER

"The Old Country!" Buffy said. They were still standing but would have risen if they had been sitting down.

"To Home. Here's to Home. Down the hatch. The Old Country!"

"The Queen!" Buffy was inspired. "God bless the Queen."

"I'll drink to that," Tuppy said. "God bless the Queen." Edwin, in silence, drank his share. With toasts it was impossible not to. In a minute, he thought, he would slip out and fetch Leila from the very awkward position she was in. A stranger in the yard, yet familiar. He looked at his guests. They were very good-looking and very good-hearted people. They would never knowingly hurt anyone, but Leila would be frightened of them. They were toasting their old regiments now. It seemed inconceivable that he belonged with these people. He never spoke or thought of England as the Old Country. He never thought of it as Home as they apparently, after many years, did. He believed this was described as a migration syndrome; he had heard the phrase. What was home anyway other than a place you lived in and came back to every night?

◆ ◆ ◆

"Leila dear," Leila's mother said, "we shall be running out of knickers. Remind me, dear, to do some washing tonight when we come home. Now, have we got everything? Got the tickets? Yes? Slam the door then, dear. We'll wait by the gate for our taxi. He should be here any minute now."

The two women negotiated, in single file, the red-slabbed path between wet lavender and rosemary bushes. In the misty, sweet-smelling dusk they stood close together, easing their feet, lifting one and then the other, their best shoes pinching rather. Leila's mother, feeling the weight and the expense of her coat, said in a low voice, nudging her daughter with her thick shoulder, "You know, dear, I am certain that the people next door have separate bedrooms."

"There's only one light on now," Leila said, turning with a ponderous movement to peer through thick leaves.

"It isn't bedtime yet," Leila's mother said, "and I have the feeling that she has gone away. I'm pretty certain. I saw him wave to her from the edge of the veranda. Last evening, dear, last night she left."

"She goes every day and he always waves," Leila said. "She goes to work. I think she goes in the night too sometimes."

"This time, dear, she had luggage." Leila's mother stepped to the edge of the footpath. "Luggage," she said once more. "You know, dear." Leila's mother peered down the street and then turned back to Leila. "I've seen him often," she said, "from the bus, dear; he seems to walk out from the end of that plantation of trees and he stands at the edge of the children's playground and watches the children playing."

"P'raps he's someone's gran'pa." Leila yawned.

"I don't think so, dear; he only stands and doesn't seem to own any one of the children. I mean a grandfather would." Leila's mother sighed. "A grandfather," she said, "would push the swing or run to the end of the slide to catch. . . ." She paused. "He's such a fine-looking man, very handsome, Leila, not young but handsome all the same, well-bred I should say and well-groomed, always a good sign, dear. Is that our cab? Wave, Leila, dear, wave your scarf. It's all right, the driver's seen us, he's coming back. You know," she added, half-turning again towards the house next door, "I simply cannot imagine where the bathroom is in that house."

"**H**ave you heard from Cecilia?" Edwin Page recognized Daphne's voice. He held the receiver as far away as he could from his ear. Daphne had, she explained, Haydn's Trumpet about to climax in the other room. "Can you hear it, Teddy? It's so invigorating. I'm getting more energetic with every blast." Had he heard from Cecilia, she wanted to know.

"She only left last night." Edwin had to shout the words twice.

"I thought she might have phoned from the airport," Daphne bellowed.

"Yes," Edwin said, "she did. She was homesick and she thought she had left the gas on."

"Can you speak up? Can't hear you. It's the ecstasy. An unfortunate moment of levity."

Edwin raised his voice. "Cecilia," he said. "She's left all sorts of arrangements and instructions for my welfare and comfort."

"Yes, I know," Daphne said. "She told me she was divinely inspired to make a macaroni cheese yesterday. A sort of grand gesture, a tour de force, as we say at St. Monica's—grating cheese after doing all that packing. Such self-discipline. I was ringing," she went on, "to see if you would like to totter round to share an incredible pizza. Cecilia did ask me, you see, to keep an eye on you." Daphne's voice quietened as the trumpet at her end gave way to some softer instruments. "That's better," she said. "I thought I should check on you to see how you are managing. If you'd like to come I'll put an extra plate to warm. I know Cecilia's arranged for lots of people to look after you and entertain you. I thought I'd be the first. . . ."

"No, thank you, dearest Daphne." Edwin shook his head and, realizing that she could not see him, saved his smile. Smiling, he had read somewhere, encouraged wrinkles, lines and crow's feet. "I must get on with some work," he said, "and since Cecilia only left last night . . . perhaps next week sometime?" He did smile this time when he spoke. People sounded as if they were or were not smiling, he reasoned, and Daphne might think he was being unfriendly. And he did not want her to think that he was thinking of the preservation of his face.

"If you're sure then," Daphne began. "The trumpet's back." She raised her voice. Edwin heard a muffled roar and a crash.

"What's that noise?" He strained to hear.

"I think it's something to do with the oven." Daphne's voice hit his ear. "I'll have to go. Till later then. *Auf Wiedersehen.*"

◆ ◆ ◆

Edwin prowled in and out of the rooms of what seemed, this evening, like an absolutely deserted house. Earlier, when he had come home, everything was just as he had left it. So much so that it was depressing.

— 4 —

He took the electric cleaner and vacuumed the hall and the sofa cushions in the living room. Though they, he and Cecilia, were what is called a double income family and were comfortably well off, they had only one car, Cecilia's. Edwin walked daily to his university, an easy walk mostly through a pine plantation across the road from their house. They did not keep a maid, neither did they have anyone once a week to clean through the rooms, as Edwin, who worked at home a great deal, was easily disturbed and disliked having a stranger about, especially in his study. The house was pleasantly shabby. It was the kind of house, he thought, with satisfaction, where the cat ate from Royal Doulton plates and potted plants stood on Wedgwood. He was not a snob, but the idea pleased him, and he left the vacuum cleaner to write it down, wondering if Cecilia would like a kitten—well, it would be a cat by the time she was expected to return. Ginger kittens were pretty and always looked clean. A sort of ginger surprise. A white cat was unusual and would be softly yielding to generous caressing. He had, at the back of his mind, an idea that Cecelia did not care for cats. Cats and children . . . His thoughts wandered as he bent down to follow the vacuum tube as it resumed its noisy squirming under low-slung furniture. Children would cause cats and dogs and bicycles, and she, Cecilia, would not go away to conferences and take study leave for a whole year on the other side of the world, like now, from last night. Cecilia would be away, this time, for twelve months.

"Why don't you come with me?" she had asked repeatedly during the last weeks. But always he had shaken his head, smiling. "I do have my work." He had his reasons for not going away. "The house to look after." He shrugged, and feeling self-conscious, he had rubbed both knees slowly with his palms. "My health," he said. "I would only be a nuisance to you."

"There's nothing wrong with you." Laughing, she raised her glass, squinting at the light through the almost colorless drink. "Why don't you retire early?" she said, failing to see his shocked expression. "Lots of people do, especially from your kind of work. You could go to galleries and things while I'm busy." Not noticing at all how he looked, she went on, "There's a great deal of culture in Canada, and after Canada, this time, there'll be London and Europe." The ice tinkled as she put down her glass. They were having a little farewell dinner, just the two of them, before the "Farewell to Cecilia" parties at the tennis club and at the Mary and Joseph. They were silent while the waitress cleared their plates away. Edwin remembered that he was the sort of person who, when traveling, missed seeing churches famous for their twin spires or stained glass, because of sudden longings to go back to the hotel. Once there, he would have a long hot bath and then, ringing for room service, he would order coffee and sandwiches. He was often ashamed of this need, especially when Cecilia, eating more than her share of cream-filled cakes, lamented that she had not seen the one and only perfect sunset. He felt ashamed remembering afresh about hotel rooms and how he always wanted to remain indoors, unpacking his books and asking the chambermaid or porter if it was possible for him to have a table and a chair. He always took with him, when traveling, some rags for cleaning the bath. He understood that he was merely claiming territorial rights. He had come to realize that it was of no use to explain the ritual to Cecilia when she was impatient to go out exploring.

Over coffee they talked calmly and settled finally on the plan that Edwin would fly across to spend Christmas and New Year with her in England. Many husbands and wives found themselves in similar positions, they told each other, of being apart, because of their work, for long periods. Planes were filled daily with people being carried to and from various places all over the world, to take part in passionate and strictly moral meetings in hotel and motel accommodation, which was so uniform throughout that all meetings became one universal meeting, and it was easy to forget, later, in which city and in which country the predictable embrace had taken place.

Cecilia, wanting to feel the soft coolness of cream on her

tongue, spooned up the contents of the little silver cream jug. This was not the first time they had agreed to be separate.

♦ ♦ ♦

The telephone interrupted their lives a great deal at all hours of the day and night: the general hospital, the Mary and Joseph Maternity Wing, mainly. Edwin was used to taking messages about the emerging head, where it was and where it was expected to be. He was often amazed at the precision of this knowledge. This precision and the clarity of thought and knowledge which accompanied it was something which had attracted him to Cecilia years ago.

Often he, returning home first, took a message for Cecilia which caused her to go straight back to the hospital before she had set foot in the house. He realized he was missing the nuisance of the telephone. He put away the vacuum cleaner and boiled an egg. The macaroni cheese, Cecilia said, would keep. No she hadn't put much mustard in and yes she remembered he was delicate in the throat and no there was no other frightful sauce. He tried to disguise the staleness of the egg with a touch of cheap white pepper. He wondered why it was not possible to buy fresh eggs. "Fresh apples too," he said aloud, and startled himself with his own voice. He longed to bite a fresh apple. A ripe apple full of juice and sweetness, straight from the tree and picked by himself. He wondered if he could remember the taste of an apple which had not been kept in cold storage. He swallowed the egg in lumps too quickly with lumps of bread and butter. He opened the refrigerator and stared into the cold cleanliness.

He stared at himself in the bathroom mirror, examined his tongue and clenched his teeth at his own reflection. He examined a patch of dry skin on his shin. He had to put one foot on the side of the bath and roll up his trouser leg to find it. He had meant to ask Cecilia if it was a skin cancer. He thought he would measure it every day to see if it was spreading quickly. He would keep written notes describing its appearance and what it felt like.

"Does it itch?" He asked himself the kind of question Cecilia would ask. "Not a great deal, not *yet.*" His answer, as usual, carried an implication.

"Have you vomited?" was Cecilia's direct response when he complained of crippling abdominal pains. "If you haven't vomited and you don't vomit it's probably just a little muscle you've pulled. Nothing to worry about." She often prodded his quivering bare flesh with wise fingers, smiling down at him, even kissing him lightly and quickly. "Don't die," she said to him once during one of his illnesses. "I'd have to rush out and buy a book of quotations if you died."

He hunted for his magnifying glass in order to look more closely at his skin.

♦ ♦ ♦

Edwin had three books of the body in which he kept notes. The books were the external, the internal and the intangible. The book of the skin (the external) had separate pages for different places on the body. He planned at some stage to have a series of maps like ordnance survey maps (in sections) of the human body, his body, with special methods of marking wrinkles, hair, moles, bruises, pimples, dry patches and the rather more unusual blemishes. Every page had its own legend and scale and he hoped, ultimately, to make an accurate index. All three books had stiff covers and blank pages for drawings and diagrams alternating with lined pages for the written comments. Faithfully he kept the records, three valuable collections of human data. There were no limits to the notes he was able to make. He often imagined Cecilia's pleasure at receiving the copies, handsomely bound, at some time in the future, after he was dead.

Admiring and emulating the ancient Italian mathematician Girolamo Cardano, Edwin felt there were great possibilities in what could be written if the writing was about oneself. Cardano was remembered in encyclopedias because he perfected a method of finding cube roots and was physician to the kings of Scotland. But it was his self-revealing passages in his autobiography which made an even greater claim. Edwin felt at once an identification with this man who, in his own self-portrait, followed a description of his height with an immediate descent to the problems he had with his feet. Cardano further endeared himself by his amazing habit of looking for some sort of illness when he discovered that he was not ill. It seemed that happiness lay in the relief of being without pain. Perhaps happiness was in reality simply the state of being not unhappy. The discussion was endless; Edwin enjoyed the reasoning. It was better in fact to have some sort of pain, a mild headache for example, because without physical pain anxiety and worrying were more in evidence and were more distressing.

Certain passages in Edwin's books of the body were modeled directly on the writings of this self-absorbed, self-preserving scholar. The Renaissance period, he was sure, was not far removed from his own life. This thought often provided consolation.

♦   ♦   ♦

He surprised himself leaning over the kitchen table rereading the newspaper as if he had never seen it or any other newspaper before.

Resisting the temptation to sit with his freshly soaked senna pods in front of the television to watch a film described as a movie looking into the innermost thoughts of a middle-aged, happily married man who has an affair with a fifteen-year-old girl, he went into his study and read Plutarch's essay "Advice on Marriage" in the same gulping way as he had eaten his egg. He put the book aside, knowing that he was not noticing what he was reading. He thought of Cecilia and the long journey she must make. He had no idea where she was by now. Perhaps she was at this very moment, during a far-off and unbelievable sunrise, flying over the sugared peaks of some distant mountains. She would be looking down into an amazing pink light beneath which bandits, lying in wait for poverty-stricken peasants, would leap upon them as they patiently tried to grub a living from impossible rocky and desolate slopes. Of course she would not be able to see any such gruesome scenes from that height. She was still, he thought, several hours from the fog-bound descent into London. He knew the feelings of real fear it was possible to experience during what seems like an entirely blind landing. He could remember very well the sensation of being held hovering, at thirty thousand feet, before the plane begins to lose height. Suddenly, from the impenetrable thickness of the fog, hidden perils begin to appear, steeples and towers and tall blocks of buildings, the roofs of innocent dwellings, and then the even more innocent and simple back gardens where a man might be mowing his lawn or a child might be playing with her doll. Cecilia had written to him once, "how fear can seize you somewhere in the throat, in the head and in the heart, that it is possible to be completely afraid." It was unlike Cecilia, who, outwardly, never showed any fear. She was never frightened, but she knew about fear and did not belittle his. He hoped she would not be afraid landing in England. She would have to land again, quite soon after being in England, in Canada. There would be many such landings. Thinking about her, as he often did, he renewed his feelings of reverence for the way in which she took lives, one after the other, in her hands. He knew how she held them, these lives. He often imagined her hands, capable in rubber gloves, cradling the tiny bodies and the little limbs. He could imagine each tiny head having to be steadied as it rolled on its stalk-like wrinkled neck. She held these lives in the palm of her own strong hand. She had an intimate knowledge of human life, of birth and death and of illness and cure. This knowledge was combined with a hygienic and, he thought, a clinical prettiness. Edwin, liking a certain antiseptic fragrance which hung about her, once asked, "What's that smell?" She explained it was a special liquid soap they had to use. He discovered quite soon, though he did not want to think this, that it had a masking quality. He discovered too, quite early on, that her own appearance mattered very much to her. To look young was all-important.

His curiosity about the things she knew was no less now. From the beginning he wanted her to tell him about the human body. Where is the prostate gland, he wanted to know, after seeing an advertisement for pills. He could never hear enough. Oh, you're being so morbid, she said then, laughing and putting a long-drawn-out emphasis on the word "morbid." Tell me, he often asked, about Vorwickl. Perhaps he was teasing, he tried to make it sound like teasing, this questioning about a friend of hers, an ugly woman, he thought privately, but clever, a colleague as deeply involved as Cecilia was herself. What did you and Vorwickl do together and how? What was it like? He took the chance when she was in a good mood and provocative. There's nothing to tell; she had a way of laughing as if there was. Of course he knew really there could be nothing to tell about Vorwickl. She was stout and wore, even then, years ago, thick-lensed spectacles, and her hair was drawn back into a heavy unbecoming bun. With all his ideas about his own knowledge of how a woman could improve herself, make the best of herself, it was impossible to apply any of these ideas to Vorwickl.

They would be meeting soon. He could envisage them, as able as ever to make the best of a dreary hotel room somewhere during one of the pauses in the tremendous journey. They would just talk, he supposed. After so many years there would be a great deal to say. Vorwickl had the power of speech and Cecilia of laughter.

On his desk there was a small blue vase crammed with white rosebuds. Moisture, like tears, glistened on the dark green leaves and on the full lip and curve of the plump little jar. Cecilia said it was a jug really and disgracefully potbellied. She had put the roses there. It was the last thing she did before leaving. While they were waiting for her taxi she had exclaimed, with an excited joy, that she had been so busy she had never noticed the Iceberg. The light from the veranda caressed the rosebush. Cecilia ran indoors then for the kitchen scissors. "To remind you of me." She laughed, and with quick nimble fingers she made the little arrangement. As if he needed to be reminded. He pressed the rosebuds gently between his thumb and forefinger, feeling the cool softness of the tightly closed and layered petals. They did remind him of Cecilia. It was their small, neat prettiness, tightly closed. He fancied too that the green and white would have been a choice of colors in the Elizabethan court, one of his chosen areas of study. The colors soothed him. Iceberg roses; she said she loved them. While he was fetching a light coat for himself, she said he was to stay at home and look at the roses and not come to the airport. "There's no need," she said. "So many people there, no chance to talk." All the others would be there. She would rather say goodbye like this, at home with the roses. He remembered other times, when, surrounded by kind and well-meaning friends, he had tried to say one last thing to her before she boarded the plane. It had not been possible. He knew too, from his own travelings, that she was already, in her mind, part of the way on her journey. She knew he would understand, she said; she would rather go off on her own. The taxi came quite soon.

Planes crashed or broke up on takeoff, he thought as he sat alone by his desk; they did not often crash on landing.

He stared at the silent flowers.

There are two types of novels, Edwin wrote, bending over his desk, *those which end with the characters getting married and living happily ever after and those which start with the characters married and living unhappily.* Not sure whether this was his own remark, he put it in inverted commas and followed it with a quotation from Euripides, from Jason in despair and in self-justification.

> *If only children could be got some other way*
> *without the female sex! If women didn't exist,*
> *human life would be rid of all its miseries. . . .*

He hoped the quotation would interest the students. Four-thirty was a bad time for a lecture. They wanted to get away to their work; many of them worked in the evenings. He suspected they worked all night. Nine o'clock in the morning was a bad time for a lecture for this same reason. Perhaps there were no good times for lectures now. Sometimes he wanted to blame someone. The Tranby woman and her friend and colleague Bushby, or was it Burton? What did either of them know about the Elizabethan court. He felt they were waiting for him to retire. Probably they wanted to replace him with a computer. Tranby had no feeling for the Elizabethans. She positively scoffed at his idea of green and white. How did he know for certain? she once asked in the staff tearoom. The room was in the basement. He had tried to get up the stairs too quickly that time. Had he a quotation, Tranby wanted to know behind him on the stairs, to support his statement? Her angora twin set close behind him had caused him to hurry more. He could hardly breathe. Watch the old ticker, gran'pa; he was sure he was not imagining her words. How did he know for certain, she kept on behind him, what the colors were? Was he sure, she wanted to know, or was it simply a romantic and fanciful idea from the imagination of an aging man? Both Tranby and Burton, or was it Bushby, should in his opinion have been got rid of years ago. That was his private opinion. He never spoke to either of them if he could help it. He was unable to understand, when he thought about it, how everyone else seemed to like them both so much.

As he tried to think of the next point to make in his lecture, he was aware of a rustling sound outside his uncurtained window. He raised his head and listened. All was quiet as it usually was at midnight. He tried to concentrate on the pages in front of him. He had stopped for the time being, wishing that Cecilia had not gone away. He would miss her later and keep on missing her. As a rule he was still in his study writing and waiting when she came in late from the hospital. She would perch on his knee and pour whisky without measuring it, and she would begin to tell him things. She needed, he knew, to tell him everything, especially what people had said and what she had said to them. He would wait now, he knew, by the telephone at times when she could not possibly phone. He would forget what the time would be in Toronto, Montreal, London, Paris, Vienna and Rome. All the same, he would wait expecting her to call, reverse charge.

He heard the rustling sound outside the window again. Earlier there had been a moon but now heavy clouds made the night black. The rustling was once more followed by silence. He listened, trying to follow Jason's lament with a good sentence, and knowing that his concentration was disturbed, he allowed himself some bitterness. Part of Cecilia's conference was to be an investigation of infertility. Was it ever mentioned (he sat back in thought) and talked about (he began a lecture in his head), this game, this archness and evasion (the lecture was not for his students), this flirtatious sighing and flickering of the eyelids and the endless talking about "making love"? Some people even called it rape when they did not mean rape. Is this one of the causes of the problem? How many people (he warmed to the subject), how many people playing and pretending, changing partners, even with their lawful partner, how many of them would be fertile if they did the thing properly? He flinched at the words "the thing." Cecilia played all too well this game; she had all the mannerisms. He was sure she would not contribute to the conference from her own experience. Dippy Fairfax had once said something about this very subject and they had all hooted at him. Edwin included. Remembering this he stopped composing; it was pointless anyway.

One bitterness led to another. Bitterness is destructive and hard to control. With fragile honesty he knew he was feeding bitterness. A few weeks earlier he had delivered a guest lecture. The invitation to be one of three guest speakers had pleased him. A former colleague, ignoring his later research and writing and his notable prize, introduced him with a quotation from an article, his first, published in a journal current thirty years ago and now no longer in existence. This introduction was a shock (he wondered if Tranby had written it) and it took a great deal of energy to try to make a joke about the youthful article, suggesting that since it had been out of print for so many years it could now be considered rare and therefore could be offered for sale in aid of a favorite charity. It should be possible, he told his audience, to ask a favorable sum for an original copy. Trying to hide the indignation which trembled in his voice and at the backs of his knees, he had given the lecture unable to help noticing an exchange of what seemed to him supercilious looks between younger members in the auditorium. Thinking about these people now, at his desk at home, he reflected that he did not even know their names or the subjects in which they specialized. Allowing his thoughts to become more and more wasteful, he dwelled on his performance. He was afraid that his lecture, from which he had left out a part because of the lengthy introduction, may not have made sense. While he listened to the ramblings of his onetime colleague, his energy had ebbed. He had felt then that all his prepared work was worthless and that it was conceited of him to have accepted the invitation to speak. He felt too that the audience were really waiting for their promised refreshments and that it was up to him to be as brief as possible.

Tormenting himself, he thought it would be sweet to be able to ask someone now for mercy and relaxation, for pity and for soothing words, as if he could be at the receiving end of a beautifully composed and well-performed mass. These thoughts and the accompanying swelling ache in his throat, which made him gulp painfully several times, alarmed him.

I must be ill, he told himself. Surely I am not, at my age,

crying somewhere inside. He reached for his books of the body; his hand hovered over the intangible.

There was another rustling sound in the blackness outside his window. He was feeling quite sick: the stale egg and that awful pepper; he could taste them still. He heard the sound again and a tapping of soft fleshy fingers on the lower part of his window. He rose slightly in his chair and peered at the glass, which only presented a reflection of himself and a part of his room. The house was sheltered by trees and bushes. A little path, frequented only by girls chasing runaway dogs and the man who read the meter, went down that side of the house. Beyond the uneven and sometimes flowering hedge there was a similar little path and then the next house formed a dark, solid shape which at times, as he made his notes in the evenings, seemed very close to him. No one, he thought, would be on the little path at this hour. He leaned back in his chair and opened the notebook of the intangible. One of the later entries, written one night when Cecilia had been called back to the Mary and Joseph, encompassed a vision of old age. The vision offered four alternatives, all with brief and honest, quite courageous descriptions. They were all possibilities, Edwin felt, for himself. His own old age, which came nearer every day, carried these possibilities: Alzheimer's disease, Ménière's, Parkinson's and Paget's. He turned to a fresh page.

He began to write a sketchy description of the people who had been at his lecture, the younger men who were now his colleagues. They all seemed to have round smiling faces, eternally healthy and boyish, retaining the sparkling, intelligent schoolboy eyes which must have captivated first their teachers and later the members of the appointments board. He sometimes wondered if they were vegetarians.

Once, recently, he had lent one of his books (he did not lend his books as a rule) to a younger colleague. The book was not returned immediately, as, apparently, others had wanted to consult it. When it did come back to him, a birthday card, used as a bookmark, fell out. The inscription *Happy Birthday Shithead from Nympho* had shocked him, and for some time afterwards, he found himself looking at the boyish faces in the staff tearoom, wondering which one of them had been addressed with such vulgarity, especially on the sacred occasion of a birthday.

There were young women too, some of them quite ferocious, coming into the department, late, with their small children. He had been surprised, in the face of fierce feminist demand, how easily these women burst into tears. He kept a box of tissues on his desk and, not knowing what to say, pushed it shyly forward. He was incapable in the presence of such displays of grief to do more than this.

"Give yourself a seven out of ten, dear, and buy yourself a new hat." He had the sentence written out in readiness for an overwrought mature-age student but was unable to say it at the appropriate moment.

Seen from a little distance these people all looked alike to him. Their clothes were like a uniform of denim and Indian cotton. There were several beards and a great deal of hair. The hair, he thought, caused half-hidden eyes to be bewitching and treacherous. From their positions they made pronouncements in a language which was unfamiliar; a nightmare of fashionable and, to him, false scholarship. When he was not depressed and negative (one of their words) he, in a fairminded way, was sure that they, in turn, would have their opinions of him. At times he tried to be agreeable and went down to the tearoom on purpose to try to follow discussion, nodding his head and smiling kindly. He knew and wrote all these things about himself and often read through what he had written previously. He felt this made him suitably humble.

He took up his pen again, having let it drop while his mind wandered.

A ragged cloak upon a stick . . . He wrote the quotation on a fresh page, following it with *a world of disorderly notions, picked out of his books, crowded his imagination.* It would come to him later who had said or written these.

The sound from outside came again. It was a soft tap-tapping on the lowest part of his window. The sill was quite high off the ground. Someone knocking, unless he was very tall, would have to stretch to reach.

A sudden sweetness from the white rosebuds made him glance at them. A few of the buds were opening. The room was warm enough to bring on this sweet opening. The books lining the walls, together with his solid desk by the window, made the room rather like a fortress with double walls. The large bed covered with red rugs gave an impression of comfort. Again he heard the rustling and movement outside the window. He glanced quickly round his room. The warm rugs on the bed, the books and their brightly colored covers and the wisdom and entertainment in their contents, the masses of words expressing so much of human life, were an insulation.

Edwin stood up and, leaning over his desk, raised with difficulty, the wood being old and swollen, the bottom sash.

"We are locked out of our house," a woman's voice said from the darkness immediately below. He leaned forward, his stomach resting on his lecture, and saw them, two women, squeezed together huddled in the narrowness of the service entrance. "We are your new neighbors," the woman said, "next door."

"Ah yes, of course! Page," he said, "Edwin Page, allow me, let me help you," his quiet voice and his words encapsulating a whole lifetime of that endless chivalry which makes men available for climbing up, and for penetrating and forcing ways through impossible cracks and apertures in order to enable forgetful or lost women to be rescued. "Just wait a moment, please," he said. He put on his dressing gown, tying the magnificent cord carefully. He never liked to appear partly dressed. Quickly he smoothed his healthy bright hair and made his way through the front door across to the side of the house where the two women were.

"Oh, Dr. Page, I am very much afraid," Leila's mother said, crushing the smaller bushes and snapping little branches in her haste to leave the little path, "it is impossible to break into our house. As you know, we have only recently moved in. It's absolutely burglarproof: metal grilles, locks and bolts on the doors and the windows. Oh!" she gasped. "I feel we are going to be a terrible nuisance. We have been going round and round the house, and you know how dark it is, trying to see if there was one teeny weakness, one teensie-weensie little place where we could break in like burglars." In spite of being breathless she laughed and held her arm, fat in the sleeve of her fur coat, for Edwin to take. He helped her up onto the veranda of his own house. Still holding her arm, he led her to the front door. "We've been to the play," she explained. "We joined the Theatre Club; I want Leila to meet nice people." Her sharp heels pierced the soft old boards and then pitted the linoleum in the hall.

"There was this man in the play." She looked up at Edwin. "Could be," she said, "the spitting image of yourself if you had an Afro hairdo. He was handsome, wasn't he, Leila pet? Had all the women after him, didn't he, Leila? Quite the Dong Choon. A real heartbreak and a scream really. I enjoy a good laugh. Of course this was Russian; they're so morbid, as a rule, aren't they? It was just when the man—not the one with the Afro, the other one—when he gets run over on the railway line—how they do that on stage beats me—it was ever so real: it was then that I remembered seeing our keys on the kitchen table where I left them. I never picked them up! So near and yet so far!" She sighed.

Leila followed her mother. She looked pale and was dressed in what surely, Edwin thought, must be her best clothes. She had a fur coat too. Her handbag was white and purple. Cecilia, if she saw the bag, would hardly be able to conceal her mirth. She would shake with silent laughter and whisper somewhere, in the kitchen probably, that it was hideous and how could anyone bring themselves to buy it, and at the same time she would be sorry for having found the bag laughable. She would be sorry for the girl and she would try, in some way, to atone. Perhaps take the girl on one side and say something kind about her appearance and share some feminine secret with her so that the girl's face would light up with her smile, as only a plain girl's face can.

"So stupid of me," Leila's mother was saying. "I am afraid we are disturbing you, Dr. Page; I don't know at all what we are going to do."

"First of all," Edwin said in his kindest manner, "you must sit down." He leaned over to switch on the light. "Do come in."

"Oh. No, no," Leila's mother cried. "I don't want to disturb your household more than we have already. Your wife?" She glanced quickly at the closed door on the other side of the hall.

"My wife is not at home," Edwin assured his unexpected guests. "Please do come and sit down." As Leila's mother entered the room he could see reflecting in her eyes the cottage quality of the furnishings, disappointing after an expectation of a desirable wealth and fashion. He saw, perhaps for the first time, the haphazard collection of chairs—cane, chintz and colonial.

"Really, as if different women had chosen them all," Daphne had said in her loud cheerful way more than once.

Edwin, still smiling, wondered whether he should quickly drag the dear little Regency sofa from Cecilia's room so that the present selection of chairs could benefit from the delicate blue velvet and the gilded woodwork. He saw Leila's mother recoil in a controlled way from the walls, which he knew, but had stopped noticing, were decorated with red cabbage roses nestling in vague foliage. "Lettuces": often Daphne filled in pauses during conversations, startling those guests who had carelessly failed to pay homage to the ancient wallpaper. The bookshelves too, suddenly as they became victims of the scrutiny, appeared to be filled entirely with tattered worthless volumes. The standard lamp leaned, the silk shade was faded, scorched and frayed, and he saw, and again it was as if for the first time, how threadbare the carpet was.

"You don't have telly then?" Her glance had come full circle.

"In the other room." Edwin moved as if to the door.

"Leila needs to pay a call," Leila's mother said. She leaned back with a contented sigh in a chair which looked as if the wallpaper had spread.

"Sorry?" Edwin turned. "Oh, of course, this way. I'll show you where the light switch is. Down the passage, second door on left." Gently he guided Leila, his fingertips hovering over her thick shoulders.

"Your wife's a doctor?" Leila's mother seemed to approve as Edwin, returning, picked up a small cushion designed and embroidered by himself during a convalescence once. "Pea-cocks," he was about to explain at random, his nerves some-what shattered by two female visitors in the middle of the night. "Peacocks," he repeated in an almost apologetic way, searching for the best words to describe the Elizabethan motif in the elaborate design. But Leila's mother leaned forward. "Oh, thank you," she said, "thank you ever so much; just slip it in the small of my back." The peacocks disappeared, as if forever, as Leila's mother flattened them. "Our agent," she said, "did explain we were next door to two doctors."

"Only one at present. For the time being. I am deserted." Edwin gave a little shrug of dejection and matched it with a suitable grimace of mock sorrow.

"Aw, that's a shame. Fancy anyone leaving a lovely home like this." The cracks in the ceiling seemed to grin as Edwin turned away from Leila's mother's attempt to praise the room with a critical glance. "P'raps she's bored," she said, "needs a change. Change is as good as a feast, so they say. P'raps she's been working herself too hard. A woman needs . . ." She seemed to be sucking a tooth as if extracting the last shred of something, a lamb chop perhaps; meat did stick in the teeth. He began to brood on teeth. He should, he knew, make an appointment with the dentist.

"Any kiddies?" Leila's mother was speaking. "I suppose if you have children," she continued, "they'd all be up and away, but then again"—she smiled in a comfortable way at him—"there's sometimes a late little littly pattering around the place." She paused as if listening for these little feet some-where in the distance.

"No," Edwin said, leaving the idea about telephoning the dentist. No one would be in the office at midnight. All the same it was something he could get done during Cecilia's absence.

"Unfortunately, no," he added sadly, knowing that Leila's mother would expect a degree of regret.

"Aw well, what will be will be, as I always say." She nodded wisely. "They seem to go in these days for sugared mothers, don't they?"

"Sorry?" Edwin paused. "Ah!" he said. "Surrogate." He laughed in his most charming way. "Not sugared," he said, "surrogate."

"Yes," Leila's mother said, "that's the word. With no family"—she pronounced it "farmily"—"a woman can be very lonesome."

"Ah no." Edwin smoothed the silver richness of his hair with the palms of his hands, first one temple and then the other. He was surprised that he was suddenly nervous. The woman, in her vulgar curiosity, seemed sinister. "No, no," he said with the extra charm he used in the face of what he felt to be vulgar, "she is not at all lonely, not in the least. Her work is tremendously important to her. She has gone—"

"Aw, fancy!" Leila's mother, not listening, stretched out a well-bandaged leg. The bandage was very obvious beneath a bright flesh-colored stocking.

"She"—he paused—"my wife is—her work is obstetrics and gynecology." He felt he must explain, and at the same time it seemed to him that he was actually apologizing for Cecilia's vagrancy.

Cecilia would know about leg bandages of course and would, in the circumstances, be concerned and might even ask a sympathetic question or even two. He wondered whether to mention this now even though her concern was mainly for those fruitful women whose legs might become, at any moment, a part of their interesting condition.

Leila's mother tried again. "All the same," she said, "it must be dull for Dr. Page—I mean, no farmily. Always other people's kiddies—not the same as having your own."

"Cecilia," Edwin corrected gently, having no difficulty or embarrassment with his wife's name. Patients often used her first name, perhaps those of the higher income bracket. . . .

"It must be dull for Dr. Sissilly." Leila's mother was not to be stopped. "I mean it's always the same old story; childbirth is so repetitive." Her sigh was laden with all the long-drawn-out hours of labor, first and second stage, from Eve onwards. With a weary look she lifted the bandaged leg onto the small stool which Edwin, with courteous attention, placed in front of her.

"Not really," he said. "You see, Cecilia really feels the individuality, the special light, she calls it, which surrounds every newborn baby. Every birth is an event, a miracle." He bent his handsome head kindly towards his visitor. "Every time," he said, "she comes home radiant." He paused, and as his visitors seemed to be waiting for him to continue, he, aware of being nervous and pompous, said, "I often see this radiance give way to a wonderful calm expression, an *exquisite tenderness and purity.* I'm afraid I'm quoting now; it's a bad habit of mine. But do you, by any chance, know Hans Memling, *The Virgin and Child,* or Albrecht Dürer? They can and do explain far more satisfactorily . . ."

"I don't think we have met them—have we, Leila? But we both love ickle babies, don't we Leila honey? Come and sit down by Mother. She's so shy," Leila's mother explained, "and we've had a fright at not being able to get in. Just think, Leila," she continued, "we are next door to a house with two doctors. Remember *The Young Doctors?*"

"Only one real one," Edwin said. "I deal only in words and phrases and not with the body. And alas!"—he became a little theatrical—"I am no longer young. I am—how shall I put it?—*a tattered cloak upon a stick.*"

"Come again?" Leila's mother said. "I beg yours?"

"Mostly I . . ." Edwin swallowed. "Cecilia is away for a year." Leila's mother, showing no reaction, simply arranged her face for her next question. "And what is your speciality?" she asked in a bright way, her tone dismissing Cecilia and her devotion to her work. "Do you carve people up or are you a bedside man?" Her full red lips, pursed, seemed to wish for both.

O mater pulchra filia pulchrior. Edwin, smiling, surveyed

—— 23 ——

his visitors, changing the subject and changing the quotation in his translation, "What a beautiful mother *and* a beautiful daughter," feeling that any sort of comparison or grading of beauty might be out of place. "Unfortunately for the purse, neither," he said, going back to the question and glancing with pretended shame at his laden bookshelves. "To have books in more than one room in a house is positively gross," he said. "But I am helpless!"

"Well, never mind!" Leila's mother said. The compliment had pleased her. "Mercy buttercups." Yes, she would fancy a glass of port. She had always been fond of a good port. A nice port could do wonders, and being locked out was quite an occasion for a little celebration, wasn't it?

"It's no use our trying to get into that house," she said over her second glass, "is it, Leila pet? We know! The agent when we rented it off him stressed emphatic that it was burglar-proof. 'Can we get raped in there?' I asked him, and he made a point of that. 'No, my dear,' he said, 'you can't ever be raped in there.' That's what he said. 'No one can break in there and you cannot be raped and burglarized. Two ladies on their only,' he said, 'need protection.' Mr. Bott. Take Mr. Bott: he would have said the same thing, wouldn't he, Leila? Your daddy, Leila, he always said, 'If I'm not spared, if I'm took, be sure to choose a house as you can't be raped in.'" Leila's mother sniffed and blinked. "I am sorry," she said. "Have you a tissue?" Edwin fetched some from the bathroom. "So, Dr. Page," she said, dabbing her eyes, "we are so to speak completely at your mercy."

Edwin, knowing that he was unable to sleep if strangers were in the house, and immediately regretting his words, said, "Perhaps you would sleep here?" He began at once to feel, in advance, the uneasiness in the house.

If Cecilia had been coming home from the Mary and Joseph it would have been different. He would sit in her room after Leila and her mother had been seen off to bed, and Cecilia would brush her hair, and giggle, and say that she could hear the guests doing dreadfully sordid things in the spare bedroom. She would giggle again about Leila's clothes, "that awful long red and blue checked skirt! Those cheap boots—did you see the heels? And that purple and white vinyl bag. Oh, I don't mean to laugh, but her gear, it's too terrible!"

"We have a comfortable spare room," Edwin said, sternly silencing Cecilia's laughter, which was so shrill in his head he felt that the visitors must be hearing it too. "And in the morning," he said, "we can sort out the problem of entry."

"Now that would be nice." Leila's mother put her other leg on the stool and agreed that a cup of tea before bed would be very acceptable.

♦ ♦ ♦

Leila's mother was to have the bathroom first and Leila was to be second and Edwin, as host, would do the locking up and be last.

"Mr. Bott always locked up," Leila's mother said. Edwin, not knowing what this Bott looked like, tried to look as unlike him as he could. He limped across the room. Mr. Bott would never have limped, he thought.

Leila's mother would be a long time in the bathroom. She made the announcement beforehand. She had to rinse out a few things. "Our lingerie," she said to Edwin in the hall, where he seemed to be caught. She even suggested that he might like to go first, as she never liked to keep a gentleman waiting, especially in his own house. She had not lost sight, she said, of whose house it was. She did not want to hold him up, she said. But he, with repeated little bows and small words of insisting, said, But no, she must be first. He was sure she was tired; hadn't she said the play was very long? As for himself, he never went to bed early but worked late at night. There was, he said, simply no hurry.

"Yes," Leila's mother said, "we have often seen your light." She held, in both hands, nightdresses belonging to Cecilia. She thought she was too large herself but perhaps Leila might . . . Edwin hoped the night would be a comfortable one for them.

"Thank you," Leila's mother said, taking up all the space in the hall. "It's a funny thing about lingerie," she said. "Lingerie": she let the word roll on her tongue before she finished saying it. "Lingerie," she said, "seems to be based on the idea that we are attracted to clothing which reveals a great deal but not our all. Not everything about the human body. We enjoy," she said, "the suspense of peeking at each other even though we know, often very well, what we are peeking at." She moved slightly, Edwin hoped in the direction of the bathroom. She shook a plump finger at him. "No peeking," she said. She seemed to savor the idea.

◆　◆　◆

The water was running in the bathroom for a long time. He sat at his desk and stared at Jason's despair: *If only children could be got some other way . . .* Leila's mother certainly had some ideas on underclothes. Surely she could not have read Donne quoting Pliny. It would be amusing, perhaps, to read the passage aloud to her, perhaps at breakfast:

> . . . that when their thin silk stuffs were first invented at Rome . . . it was but an invention that women might go naked in clothes, for their skins might be seen through those clothes, those thin stuffs . . .

It was one thing for Leila's mother to talk about what she called lingerie; he was sure she would be outraged and her respectability wounded if he quoted Pliny. It was quite in order for women to say certain things. If a man said them, then a woman would set about accusing him.

In an attempt to soothe himself and to make the night as ordinary as possible, he gazed upon the pensive and gentle faces of the Madonna. Because of his lecture preparations he had several on his desk. Uppermost were the Hans Memling, the Dürer and the Van Eycks. The children lay there in complacent repose, each with innocent limbs and a babyish head which contrasted with the facial expressions of wisdom more suited to those of an old man. This contemplation of the representation of the human individual as a naked, plump, contented child, the subject of countless acts of adoration and contrition, never ceased to fill him with indescribable longings.

Perhaps, as others had for centuries before him, he would meditate, keep to his quiet existence and dwell in the peacefulness reflected in the patient expression in the face of the blessed Mother as she holds her child.

He heard the regular beat of the water meter. Perhaps they, Leila and her mother, were both in the bathroom. The throb of the water in the pipe as it passed below his window seemed to echo in his head. Women, he knew, were often sociable in bathrooms, flipping up their skirts to perch, chatting, on the lavatory and removing clothes shamelessly to step one after the other under the same shower. Often he'd heard peals of silvery laughter (Cecilia's) from the bathroom when she had a friend, not Daphne, to stay. Sometimes he'd heard snatches of songs and conversations over the noise of running water and filling toilet tanks. Women, he knew, continued to talk even while they cleaned their teeth. He preferred having the bathroom to himself.

He thought he would examine the dry patch on his shin. He found it with difficulty. It looked the same as it had looked earlier. There was not much point, he thought, in recording a measurement, as he had not written down, though he meant to, the earlier size. At a guess it did not seem to have grown bigger. He wished he had asked Cecilia what he should rub on it. He folded back the cover on his bed, neatly, and put his pajamas out. Cecilia always thought this action of his cute and said so every time she came into his study and saw his pajamas spread out ready.

When they were first married she laughed so much when she saw him fold up the hotel counterpane, and when she saw him shake out and put his pajamas on his side of the bed, she had laughed even more. It had seemed as if she was going to cry. Later, in the night, she said she was sorry for laughing, that it was all her fault, laughing the way she did. All her life, she explained to him tenderly, she had been a nuisance, laughing at the wrong times, at school in particular. Daphne could tell him.

"Good heavens, yes," Daphne's deeper voice bore witness on many occasions. Daphne was not given to shaking with helpless mirth during times of crisis. Edwin thought she bore up wonderfully well under Cecilia's often inexplicable behavior. He often relied on Daphne. He, though he would never have asked, wondered if Cecilia had ever had to leave the labor room or the operating table when, just for an example, she was removing something internal and vital, doubled up with the giggles, as she sometimes had to leave their dining room when visitors were present. Like the time he was helping the wife of his own head of department to dislodge a king-size prawn from where it had dropped. Cecilia's unsuccessful attempts at smothering her laughter (she was hidden, her face buried in her old Girl Guide uniform, behind the kitchen door) were fortunately drowned by Daphne, who, rising to her feet, proposed in immense tones a recitation from Shakespeare and a toast to the Great Bard, as he was called at St. Monica's. The prawn ultimately escaped from its temporary mooring and the meal continued, Cecilia, demure, solemn and pretty, placing Icebergs, exquisite chocolate-coated buds, in front of every guest in turn as if to make up, to appease.

Dear sweet Cecilia, how sweet and kind she was their first night together, all naked and new and young, saying she would love him forever. Edwin often turned to the relevant pages in the notebook of the intangible. He enjoyed rereading all the sweet things Cecilia had said when they were first together. He had noted them all, word for word.

The telephone started to interrupt them immediately, for she was always on call. They blamed the phone.

"Oh! Stupid old phone!" Cecilia said. And, singing, she dressed so quickly Edwin was hardly aware of her leaving the room. Though he recalled on all subsequent disturbed nights the sound of the car in reverse as he had heard it on their first night in their own house, after the honeymoon.

All good gifts around us are sent from heaven above. Edwin thought he heard the words when Cecilia sang. He never heard more words, as she hummed the rest. If she had shown a tendency towards religion, he thought, she could have been praying or singing inside herself with angels, a sort of hidden choir.

"What is it you sing when you go out?" he asked her once.

"Oh, do I sing?" Cecilia, suppressing mirth, was surprised. "Perhaps," she said, "it's something I sang at school. I can't remember." Perhaps, Edwin thought, she did pray as she set out to deliver another child. He respected her privacy too much to question her more.

He looked at the quotation from Jason and at the passage he wanted from a certain novel, where a father lifts up his naked baby son to his lips in the presence of a woman who has come to take the baby, to buy him if necessary. Finding material for his lectures sometimes made him the more aware of his loss. Life seemed altogether brittle and without meaning then and he longed to give up, once for all, the habits of pleasure, which included overeating and stupid excessive drinking. Some literary references made the idea, the idea of having children, very desirable. It comforted him to linger near the children's playground on his way home from the university. He often stood for some minutes watching the children as they climbed and jumped and scrambled. Children's bodies were loose and free in their clothes, he thought. He liked to hear their excited voices.

Suddenly, like the symptoms of an illness, the bitterness returned. He trembled as he thought again of the way in which he had been introduced by his colleague before giving his lecture. It was as if he had achieved nothing in the last thirty years. The bitterness was like a symptom which comes at intervals, growing in intensity, as a pain grows, and fading as a pain fades. Always it left him worn out and depressed. Cecilia, when he spoke of it to her, had said not to keep thinking about upsetting things. "Think of something else," she interrupted his complaining. "What shall we have for dinner? I'm starving," she said. And he felt ashamed because he saw himself on these occasions as small-headed and with the petulant mouth of a disagreeable child.

Cecilia loved food. He could hardly bear watching her eat broccoli. "Pass the butter," she asked him, with her mouth full, and spreading the melting mass with her fork, she positively stuffed herself. He was afraid she would burst something, she ate so much. But she never did and she remained slender whereas he, picking and choosing and being careful, was bulging horribly in places where he wanted to be neat and flat.

He thought the water had stopped. They must have finished in the bathroom. He stood uneasily in the middle of his study, failing to feel protected by the extra wall provided by his books and journals. There is no greater annoyance than being annoyed with oneself. He wished that he had never invited them, this Leila and her mother. But what could he have done in circumstances like these? He opened his door a crack. The hall was deserted. The light was still on, for him presumably. There was no sound from the room opposite. Not even a murmur of voices as the two women might quite expectedly have comforted each other with the better memories of the day and the hopes for tomorrow. He set off along the hall. He would not be able to sleep; he would not even contemplate sleep. A warm shower would be relaxing. It was almost as if Cecilia was prescribing a shower, a long warm shower. He saw Leila coming out of the bathroom. He was too far along the hall to turn back. He saw that her blouse was unbuttoned. She gave a shy half-smile and slid by him sideways; her full youthful breasts, pinkly innocent, moved slightly in the opening of her garment.

"Good night," Edwin said and pretended to be looking along the hall for a cat to catch and push out of the kitchen door. Leila, without attempting to pull her clothes together, disappeared into the guest room.

Edwin, deeply moved by the sight, the glimpse of the girlish pink body, unseen, he thought, by anyone except herself and her mother and, now, him, stopped at the door of the bathroom. Voluminous undergarments hung dripping from the shower curtain rail. He turned abruptly and fled from Leila's mother's washing.

The pink mounds which were Leila were sweetly inviting. He searched along his shelves for poems which would recall what he had just seen. It was a hardship not to be able to use his own bathroom. He, in spite of this, became quite excited as he sat down at his desk with John Donne and Goethe.

"Anyone for tennis?" Somewhere, as if in his dream, Edwin thought he heard Daphne calling. It was hardly light. He realized he had been asleep, still partly dressed and in his dressing gown. He sat, full of sleep, on the edge of his bed. "Anyone for tennis?" It was Daphne, immediately outside and below his open window. Usually he closed his window. He remembered now why it was open. Daphne must have come down the side of the house. "Three times round the oval and a jog-jog-jog through the pines," she bellowed pleasantly. "I promised Cecilia"—she lowered her voice as Edwin leaned over his desk towards her—"I promised Cecilia," she said, "that I'd exercise you every day."

"Daphne," Edwin said, "whatever time is it?"

"Six, or just back or front of six," she said.

"Sssh! Do keep your voice down." Edwin was breathless and agitated. "I have guests, you know, houseguests."

"You what!" Daphne's attempt at a whisper failed.

"Yes; Leila and her mother, forget their other name . . ."

"Good heavens! But how! Does Cecilia know?"

"Of course not; they only came last night. Locked out. That house, behind you; left keys inside."

"What a hoot!" Daphne said. "But why on earth, Teddy, didn't you pack them orf to the El Sombrero or that darling little chez nooky nook, the guesthouse, Pilgrims Roost?"

"I must say, the wise thought did not occur to me." Edwin yawned.

Daphne thought for a moment. "You'll have to get rid of them, straight away, otherwise you'll be stuck." She pulled the brilliant hockey colors she wore as a belt into a tighter knot. "Well, come along. Leila or no Leila, we'll do the oval." She began running on the spot, her large feet pounding on the earthy path. "High knee-raising," she cried, "one two, one two."

"Oh, I can't, Daphne," Edwin almost whimpered. "I haven't slept!"

"Rubbish," Daphne said. "Ten minutes in the fresh air is worth an hour of sleep. Let me into the kitchen then. I could do with a pot of tea."

"Oh, I don't think you should come in . . ." Edwin began, but Daphne had disappeared. He could hear the thudding of her feet on the damp ground as she made for the back of the house. He retied his dressing gown cord and went as quickly as he could to unlock the kitchen door before she, with her hunting horn voice, roused Leila's mother and Leila.

◆ ◆ ◆

"Oh yes, we were on TV, the both of us," Leila's mother said, "the both of us interviewed by ever such a nice young man—remember, Leila? That nice young man—not the one with glasses; the other, gingery one. Well, we made a complaint, you see, about this holiday tour we'd been on. Really dreadful it was." She pulled her cardigan closer, seeming to Edwin to cuddle herself in the inimitable way some women did. Leila was still in her nightdress, the one Cecilia wore when she was not well, a sort of stretchy material; it always made her look appealing when, flushed with a temperature, she lay in bed and put her hot hand in his. Edwin supposed that the stretchy stockinette fitted Leila, who was definitely plump, the best. He wondered whether Leila's mother had stayed dressed or slept raw, as Cecilia would have said. He thought again, as he sat at a corner of his own kitchen table while Leila's mother poured tea, of the tremulous untouched pinkness which was Leila when she was unbuttoned. Without meaning to, he remembered the delphiniums, years ago in Cecilia's mother's garden, with their intense blue flowers reaching up into the small branches of an apple tree where the little apples, ungrown, were like nipples hidden among the leaves. The flowers of the delphiniums seemed to be apple-tree flowers then. Lying on the grass between spindles of rosemary, he sketched Cecilia as she sunbathed. When the pencil (2B for drawing) rounded the curves of her neat white breasts, the sensation which darted through his body made him catch his breath and exclaim, "How lovely you are! I do love you!"

Cecilia's mother never commented on the sketches. "Daddy will cover them up," Cecilia said, which he did, with several old copies of the *Radio Times*. At the time Edwin thought it odd that an art dealer should cover nakedness. "I suppose it's because it's me": Cecilia provided the simple explanation.

The morning now seemed like the morning of an English summer, Edwin thought, as he glanced through the kitchen window across to the mist-shrouded pine plantation. Every moment the trees became more evident. The distant sound of crows, high up in the trees, suggested the spaciousness of open fields and paddocks as though, overnight, the quiet suburb and the locked house next door could have disappeared.

"We never ever knew where we were going to sleep," Leila's mother was saying, "and you *know* what Spain is!" She turned her eyes up to the ceiling so that only the whites showed. "And once," she continued, "the coach left without us and there we were, stranded!"

"Good Lord!" Daphne said. She cradled her mug of tea in both hands and gazed with her honest sort of sympathy at the two visitors.

"Delphiniums," Edwin said aloud, but no one heard. He thought of the blue, like china blue; it—the china—was meant to mean something, he supposed. When Cecilia was near delphiniums, her eyes seemed even more blue, bright with a kind of blue fire if there could be such a thing. "Blue eyes is oversexed": he'd heard this unforgettable remark once; he thought it was said behind him on a bus. Now he wondered how to correct it grammatically without altering the impact. He was enjoying his tea. He had not expected to like it, having been dreadfully put out to find Leila's mother already in the kitchen, with the kettle on, when he went through to let Daphne in. Unable to let her in secretly, he had opened the door with a flourish and now they all sat, a curious assortment of people in curious clothes: Edwin still partly dressed, as he had been all night, under his dressing gown; Daphne in her old school hockey tunic; and Leila with her clumsy skirt pulled on over Cecilia's fever nightdress. The skirt was obviously meant to hide the way in which the clinging material was stretched round her plump body. The skirt only covered the lower half and Edwin, though he tried not to, noticed how Leila kept her arms folded as often as she could over the revealing quality of the top part of the gown.

Cecilia never made the tea because of his little ways with the teapot. In the early days of their marriage he had once tried to expound on his theories. Freshly drawn water and the right size of the special scoop, not used for anything else, but kept especially for the purpose in the tea tin, which, he explained, must have a well-fitting lid. Cecilia, concentrating, he thought, narrowed her eyes so that they looked like splinters of blue ice. Suddenly she had started one of her laughing fits. She laughed till tears sprang from the corners of the half-closed eyes. He thought she was crying.

"What's the matter?" he asked then. "Are you all right?"

"Oh, quite all right." She was positively howling, he remembered.

"Do go on"—she was gasping—"but do first tell me what formula did you have, or"—she could hardly get the words out—"or were you breast fed?" She exploded in further mirth.

"What d'you mean?" He could remember all too well his perplexed feeling. "Mother was most particular about . . ."

"That's just it." Cecilia was calmer. "But never mind!" And she had rushed out of the kitchen, leaving him with the tea tray. The happy notion of taking the tray to her bedside seemed to be the answer that morning and for all subsequent mornings. Later he began to drink his tea alone in his study, as it suited his bowels to do this.

It was Edwin's policy to take the teapot to the kettle and he noticed, with a surprising feeling of approval, that Leila's mother did this and that she had the water at an unsurpassable boiling point. "On the boil!" she said, when it came into forceful contact with the tea leaves.

"Who's for eggs and bacon?" Leila's mother was looking into the refrigerator. She managed during this examination of the contents to extend a questioning look towards them all.

"Oh, rather! Scrumptious!" Daphne seemed eager. Good manners caused her to raise her eyebrows in the direction of Edwin. He nodded, not quite certain what he wanted himself, and went on sipping his tea, looking across to the window as if studying the sky for a weather warning. The pines, as if they had stepped away from the last shreds of the rain mist, seemed suddenly closer. The crows had moved on. The pine plantation was, after all, only on the other side of the road.

"More tea, Doctor?" Leila's mother had the teapot almost level with his head. She liked to pour from a height, she said. "Airyates the tea," she explained. The pines, as Edwin accepted his second cup, seemed taller and blacker and he began to feel shut in by them, closed in in the suburb and in his own house.

Leila's mother rattled about in a cupboard and emerged with a frying pan.

"Housekeeper's sitting room, billiards room, pink parlor,

rose room, green room"—Leila's mother was nodding her head, counting—"the yellow drawing room, the blue room, the music room"—she thought for a moment—"the vestibool, the nursery and the schoolroom, the master bedroom, the bathroom and the dining room." She turned the bacon with deft movements. She was describing the Botts' house and was pausing on the panel of bells which was, she said, smack bang right over the door of the pantry. Seeing her by the stove, Edwin felt that she had always been there.

"Then there was the other bathrooms and the north entrance and the garden room and the south entrance . . ."

"Good heavens!" Daphne said. "We must each have been given identical wiping up clorths for Christmas. Miss Heller . . ." She paused. "Good Lord!" she said. "It might have been Miss Hearnsted . . . One of them gave me mine. It's got a greeny background with little pictures of bells and all the names of the rooms made into a delirious pattern; an ancient manor house I thought was the nearest thing to it. What color was yours?"

"Yes." Leila's mother continued with an excessive calm in the face of Daphne's lack of tact. "Mr. Bott had a tea towel, pure linen, designed as a reminder of our lovely home before we had to part with it. It was, if my memory is not playing tricks today, one of the last things Mr. Bott did. What was the very last thing your daddy did, Leila pet? Can you remember? He was always into something." She smiled at the assembled little company and began to break eggs, one after another, into a cup, passing each one under her nose with a knowledgeable look before tipping it into the appetizing contents of the frying pan. "Pass up some plates to warm, Leila," she said, "and put out the knives and forks. Bread, everyone?" she asked. "Or would anyone prefer toast?"

◆ ◆ ◆

"I must walk Prince before I go to school," Daphne said as Edwin accompanied her to the front gate. "Are you coming? I'll meet you in the pines. . . ."

"I'm going for water," Edwin said. "You know, to the spring. I always fetch it. I've got the containers ready. Like to come?"

Daphne shook her head. "No," she said, "must take Prince. Honestly, Teddy, I don't think it's worth all the trouble you take—going to that so-called spring. Every time I pass there, in the car, you know, and I see you crouched there, in the rain sometimes, filling all those dreadful plastic things, I feel I must tell you that it isn't a sacred spring at all and you shouldn't kneel there, getting your knees wet. That water, honestly, Teddy, I bet it seeps down there from all sorts of horrid places, factories, septic tanks, the cemetery is not all that far away and the dogs' home. I wouldn't touch it. Honestly, Teddy!"

"You sound just like Cecilia," Edwin said.

Daphne paused on the path. "Well, I did promise to do my best to look after you," she said, "to convert you if necessary. I'm only trying!" She glanced back at the house. "However will you get rid of them?" she said.

"Supposed to be phoning the agent now." Edwin glanced too, with some uneasiness, at his own house, which had a secretive look about its front windows. He felt as if he were looking at his house for the first time and perhaps seeing it as a stranger might see it. "The owner's away," he said, moving his head slightly in the direction of the house next door. "Place has been let, on and off, for some years."

"Pity Cecilia isn't here," Daphne said. "She would straighten things."

Edwin sighed. He would have to manage, he told Daphne.

"That was a huge breakfast." Daphne changed the subject, but only partly. "I'll have to get Prince. I hope," she added, "you don't have troubles."

"I hope not," Edwin said.

♦ ♦ ♦

Leila's mother removed her washing from Edwin's bathroom. The two of them, Leila and her mother, carried the wet clothes to the neighboring garden, where they threw them over the clothesline. Edwin, watching from his study window, saw glimpses of Leila through the thick leafy bushes. She was walking about, eating. She seemed to have something in the palm of her hand. She ate quite hungrily, he thought, even though it was not long since breakfast. Her mother, as if unable to resist, began pulling up long grass and the tough stalks of weeds. These came up from the wet soil easily. He wondered how anyone could be enthusiastic enough about a garden belonging to someone else to pull out weeds.

Because of being disturbed, he had not followed his usual morning ritual. He thought about his violated bathroom and shuddered. When the telephone rang he thought it might be the agent. Leila's mother had said, before leaving with the washing, that she had left a message with the secretary, the agent not being in yet. She would wait at the house, she said, and not trouble Dr. Page with their presence a minute longer.

It was Cecilia. What was the time over there? she wanted to know. How was he? she wanted to know. Had he eaten the macaroni cheese? Yes, she was homesick as she always was. Yes, she was wanting to come straight home. She always felt like coming home, even before the plane took off. He heard her voice as plainly as if she were standing beside him. He almost put his hand out to touch her because of the sense of nearness. He tried to prolong the conversation, to hold on, somehow, to her voice. She wanted a quotation if he had something suitable. It was to match something in contemporary life, to sum up something about relationships. Yes, sexual. She was working on her paper during the journey. She was having a one-night stopover in London. Yes, the plane left midday tomorrow. Imagine, she wanted Edwin to imagine, after all this time what it was like to be back in London. She had forgotten the wet pavements and the smell of wet coats and wet shoes, the smell of wet people. So many people. Did he remember how many people? Crowds of people in the drizzling rain. No, not afraid coming down in the fog. Practically asleep then. He heard her laughing. She had upset a glass of Coke in her lap. Yes, in her lap. Cecilia laughing. Yes, it dried all right. She wrapped a British Airways blanket round herself and she dried while she was flying over the white sands of Saudi Arabia. Yes, salmon pink in the sunrise, or was it sunset; she was confused. Yes, she was warm. Yes, mostly she slept during the flight. Yes, she was afraid of landing. Yes, the plane stood still, dizzy as always, standing on nothing. Yes, dipping from one side to the other and then dropping down and down. Yes, hovering and sinking and then dropping down, and yes, the back gardens, emerging from the fog, rushed to meet them as they always did. Her bag, stuffed under her lap, was drenched with Coca-Cola too. It was all a huge joke. Yes, she'd bought a bottle of whisky on the plane. No, not a good one, not the one he liked. The plane was enormous. Only one kind of whisky, only bought it because everyone else was buying it. Laughing. To drink at home in the wardrobe. Plane full of Indians, Eurasians and English. The stewards were mainly elderly; they needed new uniforms but were very kind. Yes, mainly men. She had never imagined the plane would be so big and so full of people. She had forgotten, she said, how many people there were in the world and how many different kinds. Did he remember Vorwickl? she wanted to know. Ilse Vorwickl? She was glad he remembered. She was meeting Vorwickl tomorrow and they were traveling together on to Canada. Vorwickl was now Frau Doktor in . . . Edwin missed the name. But the quotation—could he find one for her?—was to fit the idea and don't be horrified, she said—she began to laugh again—but I'm dealing with snatched sex across the corner of the kitchen table, the unwanted pregnancy, the repetitive nature of the event, from the woman's point of view, the man, unwashed, not even taking off his clothes nor hers and having one hand reaching into the fridge, groping. Yes, groping for a beer. She wanted, she said, something literary, some metaphor or an image which would say all this by implication so that her paper, while being truthful, need not be too horrible. Yes, a point—to make a point of something all too familiar. Perhaps, she said, Euripides, something from the chorus, it did not need to be the hero or the heroine. Edwin, racing in his mind along his bookshelves, promised to look. The next minute Cecilia was saying little words of farewell, fond conventional words, and with a click she was gone.

◆ ◆ ◆

Leila's mother, who had come back into the house to strip the sheets off the spare bed, told Edwin that the agent had turned up with spare keys to let them into the house next door. She was, she said, going to wash the sheets and remake the bed nicely, and it was ever so good of him, she added, to have had the two of them to sleep the night. She would never be able to thank him enough, she said. "Leila would've come to say thank you," Leila's mother went on explaining, "but she would eat those radishes. I said to her, 'Leila,' I said, 'they're not digestible,' but would she listen! She's fetched them straight up, pardon me for mentioning, but that's why she's not come back over to say thank you. Really, young people! They will not be told! Especially if there's a craving!"

Edwin, with the half-smile of politeness still frozen on his face, went to his study. There was a sweet fragrance in the room. The white roses, the little Iceberg buds, had opened. Their perfection was enhanced, he thought as he bent over them, by a slight flaw. The delicately perfumed petals were beginning to turn brown along their crinkled edges. Of course he remembered Vorwickl, one of Cecilia's friends when she was a student. He had tried at one time to help her learn English. They had all tried. In desperation Edwin paraphrased, against his inclinations, one of Shakespeare's sonnets. Vorwickl's eyes, bulging behind her thick-lensed spectacles, were eager and intelligent. She grasped the meaning immediately, asking:

"Bot vy some many vorts und fourteen lines to tell soch a small ding!" Edwin, cursing the organizers of the English course, did not try to explain. He was dreading her reaction to the ballad which was included in the next exercise.

He hid in his study until there were no more sounds of other people in his house.

"**M**edievalism meets the Renaissance!" Daphne called as she strode towards Edwin. Prince, in a kind of mad ecstasy, bounded forward. The plantation resounded with his joyful barking.

"Heel! Prince!" Daphne bellowed. "Here, Prince! Heel!"

Edwin thought they could not know the full strength of her voice at St. Monica's.

"I was hoping you'd be having a walk," Daphne said.

"I was hoping I'd find you too." Edwin had more in his voice than mere good manners. He had hurried from the university and had not stopped in the little park to watch the children playing as he sometimes did. He wanted to be with Daphne and, because of this hurrying, was out of breath.

Walking in the pines was something they all did, Daphne, Cecilia and Edwin. Edwin jogged there too on the days when he particularly noticed his stomach. Now, because he was trying to think of Cecilia, he hoped that being with Daphne he would, in her forceful company, be able to discipline his mind. Daphne hurled a stick for Prince, who went after it willingly. She shivered as a cold wind rushed between the trees.

At all times of the day the pines had their own variation of color and atmosphere. In the mornings they were green in the misty sunshine, and the tufted grass, from a slight distance, sparkled with moisture and looked smooth, like a carpet, spreading over little slopes and rises between the trees. The pines, uniformly apart, all grew to the same height, though here and there one a little taller topped the others.

In an effort to recall and think about Cecilia he remembered the silver-backed hairbrush, a present from her on his last birthday. "Real bristle, not nylon," Cecilia said. Unwrapping the brush from folds of white tissue paper, Edwin caught in his left hand a little piece of ornamental card which bore the statement *Anthrax Impossible*. Moving the card to his other hand, he stared at it. The possibility had never occurred to him. He looked up "anthrax" in the dictionary, his birthday egg getting cold. " 'Malignant boil. Disease of sheep and cattle.' " He read it aloud.

"Wear your wig then if you're worried," Cecilia said, "and you can use the brush on that and observe it for symptoms." She began to giggle. "Wig," she said. "Nothing abnormal discovered." She was helpless with mirth and upset her coffee.

They both possessed wigs for those occasions demanding change. The parties they went to, their social life as Cecilia called it, in italics, she said, consisted often of people who were not being themselves. Being someone else and not being themselves, they often threw off their clothes, or some of them, between two and three in the morning. They gave each other pet names and pretended relationships. They dressed themselves in Glad Wrap and said they were sure to get AIDS and stayed on for breakfast. Edwin's conclusions on the way home from these events were usually written up at great length in his notebook of the intangible. He intended one day to read this notebook, and the others, aloud to Cecilia or perhaps, later, to have them published and left as a gift to her.

Cecilia, whose own hair was bright and blond and curly, had a wig which was streaked with gray. "It's called pepper-and-salt," she said, laughing, to Edwin when he protested. She declared the wig made her into a bird of prey. "I'm an eagle, a hawk, a falcon about to swoop. That's my new image."

Edwin's wig was white-haired; the wispiness, he thought, made him look like a poet. "I'm a poet," he said. The white hair enhanced his suntanned look.

"More like the head of my old department," Cecilia said, looking closely at herself in the mirror. "Remember old Stirrups?"

Often Edwin grumbled about his thickening bulging waist. "A corset is what you need." Cecilia poked at his flesh with capable fingers. That was why he liked the bathroom to himself. Sometimes he forgot the little corset and left it hanging on the back of the door. Cecilia had something also; she called it a merry widow. She did not wear it often.

The pines always reflected something different. He forgot about their fragrance until it surrounded him on hot days. When it was hot, and a small scented wind caressed him gently, he did not remember the rain dripping through the branches at other times of the year.

The wind, rushing, sighed and seemed to moan in the dark tops of the trees. Daphne's face was quite red. Their feet seemed to sink and rise as they walked on the yielding pine-needled ground. Raindrops, left from a recent downfall, hung above them and fell in scattering little showers from time to time. The plantation was deserted.

"Father was awfully foolish about Miss Heller, you know," Daphne said as they walked side by side where the path widened between the stiff black trees. Because of the delicate nature of the subject, she dropped her voice. She slackened her speed. Edwin was glad to adjust his step to hers.

"I don't talk about this as a rule," she said.

"Of course not," Edwin replied in the voice he kept for occasions which required tact and tenderness.

"It's all over and done with now, but it was a very painful thing. I don't mean that Father meant to deceive me, but anything like this does deceive someone. It was because he did not want to hurt me, I quite see that. He simply never said anything. He never told me and I had to"—her voice seemed to give way—"I had to make certain discoveries for myself," she added.

Edwin cleared his throat. He had not intended an emotional conversation. He realized he should not have expected to escape from Daphne's feelings when he, after trying to think and talk about Cecilia, began to tell Daphne about Leila.

"I find I can't get her out of my mind." He wanted to talk about Leila but was surprised at his own words, wishing to check them and to go on saying them at the same time. There were so many things he wanted to say about Leila. It had been a shock to realize that for a few days he had forgotten to examine himself for blemishes and symptoms, though he had taken trouble with his hair and eyebrows. The dry patch on his shin, for example: he had not made any further notes on it. He was not even sure, as he walked, whether he still had the patch of dry skin. He had no idea whether the condition was spreading. His book of the body was absolutely neglected.

"It isn't," Daphne was saying, "that Miss Heller wasn't awfully kind or that she wasn't a good housekeeper. You remember what she was like, of course?"

Edwin did remember a faded, grayish woman who sat, with quiet patience, at old Dr. Hockley's bedside during his final illness. Miss Heller had blossomed, if it could be described like that, into a very different Miss Heller now. He thought Daphne was crying. He had not meant to upset her. Glancing quickly at her, he saw that she brushed her cheek with the back of her yellow string glove.

"The wind," she said as if to explain the tears. "It's getting dark; we must be turning back."

"Of course," Edwin said quickly. "I must explain it is all because of how Leila feels towards me: it is entirely . . ." He looked at Daphne, wondering if she would understand. "She is unawakened; it is a presexual feeling she has for me. Perhaps she is looking for a father figure . . . I don't know." He paused, knowing he was falling into despicable jargon, one of the many phrases Cecilia used and mocked. Phrases which could be used to dismiss someone else's relationship could not be applied to Leila. The word "relationship" was not even correct.

"I understand," Daphne said. "I do understand." He was grateful for her fervor.

"For three days," he said, "Leila . . ." He paused, awkward with the name, knowing that he was self-conscious. "Leila," he went on, "has been coming with all sorts of reasons for coming. The first day was because the oven in their house was hopeless and could they put a cake in my oven. It was all mixed and in the tin; naturally I said yes. It's a terrific cake; it's taken Leila's mother three days to ice it. 'It'll be a lovely cake,' Leila said to me. 'It takes Mother three whole days to ice this kind of cake.'"

They walked in silence as if they were both occupied with an unspeakable vision of this troublesome cake. "And then," Edwin said, "they wanted to invite me to a meal because I had been so kind to them, and as my oven was the better one, Leila's mother asked if she could prepare the meal in my kitchen."

"So of course you said yes." Daphne threw a fresh stick. "Here, Prince!" Her voice rang through the trees.

"That's right, I did." Edwin in an absentminded way watched Daphne's dog. "And then Leila's mother," he said, "thought that the cutlery provided in their house was awful, 'cheap and nasty,' she said; she wouldn't want me to eat with it. So I then said to her to use mine, and so it seemed simpler to eat the meal, which was by the way delicious, in my house. And today when I came home Leila was playing records. . . ."

"In your place? Your house?" Daphne stood still. They both stood still and watched while Prince ate the stick he had retrieved.

"I've said all along he's insane," Edwin said.

"Yes, I'm inclined to agree with you." Daphne found another stick and threw it. "Playing records," she said, "in your house on your player in your . . ."

"Yes," Edwin said. "The hot water system in that house is apparently quite useless, and her mother was sure that I wouldn't mind if she, Leila, washed her hair in my bathroom. And there she was curled up in an armchair with her head in a towel and the whole house full of what the dear child calls music. It was only one record; she'd bought it the day before and wanted to hear it. She must have played it a dozen times, over and over again."

"No record player in the house next door," Daphne said.

"Yes, that's right." Edwin paused. "She kept playing the

record and then she told me she hoped I wouldn't mind her saying what she was going to say and of course I said no of course I wouldn't mind and she then told me that she liked me very much. She had really liked me straight away. She had never in her life ever really liked anyone as she liked me. She said she felt more at home in my house than in any other house. . . ."

"Oh Lord!" Daphne said. "All I know is that Father was most awfully foolish, Teddy, over Miss Heller. He was completely taken up in a sort of splendid insane self-exaltation. He thought he could do and have anything and give it all to poor Miss Heller, who, as you know, did not turn out to be all that poor. I would not be in the rather straitened circumstances . . . That reminds me: Miss Heller's new bank—she's always falling out with bank managers—her new bank has a name which sounds like some kind of sensible tampon. I have to take her to see the new manager . . . can't remember the name. Anyway that's not what I'm trying to say. . . ." Her voice broke and she turned away, calling, "Prince! Here, Prince!" her voice recovering as voices do when in command of wayward dogs. She turned to Edwin. "I feel sort of responsible, Teddy, while Cecilia's away," she said. "You will have to be very firm. You must not be available. You must try not to be available and the house must not be available. Have it painted throughout, or something, to make it thoroughly uncomfortable. It's the only way. Sometimes," she continued, "men are flattered by younger women. Miss Heller, d'you see, was so much younger than Father, but the youthfulness was not only in years. He could teach her . . . all sorts of things, and . . . oh well! Never mind all that. How old is Leila?"

"I don't know," he said.

"It sounds to me," Daphne said after a moment of consideration, "very like what we, at St. Monica's, call a crush. You know the sort of thing. One of the girls feels very passionate about one of the mistresses. For a time—while the crush is on—the girl in question wants to praise the mistress in all sorts of ways. She wants to pay homage to her and do things for her. All very ennobling. Quite embarrassing!" Edwin, turning, noticed Daphne's slight blush, which spread deepening on either side of her neck. "Fiorella," Daphne said, "is at present, at the present time, addressing all the poems she writes to me. She writes several every day. Naturally I do not want to hurt her feelings, but I do take care not to encourage her too much in the direction her poetry is taking. It's one of the problems of boarding school. Fiorella's mother too." She sighed. "She has done that thing in Venetian needlepoint. It must have taken her ages. It's for me. I think I'm supposed to wear it, but I'm not sure if it goes on top of my clothes or underneath like a vest—an English vest, you understand."

Edwin glanced quickly at Daphne. He saw that she was not in the least critical and felt relieved. She had a kind face. He had always thought that. Her chin was large and rather square; her features, though heavy, were handsome.

"So you don't know her age." Daphne was thoughtful.

"No, I haven't any idea," he said.

"Cecilia's good at guessing ages," Daphne said. "It's a pity she's not here."

Edwin was not sure that he wanted Cecilia just now. He said nothing. Leila's mother was cooking a dinner. "I'll pop a roast in," she had said. "Roast pork and applesauce—how does that sound?"

"It sounds very good," Edwin, who was usually nervous about pork, had replied, with one of his most charming smiles.

As they came to the edge of the pines they paused before crossing the road. Edwin looked forward, he realized, with eagerness to standing at the head of his dining table, stripping off the crackling and carving the meat, and asking Leila and her mother in turn (they would be on either side of him) how they liked their meat and one potato or two? He was hungry. He smiled slightly at the thought of the fruit pie which was to follow the pork.

"You could get the painters in," Daphne was saying, "and have the house rewired at the same time. That really makes a terrible mess."

"I'm not sure that Cecilia would like that," Edwin said, with his practiced slow gentleness. He could imagine all too easily the discomforts: Leila's mother in the bathroom or that awful man Hodd, or whatever his name was, the endlessly talkative electrician. "Cecilia might not like the house done while she is away. It wouldn't be kind to her to do something she wouldn't like," he said.

"No, I suppose not," Daphne said, "and she really is attached to the cabbage roses. You wouldn't want to do anything that might upset her."

"No," Edwin said.

They crossed the road.

She looked like a poached egg, her daddy said, when she was born, but everybody else saw Queen Victoria. 'My!'—they all said it—'She's Queen Victoria.' Well, it's funny, isn't it—I mean Queen Victoria, dead all these years and not even a relation. You must miss a lot not having kiddies of your own. Dr. Sissilly must in her most secret heart wish for a little boy or girl just like you. All of us ladies are mothers in our real true hearts. . . ."

Edwin, waking suddenly, seemed to be hearing Leila's mother still as he heard her, filled with roast dinner, over the coffee cups. His own replies came back to him, word for word, his pillow suddenly uncomfortable and something about the bed making him turn over, trying to put aside the words he'd said. Yes, he'd said, he agreed they, he and Cecilia, did miss awfully having children, expanding, children led to pets and

— 48 —

sports and parties and hobbies—all sorts of things and places and holidays one would never have thought of. It was so sad, he explained during Leila's mother's third glass of port, Cecilia having three abortions—miscarriages. Quickly he changed from the more technical to the popular, thinking that he saw Leila's mother stiffen slightly at the implications carried in the word "abortion."

"Aw! Lorst three little ones; that is sad, very sad!" Leila's mother squinted at the ruby liquid. "Goodness, I am clucky this evening." She rustled and settled more comfortably in the nest of cushions Edwin had made for her. "Funny thing—I seem to hear a baby crying in this house," she said. "I wonder if the tea leaves would tell me something tomorrow. Remind me, Leila: tea leaves in the morning." She sighed. "Nursery ready three times." She shook her head. "Children," she said, "they're like teeth, all trouble. Trouble coming, trouble while you've got them and trouble when they go. But for all that who'd be without them!"

He thought Leila was smiling at him during this conversation. She was turning the pages of a magazine and gazing, with her head on one side, at pictures of royal wedding dresses. "Beautiful Brides": Edwin read the heading; it was upside down for him. He thought Leila glanced at him several times with quick little shy smiles. To enter a conspiracy he returned the smiles, but each time Leila seemed to be turning another page, absorbed afresh in a world of white lace and demure expressions. Now he was not certain if her smile was for him or simply for the happiness of the queens and princesses on the thick pages. Leila's mother, her mind clearly on blue and pink cradles, was having her own smiles over real or imagined little bodies and limbs—dressed of course in pretty clothes. She enjoyed, she said, just talking about baby clothes.

Edwin turned over again, in that curious restlessness which accompanies the self-torture of going over things said in conversations and the wish, later, to be able to unsay them. While talking to Leila's mother it was not difficult to imagine Cecilia, delicate and thin-fingered, crying and crying in a hospital bed,

— 49 —

not at the Mary and Joseph, of course, but in a place some-where in the mountains, near Zurich or not far from Vienna, so that a world-famous obstetrician could be in attendance. While talking to Leila's mother he had imagined easily the way in which Cecilia, hot with an unforeseen complicating infection, would have put her small but capable hands into his. The first time and the second time in similar circumstances, but the third perhaps different, perhaps in a hospice run by an obscure order of nuns on the outskirts of Budapest, where they, he and Cecilia, would have been on holiday, the con-finement coming upon them before time—not full term, he corrected himself. This time, no crying and no tears, only something like a pretense of not minding. That it was better this way. The whole sad thing bundled up in a small sheet and carried away in the gnarled hands of an ancient nun, leaving them with endlessly empty freedom to do all the things they were supposed to like doing. Having children, they decided, wordlessly, really meant there was never a time without some kind of anxiety, and always there was the responsibility.

With all the care in the world you could never know how your child would turn out. Euripides knew what he was talk-ing about when he gave the words, *They can never know whether all their toil / Is spent for worthy or worthless chil-dren* to an old woman in the chorus. And Cardano (Renais-sance lecture number 1), relentlessly honest, made it quite clear that most of his own misery was brought about by the stupidity of his sons.

It was impossible to sleep with so many thoughts crowding one after the other. He was absolutely awake. He thought about lace. Leila liked a wedding dress which was decorated with it, a square of heavy lace on the bodice of the dress. She had drawn attention to it. He thought the thick lace made a sort of breastplate, an armor, but did not say so. Now he won-dered did Leila know about lace? Mechlin, Honiton, Chan-tilly—there were so many elaborate designs and patterns. Leila and her mother liked clothes, it was clear, but they had no taste. Green and white. He thought he would like to dress

Leila in the colors of the Elizabethan court, the area of his thesis years ago, and now rather in obscurity like so much of his work. Leila in these colors . . . he would make the suggestion at the right moment. He sat up.

"Pork takes five hours to digest." He remembered reading this in a pamphlet on the human body, or was it, he pondered, in a recipe book? He often read recipe books. He had read too, in another book, about a man industriously eating an enormous meal one night and then waking up, a few hours later, completely crippled with arthritis. Carefully he tried to move his legs. They moved and he felt no pain. He switched on the light and studied his hands. They did not look gnarled, though the veins were enlarged as if sluggish. Perhaps, he thought, turning his hands over, he should note in writing the condition of his veins. He reached for two of his body books. He opened the one for the internal. He sat tense and upright in bed, wondering what his symptoms were.

> *You're my only occupation*
> *   my only situation yair yair yair*
> *everything I hold so dear huh huh huh*
> *only because you are near yair yair yair*

He tried to scribble down the words of Leila's record, what he thought he'd heard. He had the tune in his head. He sang what he heard in his head. It was not as it should be, but pleasing all the same to have something to sing.

> *The words you say hula hula hup*
> *   in your own way yuppy tuppy yair yair*
> *can fill my heart with sunshine huh huh huh hula hula hup*
> *   huppy*
> *and then I know you'll always be mine huh huh yair yair*
> *you're my only occupation yair yair yair*

Leila's record was played several times, and Leila's mother had shown him a photograph album containing pictures of

Leila as a square-shaped little girl with a solemn face.

"She was always sturdy and very healthy," Leila's mother assured him, "the biggest little girl in her class."

Thinking about Leila, Edwin wished he could take her for a long walk somewhere, not too far away, secluded and pleasant, where he could talk to her and encourage her to talk to him. Her mother did all the talking when they were together. He wondered about the plantation. There they would be sure to meet Daphne. She took Prince for walks twice a day, sometimes three times. Other people walked in the pines too. Littering the sandy tufts of grass and the paths were squashed chocolate-milk cartons and the remnants of more intimate things discarded, the relics of human relationships, as Daphne had once described the rubbish. She chose times to walk when other people would be cooking and eating and safely at home watching television. If Edwin and Leila walked then to avoid these other people, they would be sure to meet Daphne.

At a party once everyone had been asked to write down what it was had kept them alive till the age of a hundred and one. And then they had guessed from the papers read aloud (anonymously) who had written the different recipes for a long life. Edwin reread now some of the things noted afterwards in his book of the intangible:

Taking walks with my dog every day (Daphne)
Laughing (Cecilia)

His own contribution was the raw egg diet he was on at the time and some details of ritual washing and a sort of ritual lovemaking he had studied. He was off the raw eggs but still followed the other two. As he read now he saw them in context with Leila. He decided he would give her a book of poems. She was unspoiled in the literary sense. One of the advantages of having a mother like Leila's mother was that Leila could, without anyone being hurt, be educated a little. Leila's mother, he felt sure, would encourage him.

When Cecilia telephoned, Edwin did not tell her about the visitors. What time was it over there she wanted to know. Vorwickl had missed her connection. Yes it was lonely. Vorwickl was to arrive a day late. Yes tomorrow. Look forward he told her. I'll do that she said. How was he she wanted to know. Had he eaten the macaroni cheese yet? She had two bathrooms; she was laughing. A white rose in one and a dark red rose in the other. Fresh little basket of fruit and another little basket of sewing things and a whole bottle of whisky all to herself. A present. In the bathroom he asked. He thought he heard her laughing. She had killed a cockroach. A cockeroach in the exquisite apartment. No sorry suite. She couldn't work the taps she told him. Phone the manager he said. I have she said. You can sit on the toilet and phone all sorts of people. No not on the lavatory now. Laughing again; he thought he heard her laughing. But the hotel housekeeper she said such a lovely soothing voice Canadian and polite and kind. Lovely he said. No tea she said. Drink whisky he said. I'll do that she said she missed the tea. Had he remembered the quotation she wanted to know. He was still searching he told her books everywhere. Nose in book he said. She was sure she said he'd come up with something suitable. The conference she said. How's the conference he asked. The delegates she told him some of them were in love with themselves. Self-abuse he said. She was laughing. One female she told him from the U.S. she said a gynecologist read herself into a trance with the most boring wandering lengthy paper. Good heavens he said. Yes she said this gynecologist pleased with herself did not notice the audience slowly getting up and leaving on bent legs. I get the picture he said. Yes she said this woman had to be helped down the steps of the platform, stage—whatever; she didn't know where she was. Potted palms she said. Lovely he said. The dining room she told him superb. Eat it all he said. I am she said. Bronze helmets full; roast potatoes. Bronze helmets he asked. Yes dishes she said. Roast beef and roast pork on spikes every roast has a gentleman carver. Sounds good he said. It is she said. Ornamental. Food in a colored mountain. Cakes. A tower of puff pastry balls held together in a sweet golden syrup. Maple syrup he supposed. Yes she said must be maple syrup. What about he said that remark of Jason's *If only children could be got some other way without the female sex* it could be twisted to meet the needs of her paper. Most of the papers were boring that's why she was eating too much. She had missed what he had just said would he say it again. I'll write it he said. No she had not been interviewed. Don't be sad he said go and buy something nice to wear Canadian wolf he said. She was missing him she said. He said he missed her. She would need something warm to wear she said. The wind. Also she would get too fat she said. Nonsense he said love you love you. Last night she told him the renowned obstetrician the Frau Doktor von Eppell threw a raincoat at one of the organizers. Conference organizer. Von Eppell from Vienna. Fat. It was the organizer's own raincoat which he offered to lend. Disgusted and offended he supposed. Yes yes she said the garment very shabby. Looked awful she said lying on the carpet in the magnificent lobby of the hotel. Yes she had her own coat thirty-four floors up but they were being hustled off to a reception party in another building. The wind bitterly cold she said. Yes she was warm enough. All this luxury she said need to share with . . . The Viennese obstetrician he said. She was laughing. Yes she speaks English. You could sit in a Mexican restaurant and talk shop he said. Don't like Mexican she said. Canadian he said. Yes she said. She had three lamps five armchairs a dozen shelves and cupboards six mirrors a writing table a coffee table and a king-size bed. Round. Would take three. Who shall we have in bed with us think about it she said. I'll do that he said. She couldn't turn off the telly she moaned whenever she turned the knob she got another program. Hang your towel over it he said. I'll do that she said the radio won't turn off either. Country cousin he said. He heard her laughter pealing in a far-off place. Fresh salmon she managed. That's nice he said. My room my suite she said is on the twenty-third floor. Should be a good view he said. Yes the lake a Great Lake beautiful but cold shines cold. The lake he told her is polluted. All the lakes are polluted don't drink them. I'll try not to she said. Someone coming to the door he said can hear someone coming to the door. Ring you tomorrow she said. Goodbye sweetheart he said. Trouble with being away she said I picture you as you used to be. That's nice he said. Love you love you she said and with a click she was gone.

He heard Leila's mother and Leila pitting the veranda with their heels. He told himself as he opened the front door that he had intended to tell Cecilia about the visitors.

And another thing, I simply have no real idea of her age. Leila, sixteen? Oh my God! Sixteen, fifteen? Worse! No, twenty-two surely, or twenty-three—that's more like it." Edwin, walking in the pine plantation, talking to himself, surprising himself with his own voice, waited in one place, hoping that Daphne would be coming with Prince. He was almost certain which tree Daphne would reach by a certain time. This time she was obviously late. He was about to leave when he saw her approaching, walking very fast. From a distance he was able to see her expression was grim. She seemed to be walking without pleasure. Prince ran in circles, disappearing and appearing in his usual way. She was obviously not expecting to meet Edwin.

"Teddy!" she said, her expression changing as she saw him.

"You're later than usual," he said.

"Yes," she said. "Today is my golf day as you know." Edwin had forgotten. Daphne's life was divided into her days—one for her horse, one for tennis, one for golf and four for school. They flashed through his apologetic mind. "And tonight," Daphne continued, "I have to be back at school for our rehearsal—it's nearly parents' weekend." Edwin nodded. "While I was at golf," Daphne continued, "Prince got out and ate a bikini."

With visions of solid legs beneath stocky sensible tweed skirts, large blouses, and shapeless felt hats pulled firmly over brindled hair, he said, "Bikinis? At golf? That must be a sight, Daph; where do you all strip off?"

"Oh don't, Teddy," Daphne groaned. "It was too awful. I found him with what I thought was a bit of rag. He has a weakness for clothes. I got the rag away from him and pushed it into the dustbin. You see, cloth does awful things to his bowels. Then just now, when I was about to come out, my neighbor rang. You see, she knows Prince. Apparently she'd spent the whole day trying to find something smart yet big enough, something she could actually get into. She'd come home. Left her shopping on the veranda and the next minute it, the bikini, was gone." Daphne sighed. "I went to the bin, fished out the rags, washed them and took the unspeakable remains round there and apologized. It took simply ages and here I am two hundred dollars down the drain and all that groveling. I'm worn out!"

"They must have had gold sequins on them," Edwin said in his most considerate and consoling manner.

"Everything's so damned expensive nowadays," Daphne said. "Well, enough of that," she added. "Any news of Cecilia?" He matched his walk to her stride. He shook his head. It was Leila he wanted to talk about.

"I simply have no idea of Leila's age," he said. "Sometimes she seems a mere child of seventeen or less and sometimes she's a mature young woman in her early thirties." He liked dwelling on thoughts of Leila's appearance.

"Which is still very young for people of our day and age," Daphne said, with what Edwin felt to be a rather unnecessary forthright tone. "I suppose they've come back, have they," she said.

"Yes," Edwin said. "It's rats."

"In the next-door house? Rats?"

"Yes. Rats."

"I'm not throwing sticks for anyone who eats other people's clothes," Daphne said sternly as Prince, leaping up madly, put his front paws on her chest. "Off with you!" She searched for and found a stick. "I suppose you can't get them to leave," she said. "It's one thing to be friendly to people next door, just friendly"—she seemed to be recalling her own neighbors—"and another to have them squatting."

Edwin, thinking of the bathroom, sighed. They should have had a second bathroom, perhaps even a third, when all their friends and acquaintances went bathroom mad. The Fairfaxes had had two, one each side of the master bedroom. A blue door to his and a soft rose pink for hers. Ida Fairfax, for a time, said at parties that she just loved to roll out of bed and onto the loo.

"There's only one thing to do," Daphne said. "If you won't have the decorators in, you'll have to have a houseguest turn up suddenly. Someone who'll be dreadfully in the way, in the bath all the time or on the phone for hours, someone who'll use up all the milk, preferably someone who can bring a pet, a dog." They both looked at Prince. Edwin looked away from him quickly. Had he really wanted pets? "I've even a better idea." Daphne became excited. "A weekend of sin under your roof. They would leave then. Champagne," she said, "music late at night in the bathroom, squeals from the bedroom, coming in late for breakfast, undressed still, and going back to bed till lunchtime, taking lunch back to bed, a hot lunch in bed, that sort of thing." Edwin stared at her. "You could have the music of 'Hiawatha'; it's supposed to be frightfully erotic. I've got it somewhere." She bent down. "Look the other way or something, Teddy," she said, "while I do something absolutely awful to help Prince get rid of this half-eaten stick."

Edwin looked through the motionless trees. It was beginning to get dark. No one was about. Daphne was speaking to her dog. He could not hear what she was saying. On the edge of the dark plantation, at the side of the road, on the edge of the suburb, hearing the distant noise of traffic on the main road and hearing Daphne's voice caressing her dog, he felt terribly alone. It was a sudden feeling of desolation similar to those feelings at boarding school in the time between afternoon school and tea, or that hour in the early morning before the bell rang for breakfast. Edwin pushed his hands into his pockets, a schoolboy's habit, perhaps to find the consolation of some schoolboyish treasure left in the torn lining. There would be lights on in his house. The warm smell of cooking would greet him as soon as he stepped indoors. Leila would come out into the hall, pleased to see him. He could not wait for her pleasure.

"To get rid of these people, Leila's mother and Leila," Daphne was saying, "it is essential that you have an affair. You must fill them with disgust at your behavior while your wife is away. You must do it for Cecilia."

"Yes, but who shall I have an affair with?" he asked with suitable gestures of despair.

"With me, of course," Daphne said. "I've just thought it all out. They will think that it's been going on for ages, that you are truly awful and that I'm awful too." She was excited. "I never thought I could be so creative, Teddy!" she said. "They say that man—meaning women and men—that man creates best from that which is the rejected part of him. I'll bring

Prince. What an inspiration! He can eat Leila's clothes. Will you be sure to get in the champers, Teddy? We'll need a dozen bottles, at least."

"Have you ever considered adopting?" Leila's mother asked Edwin. Every morning she studied the tea leaves at the bottom of his cup. She reported seeing money, a great deal of money, and a cradle and a boy's bicycle. In Leila's cup she repeatedly saw a ring. "Either a friendship or a wedding, Leila," she said. She even saw in Edwin's cup, one morning, what she called strife between father and son. Edwin, hearing the word "father" applied to him, experienced strange sensations. He wondered which notebook. He could not think of a suitable title for the entry and he pondered for some time on the correct way for it to be listed in the index. He had to admit to himself as he sat in the ice cream parlor (Leila's mother had fancied an ice) that lately he had not written in any of his notebooks. He had forgotten to record the external and the internal and the intangible. He simply was neglecting to keep his records up to date. Certain aspects of his life were going on as usual. He went to the university most days, gave his lectures and tutorials and spent the usual time in study and preparation. With a reluctant honesty he knew he was thinking more about Leila instead of reading the students' assignments with the care they deserved. Often the lunchtime noises coming across the grass to his quiet room seemed to him to be like the dull roar of a distant football match or the crowds waiting for a royal bride to appear on the balcony of a palace. From other directions there was often music. Listening to it, he smiled over the heap of dull essays. It was Leila's sort of music; it had a steady deep beat and a thin plaintive howling which was, he knew, the singing. Liking the sound, he often opened his window. Later, when all was quiet except for the ever-present factory-like noise of a massive air-conditioning plant, he would give himself up to his now habitual pleasant little dream of Leila. He had no right to this little dream, but its impossibility made it all the sweeter.

Quite clearly Leila and her mother admired him. It was easy to enjoy approval and admiration even without any recent practice. One morning he found, when searching among his clothes, a youthful yellow tie and some socks patterned with cream triangles. He felt quite excited when he put them on. It was like being young again to wear them.

Sometimes he pushed aside the neatly written pages he was marking and tried to think of poems which expressed his feelings. *Lovely Laura in her light green dress*—a misquotation probably, but it did not matter. Leila would look nice in green, a soft fresh green like the new leaves bursting along the almond branch. Almond blossom, that was pretty and would be like the colors of Leila's unspoiled skin. Her skin, what he had seen of it, was fresh and sweet and smooth. He often, in his imagination, saw the whole of her young body without clothes.

Once, going to the staff room at afternoon teatime, his heart and mind pleasantly occupied with Leila images, he bent down to the table, and turning the tap of the urn marked Coffee, he filled a cup which had been standing ready with a tea bag. Straightening up quickly from the urn, he was sure he had seen Ms. Tranby nudge the Head and Miss Bushby (or whatever her name was) simultaneously in their respective well-covered ribs. Tranby's elbows, he thought, seemed to jerk upwards in both directions with surprising speed and sharpness, and as he made for the door with his cup, it seemed as if a watchful silence was directed towards his mistake. He did not have to imagine much to know the half-pitying laughter which would accompany the retellings. Someone—Miss Bushby or was the woman called Burton? he could never remember—catching him by the sleeve, offered him home-made nut cookies. "Delicious, even if I, as I shouldn't, say so myself!" Trying not to be impolite, he half-turned as the plate was tilting towards him, his incapable hand missing the biscuits as they slid over the edge.

"Bad luck, Page!" He felt he must get away quickly from the inevitable words which would follow. The head of the department, a tall blond Scandinavian, as if catching Edwin's glance of annoyance, detached himself from Ms. Tranby's all too familiar way of hanging on to his arm. He moved towards Edwin, unwanted conversation beginning to drop, with chopped nuts, from his lips.

Polka dots on a yellow tie: the Tranby woman would make the most of them. A wrinkly who ought to be watching his ticker, his old ticker, trying to get up steps two at a time, showing his yellow socks. She never missed anything. His socks and his tie: he wanted to get them off at once. He wanted to get up to his room—damn the stairs, he was out of breath—up to his room and out of sight as quickly as possible. It was ridiculous having a staff common room in the basement.

Tranby and Bushby—or was it Burton?—would be sure to know he had people staying in his house while Cecilia was away. Of course it did not matter that he had guests. He would tell Cecilia and she would say it was hilarious. Reasonably it did not matter, his having guests. He knew this and knew too his unreasonable reason for not wanting anyone to know.

♦ ♦ ♦

It seemed to Edwin that Leila's mother was being careful, all the time, not to intrude. She spent her time mostly in the kitchen, either squeezing yellow and blue sponges and washing the edges of the table and the cupboards or filling the kettle. Sometimes when he entered the kitchen she was putting something in the oven. More often, she seemed to be taking something, golden brown scones or sausage rolls, out.

He noticed the little flourishes with which she placed her baking trays on the table. When she was cooking she seemed kind and wholesome and there was nothing sinister about her at all. At other times, when he was thinking about her and not seeing her, he was overcome with a kind of helpless amazement that she was in his house at all. Her way of getting into the house, by invitation from him, was frightening. At these times, unable to bear these thoughts, he turned to thinking about Leila and some of her delightful quiet little ways. One of the things she did was to look up at him with the sweetest smile. He liked to think that no other person had ever seen this smile.

◆ ◆ ◆

"These cups," Leila's mother would say in the mornings. "The excitement's almost too much. It's like going to the theatre." She tipped the cups as she read the leaves. There was quite a tension during these readings, particularly on one day when Leila's mother, peering into Edwin's cup and then into Leila's, looked up first at Edwin and then, searchingly, at Leila. Shaking her head, she looked up at the ceiling and then again at Leila and at Edwin, saying at intervals, "Well, I never!" and "Who'd have thought it!" She told them they could knock her down with a feather. She would have to watch the leaves carefully, she said, for an accident. At present she did not know what sort of an accident. You never could tell, she said; there might just be a sign, a warning, a promise. She set her lips in a thin line and rinsed the cups quickly under the cold tap.

Leila's mother did not often have ice cream, she said. She was a weight watcher and nothing in her opinion put it on as quick as ice cream. But the rat the other night had given her a shock, she said, and she was still all jittery and shaky. Sometimes she had noticed if she had the jitters something sweet put her to rights. She was ever so grateful, so was Leila, she said, that Edwin had invited them back into his house till the agent got rid of the rats in theirs. She was enjoying her ice cream even though she was overweight. Being overweight, she said, the flesh did protect the organs. She had a hazelnut whirl covered with a hot caramel sauce. The hot sauce, she said, leaning forward on the little wrought-iron chair, stops it going for your teeth. Leila had a strawberry ice with real cream and little bits of strawberries and Edwin's was green. He thought it was either almond or pistachio.

"If you don't come at adoption," Leila's mother said, "there's always whatsaname, whatyoucallit, the surrated mother, sugared whatsit, thingumajig sugar mother."

"Surrogate," Edwin said with the polite little laugh of correction. He had corrected her on this one before, he reminded her.

"Better than adopting," Leila's mother said, "like a cake you've made yourself, a home-made cake. You know what's in it. I always say home-cooked is best. You can't go wrong."

◆ ◆ ◆

In the evenings Leila's mother was quite willing to sit through Brahms. When Edwin suggested the TV in the other room, she said no, she had always enjoyed classical music. She seemed to efface herself at times, Edwin thought, as if trying not to be a nuisance. She occupied herself with her knitting, which was white, he noticed, with very small sleeves or perhaps, he thought, they were fingers for gloves. But who would want only two fingers? Leila simply smiled her small pink-lipped smile and did not offer explanations. He wanted to talk to Leila about the music.

"Have you read Ecclesiastes?" he wanted to ask. He wanted to explain to her that after a broad survey of the world, Ecclesiastes concludes: "therefore I praise the dead more than the living but above all I praise those who never were born." He glanced at Leila's mother, who was intent on her stitches. "In this music," he wanted to tell Leila, "in this third song of Brahms, the third of the Four Serious Songs, Brahms makes use of this text. And concert audiences," he wanted to add, "actually listen to it without wincing!" He had never said anything of this to Cecilia, and though this left him free to speak about it to Leila, he felt he should not because of Cecilia not knowing what it was her right, in a sense, to know first.

"What on earth are these?" Edwin unwrapped a small package. The striped paper—he recognized the local draper's wrapping—was not gift paper.

"I think they're called Playboy Jocks," Daphne said. "I bought them for you. They're more dashing than plain boxers or B.V.D.s—they have a sort of pattern, d'you see, bows and arrows—aren't they?"

"You're very knowledgeable." Edwin smiled.

"Oh, Mr. Barclay was most helpful. He is really one of those people who love their work. Imagine selling men's underwear all day and every day and being fond of it."

"Thank you for the present," Edwin said. He glanced at her luggage. "Whatever is that?"

"My portable gramophone," Daphne said. "It weighs a ton. It's ages old. I've brought it for 'Hiawatha' in the bathroom— that's an old seventy-eight. Hope it works; haven't used it for years. You have to wind it up. Cecilia and I had it in a cupboard at school. Father brought it one weekend. We used to play Wagner secretly, the 'Siegfried Idyll' and 'Wotan's Farewell.' We used to stuff a towel in it to muffle the noise. Can you imagine!"

"Oh, I see," Edwin said. "But look here, Daphne, we don't want to overdo things. They, Leila and her mother, might hear us."

"That's just the idea. The only trouble is they're not in. Whatever possessed them to go to *Murder on the Nile*? It's just about the longest film ever made and it isn't even new. It's incredibly long and rather dull."

"I told them I'd be out to dinner," Edwin said. "It seemed thoughtless, indelicate somehow, to sit romantically with you at Lorenzo's in candlelight while they prepared a dinner expecting me to come home."

"I do understand," Daphne said.

"So Leila's mother said if I was sure I'd be all right they would go out. They hadn't 'been to a cinema in a while'—those were her words."

"We'll have to either put off or prolong our lovemaking till they come back." Daphne prodded Cecilia's mattress. Edwin could see them, Cecilia and Daphne, years ago at their boarding school, bouncing on beds to test them, reserving beds and cupboards next to each other, grabbing towels, beating the others to the best showers, sharing coat hangers and eating chocolate biscuits under white counterpanes.

Daphne sat on the edge of the bed. "The Playboy Jocks," she said. "How on earth will you get into them?" She gazed in a perplexed way at the appropriate region of Edwin's body. "Will they stretch or something? They're so small." She held them up. "I can't imagine them stretching."

"Size eight," Edwin said. "Just my size once. . . ."

"Oh Lord!"

"Look," he said, "it doesn't matter; you didn't need to give me a present."

"I was afraid you might have an intimate gift for me." Daphne blushed. He knew it was an unusual thing for her to blush. He thought it quite suited her rather large handsome face. The awkwardness made him fond. He wondered how quickly he could dash down the passage to grab the orchids and carnations he had brought in the day before for Leila's mother. The stalks, he thought, might drip water everywhere and Daphne might already have noticed them in the hall. The stalks would no longer look fresh; they would even be a bit slimy by now.

"We might as well be comfortable." Edwin smiled and opened the door which led from Cecilia's bedroom through a small dressing room, which Cecilia's mother had once, on a visit, described as a walk-through 'robe, directly into Edwin's study. His glowing walls of books, his leather chairs and his own neat bed, made as he liked it, reassured him. "Let's have some champagne," he said. "I put it in here."

"Oh, rather!" Daphne followed him too quickly. "Sorry, Teddy. Sorry!" She stepped back off his heel.

"Relax," he said in his kindest voice. "Relax, Daph."

"Oh, you are a dear!" She seemed too grateful. "I'm afraid," she said, "Prince is kicking up a frightful din; he's tied up outside your kitchen door." She sipped her champagne hurriedly. They listened to the mournful barking and howling. Edwin was sure that if Leila's mother heard the noise she would predict, without the leaves and with satisfaction, a death. He knew that nature had endowed dogs with a strange strength which enabled them to bark and howl for a whole night and to have, the next day, the same endless destructive vitality as if they had had a good night's sleep. If he wanted to be rid of his guests he must take certain steps, he understood this, but he would have to listen to Prince all night too. There were other things; his heart sank: he would not sleep. He did not sleep when other people were in the house. It was Cecilia's idea to have his study as his bedroom because of her repeated nocturnal and unholy early morning visits to the Mary and Joseph. Though his health was surely being wrecked with the uneasiness of having guests, there were compensations. Leila's mother, for example, one night had made a dish of wonderfully tender beef with a sauce of wine-soaked mushrooms. Not liking to say that he did not trust mushrooms, Edwin ate them for the first time in his life. He liked them and was not even ill. He remembered now that he had forgotten to make an entry in the notebook for the internal. The awful thing was, he thought, as he poured more champagne, that he was not sure that he wanted his guests to go. He wanted his house to himself but there was something else. He tried to sort out in his mind what this other thing was.

Cecilia's smiling face on Edwin's desk seemed to approve their champagne drinking. Daphne raised her glass to the photograph. "This binge is for you, Cecilia darling," she said. There was another photograph, Cecilia's graduation year. Daphne peered at it. "Gosh!" she said. "There's old Duckbill, great friend of Father's. I'd forgotten him. Cecilia's old Head. He thought the world of her and she worshipped him. They all called him Duckbill because of the speculum: he perfected the art, it was said, of its use," she explained.

"I thought the Head was Stirrups," he said.

"I believe Duckbill and Stirrups alternated. Took turns. Gynecologists," she said, "have excellent manners. They're born with them. Father was the same. It was his good manners which prevented him from telling me . . ."

"I know." Edwin was gentle. He patted her knee.

Daphne smiled. "You can just see," she said—draining her glass, Edwin thought, rather too quickly—"those two doctors taking turns, especially as they got older and more pompous, standing aside to let the other examine or operate first." She held out her glass. Edwin poured more for them both. He wondered if having a gynecologist for a father would make a girl more knowledgeable and more well cared for "down there." He glanced at Daphne's honest face; he thought not in her case perhaps. Most certainly well cared for but not knowledgeable in the way he was thinking. Cecilia's father's attitude towards his daughter had not been one of concern for personal hygiene but was clearly that she should have the advantages of all the education that money could buy and then "get on in the world." His words. Almost his first question to Edwin had been: "And how do you earn your crust?"

"Murder on the Nile takes ages," Daphne said.

"What about some music," he suggested. "Mozart, a piano concerto."

"Lovely," she said. "It would be a pity to waste the evening with the feeling that it was going to drag."

"Number twenty-four in C minor," he said.

Daphne, knowing that she was not, felt that she was beautiful, Edwin thought, as he saw her close her eyes and listen to the piano stride across the octave before merging and rippling with the instruments in the orchestra. Music, he thought, did make people feel that they were fine-featured and noble. Their hands and feet became more sensitive too and their bodies, however ordinary, became graceful with powers beyond all expectation. Last night, glancing slyly at Leila during the Brahms, he had seen a suggestion of preening, rather like the hardly perceptible movements of a shy bird. Only something slight. It was barely noticeable but Leila had, he knew, felt special because of something in the music. He had chosen Brahms on purpose. She had looked up at him once, catching his sly glance. She had smiled in that slow quiet way of hers. During the music now Edwin thought about Leila and realized he had never heard her laugh. This made her so different from Cecilia, apart from all the other differences. Now, for no reason, he remembered the time when Cecilia, living up to her eagle wig, was called away from the Honeywells' (or was it the Wellatons') party to go to the Mary and Joseph. She had gone off to the delivery just as she was, expensively naked.

"Don't worry." Her shrieking voice filled the wide front garden (it was the Honeywells'). "I'll get given something to wear, all clean and respectable. I'll be sterilized, my dears, from head to foot." The party people were all on the steps of the porch, offering their furs and their hand-woven shawls.

"The little bugger"—Cecilia's voice must have reached the unwilling ears of neighbors—"would be far better off without my intervention." She had, Edwin remembered, simply slipped through them in a high-pitched peal of laughter into the waiting taxi. No one at the party, Edwin included, and certainly not Cecilia herself, was fit to drive anyone anywhere.

Thinking of the Brahms again, he recalled that Leila looked sweet and fresh, like something he wanted to bite for pleasure, playfully, greedily, with violence and with tenderness.

"That's a nice tune," Leila's mother often said at intervals during his records. She sat bent over her knitting, humming something that was entirely her own.

"Top up, Daph?"

"Yes, please. Oh, rather! Yes, please." Daphne sank back again, listening to the music. It was more than possible, he thought, noticing, not for the first time, her large Florentine hands, that she had never been stroked and kissed in the secret places of her body. Though, he reprimanded himself, it was never possible to be sure. She was very well made, he decided, very tall, with fine, well-shaped, strong legs. He narrowed his eyes, guessing at the quality of the architecture of her pelvis and its muscles. Guiltily he reflected that he was looking at her as he might look a horse over. He began to wonder about her in a more intimate way. Maybe, he thought, she prefers the sympathetic attention of another woman. Something slow and thoughtful, like the gentling of a horse. Daphne, herself, knew how to gentle a horse. Edwin admired this skill of hers. He knew that she approached the nervous and unbroken animal with soft little words and pattings, with perhaps only a rubdown on the first day, and then, every day, offering the horse some small new experience until an affectionate confidence was reached between horse and rider. Speculating on this, he knew his own way was both gentle and sympathetic. Perhaps some of his pride was in this study of himself. He was always discreet and unhurried. He never fell into the familiar, which he considered a danger to the art. Part of the being discreet was the way in which clothes were removed. Only some clothes should be taken off. When he had taken off some of his clothes he always put on a pleasant dressing gown of a seductive cloth with a matching quality in the choice of color.

Choosing his dressing gown, he looked across at Daphne. Her eyes were closed. It was strange, he thought, that it was possible to know someone, a friend, for many years and not really know them.

◆ ◆ ◆

Once years ago when Cecilia wrote to Edwin she put ears of corn and scarlet poppy petals in her letter. She was sitting, she told him in the letter, on the edge of a cornfield, knowing that she was going to see him the next day; knowing that they were going to spend the day and the night and the next day together. Knowing this changed and colored everything. Everything they were going to do that day, she wrote, would be seen differently because of their night in the hotel. The hotel furniture, she wrote, even before we see it dominates everything we do. He smiled now remembering how hungry she always was. They always had to find a restaurant first of all. Cecilia couldn't make love or be loved if she was hungry. In the restaurant she would talk and laugh and eat while he watched. This was the Cecilia of long ago.

Perhaps it was the champagne. Edwin wondered why he thought of these things at a quarter to midnight with Daphne sprawled ungracefully in the chair opposite. She was asleep. He heard the faint sounds of Leila and her mother when they entered the house and crept, on tiptoe, into the spare room. There was no further sound. It was as if the spare room had swallowed them both. He wondered if they needed hot drinks or if they were wanting to talk about the film but were afraid to raise their voices beyond a strained whisper. He began to worry that they might want the bathroom. . . .

Prince was still howling. Every few minutes he repeated his short sharp bark, which he followed with the dying fall of his howl. It was easy to imagine the dog's head tilted up, his ears laid back, his whole body somehow extended as part of the long-drawn-out finale of despair.

To feel depressed as he did was a sign of not having enough champagne. He knew too that champagne for him was like a massive dose of salts. There were several closely written accounts (in the notebook of the internal) of previous results. It was merely a matter of time.

He knew he must do something. They could not sit up all night. He allowed himself a charming little fantasy of Leila falling asleep, innocent and soft and warm. For the purpose of the fantasy she was not in the spare bed next to her mother but was curled up in the middle of his bed waiting for him to slide in under the sheet and the neat blankets. . . .

"Daphne, old girl." He bent down and touched her gently on her substantial shoulder. "What d'you say to hopping into Cecilia's bed for a nice sleep?" He paused and gave her a friendly little shake. She stirred, complaining that she was in no way fit to hop anywhere. "Oh, Teddy," she said, "did I tell you that Fiorella—you know, the amorous Fiorella—did I tell you that in her adoration she has copied out, by hand, the whole of Oscar Wilde's 'Charmides' in order to make a single comment on the poem?"

"Good heavens!" Edwin simulated enthusiasm. "I say," he said, "that's wonderful, Daph, but now what about you going to bed for a nice sleep." He felt his voice sounded stupid; he recognized one of the effects champagne had on him: his voice developed a tremor. It made him feel self-conscious.

"Too much champers," Daphne managed. "Too quickly."

"Go on, there's a good girl. You have first pop in the bathroom," he urged her.

"Oh, Teddy, you are a dear! I feel terrible." Daphne, trying to stand, swayed horribly. He had never realized before how tall she was. "I'm dizzy; it's terrible," she said. "I'll have to lie down. Thank you so much."

"Come along," he said, "there's a good girl; just across the passage and then into bed. You'll be asleep in no time. While you're in the bathroom I'll turn Cecilia's bed down for you." Edwin helped Daphne towards the door. She began to laugh.

"You know, Teddy," she said, "it must be the . . . what I mean is, I've always wanted to be the patron saint of a literary journal, you know, to pour blessings on learned writings. . . ."

"Yes, yes," Edwin said, assisting her through the door, which did not seem big enough for them both to go through together. He was surprised at his show of brutality. "Sorry, Daph," he said, steadying himself for the next move. Champagne, he thought, certainly had strange effects on people.

While Daphne was in the bathroom Edwin changed his mind about his dressing gown. He selected a silky one, fumbling to remove it from its hanger. He put some perfumed lotion on his hands and smoothed his face and the sides of his hair with both palms. There was something deliberate, he felt, about the action, something deliberate about short dressing gowns and the act of choosing one and putting it on. It was more an act than anything else. He was able to recognize and acknowledge in an honest way that it was only an act and had been so for a long time. He knew, perhaps because of the champagne, that the act had severe limitations.

Suddenly there was a tremendous noise from the bathroom. He listened with horror to a resonant braying sound from behind the closed door. He stood quite still in the passage but no one peered stealthily from the spare room. It was as if there were no one in there. The braying opposite continued. Even Prince, outside the kitchen door, held his howl in midair.

He crossed to the bathroom. "Daphne," he said in a low voice, as close to the door as possible. "Daphne! Whatever are you doing! Be quiet at once. They'll hear you. You'll wake them, you'll wake the others."

Daphne opened the door a crack. "It's a love call," she said, "it's the Indian Love Call to accompany 'Hiawatha.'" He heard the music. It came from an ancient record, scratching from a blunt needle, cutting across the sheer silence of the house like the rasping cry of a predatory bird along a steep and deserted cliff. It was dreadful music. He was a snob about many things and music was one of them.

"Daphne," he hissed, "turn off that noise and come out of there and go to bed."

"You should have said, 'come to bed,'" Daphne, flinging open the bathroom door, bawled in the voice she used for Prince. Behind her the music swelled.

◆ ◆ ◆

The phone was ringing. Edwin rolled over in his neat bed. It was Cecilia. She'd been to Niagara, she told him. Vorwickl, he did remember Vorwickl didn't he, that summer when Mumsie rented the cottage in the Cotswolds and he had come for the weekend and Vorwickl missing her train had to stay on over the weekend and he had to sleep on the living room floor. He said he remembered. Well, she told him, Vorwickl thought it would be a nice idea to invite the Frau Doktor von Eppell (they call her Strudell) to come to Niagara. Their German isn't the same, she said, communication a bit difficult at times. English rather quaint. Strudell, she said, had screamed when the *Maid of the Mist* headed right into the massive waterfall. Yes, the little boat goes right behind it. You are behind a wall of water. You all wear big black waterproofs and boots. The conference had a day off for trips, she said. Niagara is polluted too. You mustn't drink it. A woman, she said, is reputed to have thrown her baby into the falls. Postnatal depression. Vorwickl's thesis. What time is it over there? she wanted to know. He said he'd tell her in a moment. I'm missing you, he said with care, missing you, Cecilia, missing missing you so much and—He pulled the phone connection out from the wall plug. It was kinder, he thought, if she was cut off cruelly during his words and not during hers. A telephone fault in the middle of his words.

♦ ♦ ♦

His household, Daphne in Cecilia's room, Leila and her mother in the spare room, "Hiawatha" silent in the bathroom, and Prince, reduced to short sharp daytime barkings, at the back door, surrounded him as soon as he woke from an unrestful half-sleeping state. He had been quite unable to chat with Cecilia or to listen to her. The expected stomach cramps had started almost as soon as Daphne, tucked firmly into Cecilia's bed, was safely asleep. There had been several journeys of sheer suffering during the night. It was very early. He put on his slippers. He smoothed his hair in front of his mirror and scowled at the face reflected there. He examined his tongue. He had not noticed his tongue for some time. Forgetting everything for a moment, he ran an anxious forefinger along the sides of his tongue. He almost felt like himself, his old self, ready to report that there were no lumps. NAD Tongue NAD. He would look at the dry patch of skin on his leg later and he must remember, he told his reflection, to record the drastic champagne purge.

Though it was early, Leila's mother and Leila were already in the kitchen. The kettle was boiling and there was a fragrance of toast.

"I've fixed a nice little tray for you," Leila's mother said, slipping a plate of buttered toast from the top of the stove to the edge of the tray. Edwin, noticing the lace cloth and the two cups and saucers, glanced at Leila, who was sitting at the far side of the table. She did not look up. Her face, round the eyes, seemed puffed as if from a heavy sleep or—he had misgivings—from crying. The pain he suddenly felt was not a champagne cramp. Her eyes, he saw quite plainly in that quick glance, were like slits in her swollen face. She looked as if she had spent the night weeping, trying to suppress the sounds in her pillow or against her mother's solid back.

Leila's mother made a remark about the weather which Edwin answered with one of his smiles and some conventional words. He took the tray, continuing his smile and a self-conscious murmur of thanks. "A gentleman's got to have his little fling, Leila." He distinctly heard, he thought, Leila's mother comforting Leila as he pulled the door closed. His little fling, reposing in Cecilia's bed, had enormous long strong legs. She was taller than average and the legs, he remembered, stuck out awkwardly from underneath their owner's garment, which, she said, was a slip.

"I'll sleep in my slip," she had managed to say after one or two attempts to take it off.

Petticoats: Cecilia had extravagantly pretty things, gathered at the waist some of them and embroidered with little holes. These had a special name, some black and some white. She had an enormous red taffeta one, and several others were frilled in snowy layers. She looked so sweet in them Edwin often thought it was a pity she was not able to go out to dinner wearing one as a dress.

Daphne seemed to favor something very dull, this slip slippery enough to be useful, to stop her top clothes riding up on her underclothes. She had, before falling asleep, tried to explain something of this to Edwin as he patted her shoulder and made what he hoped were loving and soothing noises as softly as he could.

He began now to compare the long legs of his little fling not with Cecilia but with the sad, almost collapsing, Leila, hunched over her apparently unwanted mug of tea. Misery could make a plain person even plainer.

"Oh, Teddy. I've got such an awful headache." Daphne sat in bed weeping and holding her head with both hands. "I feel so utterly awful! It can't be what they call postcoital melancholy," she sobbed, "because I haven't . . . we haven't . . ."

"No." Edwin, still holding the tray, sat gently on the side of the bed and placed the tray between them. He patted the bedclothes where he thought one of her thighs would be. "There there," he said, "don't cry, Daph. You'll feel better in a minute. Don't cry, please don't be so upset. Everything's all right."

"Oh, you are a dear!" Daphne said, wiping her face on the sheet. "I am sorry to be sitting here in bed in your house howling my head orf like this. What about"—she brightened—"as one disillusioned sinner to another, what about the old hair of the dog," she said.

Edwin, dismissing quickly the horror of Prince and the disgusting things to be found on his ugly coat, said it was a good idea. "Worth a try," he said and went into his study. The sight of the empty champagne bottles, and even worse the smell of them, made him more ashamed. The double sight of sorrow, Leila and Daphne, was unbearable.

"We'll try a spot of this with our tea," he said, returning with the bottle of whisky.

"Oh yes; Father always swore by it." Daphne raised her tear-blotched face. "He maintained it saved his life—disinfecting his bowels, you know, when he was in New Guinea, and it pickled his liver and mended his broken heart. I don't know who broke it; certainly it couldn't have been Mother, and Miss Heller stayed with him till death did—" She was overcome by more weeping.

"Come on, Daph. Dry up and drink up." Edwin held out a

carefully measured dose. "Drink up," he said, "and chase it with a cup of tea." His own head ached. He did not weep outwardly. He took his medicine, both lots—the one he drank and the other his thought and realization—bravely. It pleased him to parallel Girolamo Cardano (Renaissance lecture number 1) and need a severe pain in the body, the head in this case, to help him to bear his mental anguish.

"This tea is very nice." Daphne in an absentminded way munched the toast. "I feel such a fool sitting here like this," she said.

"Don't," Edwin said. "I'm the fool, if you want to know," he said. "If you will not mind this, Daph, I'm very fond of you and very grateful to you."

"Oh, Teddy. Darling! You are being so sweet!" He thought she would cry again. Quickly he poured more tea. She did not cry but ate his share of the toast.

He thought about love and the short-lived anticipation, the accessories, the sensations, which people thought were love. He did not often think about it but recalled now Cecilia's first delight, which was also his, coupled with relief. He had been afraid of failing. "All stops full out!" she had said. As Cecilia, Saint Cecilia, she was supposed to have invented the organ. It, the idea, became their private joke. In their set it was imperative to have some remarks which had connotations, odd words which caused little twisted smiles and raised eyebrows and quick glancing looks. Edwin was unable, even in a moment of anguished truth in his book of the intangible, to acknowledge, to write the words to describe when their intimate joke had palled. The act became predictable and, quite soon, the after-effects were taken for granted. The feeling of being special and chosen and cared for was gradually absorbed, he realized now, in the more important matter of appearances. How they were seen by other people began to mean more to them and they must, all the time, have been meaning less to each other and thinking only of the next thing they were going to do. Things which would be evaluated by other people and measured against standards which were not necessarily their own.

On the voyage, when they left England, both were on their way together but separately to responsible work. Sitting by Daphne in Cecilia's pretty bedroom, Edwin recalled his vision of the university department as it was in his imagination. Brown leather chairs, polished tabletops and desks, laden bookshelves, filtered sunshine, noble minds and thoughtful discussion. Possibly Cecilia too had imaginary pictures of the Mary and Joseph Wing of the general hospital. They respected each other's appointments and spoke about them to other people with reverence during the voyage, but really only thought about themselves and what they each were going to do. They never exchanged their imagined scenery. It lay ahead, undisturbed by spoken thoughts and hopes. He thought now too about the remote scenes on either bank of the Suez Canal. He was not sure whether passenger ships came through the canal any longer. He had an idea that theirs was the last ship to make the journey.

People lived lives there quite unlike their own lives, which they felt to be so vitally important. Those people faced life and, in particular, illness in a lonely landscape where only the sky looked down on their suffering. When they had no cure, they were alone beneath a tremendous width of uncaring sky. Vividly he recalled a man and a little boy dressed in striped cloth, like something out of a Bible picture, standing on the crumbling earth. As the ship, full of apparently indifferent people, went by, the two of them stood watching its passing. There were no other people and no signs of human dwellings anywhere within sight. He was deeply moved to see the man and the boy standing quite still watching the ship. He mentioned it to Cecilia.

"Nomads," she cried. "How exciting!"

Her laughter, which was muffled in the cabin, tinkled in the various bars, bubbled in the swimming pool, and resounded in the ship's dining room at the captain's table and later in the lounge. Everyone liked Cecilia and he was proud of her. He still was, he told himself, as he looked with sympathy at Daphne, who lay back with her eyes closed. During the voyage Cecilia delivered two babies, used a stomach pump (while the ship's surgeon was busy with an inflamed appendix) on a member of the crew who had tried to poison himself, and diagnosed measles on the children's play deck.

It was during the voyage that they met the people who were to determine, from a few weeks of shipboard companionship, their future ways of living. On board were the couples: the Wellatons, the Honeywells and the Fairfaxes. All, with their own ways of seeking pleasure and relaxation, were quickly attracted to Cecilia and her laugh. Edwin, at the time, had been pleased and grateful for an insulation and a protection which was to be found in this particular form of friendship.

The new country, on the morning of arrival, stretched flatly beyond the customs sheds. They stood together at the ship's rail, feeling the hot dry air. The rail of the now safely berthed ship moved slowly above the horizon and slowly below the horizon. Edwin remembered that he wondered then about success or failure in his new appointment, and he supposed, now, that Cecilia, beside him, was silently wondering about hers.

He was impatient to get back to the kitchen to see Leila, to try to think of words to tell her he was sorry. He took up the ravaged tea tray. Daphne opened her eyes and told him that she felt heaps better. She said she'd be up and dressed in a jiffy and should they walk for ten minutes in the pines with Prince to sort of round things off—literally, a sort of hair of the dog.

"Good idea!" Edwin said over his shoulder, his need to reach the kitchen suddenly the most important thing.

Leila and her mother were not in the kitchen. On the table there was a note to Edwin. It was scribbled in pencil.

We have gone to the markets for fresh apples and veggies.
Back in a hour or thereabouts. M. Bott

He found Daphne in the back garden. "I'm most awfully sorry, Teddy," she said. "Prince has eaten all your French lavender. I do feel perfectly frightful about it." She straightened up from a ferocious fondling of the animal, who was wagging his tail, Edwin thought, as if he imagined he was providing, with this unfailing movement, electricity for the universe.

"Will you let me provide lunch?" she asked. "I'm not going to school this morning. All I have to get done is to take Miss Heller to the bank and she likes to be back early. I can promise you an incredible disaster, but"—she gave a little laugh—"better a dish of herbs where love is, and so on, or words to that effect. I'll probably never try roasting a stalled ox."

The sky through the pines across the road was pale yellow and watery. The trees seemed immense, very tall and still, as if maintaining their sentinel duties. He thought he would leave a note for Leila's mother, for Leila, telling them that he would be in for dinner. His lecture was not until four o'clock.

"I'd like that very much, thank you, Daph," he said. "I'll join you in the pines shortly."

♦ ♦ ♦

All day Edwin wished for a few minutes alone with Leila to explain to her about the stupid night. A sort of joke, he would say. He wanted her to know that the whole thing was nothing more than that. Leila's mother too, he wanted her to know, but perhaps she already did. "That woman's got a hide like a rhinoceros!" Cecilia sometimes used a cliché; he could almost know how she would see Leila's mother, and Leila for that matter, and then apologize for the cliché, but not for the thought that it expressed.

All day, except for the short time spent with Daphne eating a surprise omelet which had, among other things, olive stones in it—"The olives should have stayed on top," Daphne explained—he could not stop thinking of Leila. Daphne too came into his thoughts a great deal and his lecture, still Renaissance 1, suffered third place. Both Leila and Daphne had something in common, and this was that they had not been gazed upon naked by anyone with adoration or admiration, except of course by their mothers and, perhaps once or twice, by their fathers when they were babies. Naturally people could not be expected to gaze at other people's bodies so that the ungazed-upon need not feel slighted. It was not so simple. "Those wishing to be admired naked step this way, please." Ludicrous. He thought the reason for Daphne's weeping might have been partly because of this sad fact, unacknowledged, but then, knowing Daphne's tremendous self-honesty, not unacknowledged.

Once, in England, one midsummer, the three of them—Cecilia, Daphne and Edwin—thought they would bathe naked at midnight on midsummer eve in the river where they were having a holiday, Daphne having come to visit. Edwin remembered it all vividly. He, finding it difficult to take off all his clothes in spite of the darkness, was huddled on the grassy bank. Cecilia was prancing naked beside him. The grass was soft and wet and there was a river smell of water and weeds. Suddenly there was a rush of movement, a dash of white across the grass, and a mighty splash followed by a gasping and gurgling sound. "It's Daphne!" Cecilia, laughing, was helpless on the bank. Daphne came rearing out of the water. In the faint, partly clouded moonlight it was possible to see that she was covered in mud and slime. She pulled the sticks and weeds from her long hair. It was then Cecilia was sure they were being watched from the far bank. As Daphne scrambled out Cecilia whispered, "Those dark shapes over there—they're looking at us!" They had as quickly as possible grabbed their clothes and their shoes, and as they ran, Cecilia, almost collapsing with laughter, declared she thought it was only cows. "Cows over there," she could only gasp. "It's only some cows!"

He did not know why he was remembering something that had happened years ago except that it had to do with Daphne having no clothes on.

Daphne was unashamedly literal at times. Much later on, when her father was hardly able to leave his bed, Daphne, in the supermarket (for some reason they—Edwin, Cecilia and Daphne—were all there together), had chosen a yellow plastic pail.

"Father wants a bucket," she said simply. "He prefers to stand, do you see, and yellow seems the appropriate color, don't you think?"

Having a certain phrase of music in his head, Edwin set about a plan to play all the Mozart piano concertos in turn till he came to the phrase he wanted. His lecture had been a flop; he admitted this to himself, surprised to find that he was trembling in the seclusion of his study. He felt that he had actually run away from the lecture hall, leaping down the stairs three at a time and crossing the grassy courtyard in long running strides in order to end as quickly as possible the encounter between inability (his) and intolerable stupidity (theirs). He came home and found there was considerable time to spare before dinner. Delicious cooking smells came from the kitchen, accompanied by choppings and stirrings indicating that Leila's mother was there.

He put on the Mozart and sat down with a sherry almost opposite Leila, who was laboriously writing a letter on a pink pad on her knee. She did not look up at Edwin. Leila's mother said she would have her sherry in the kitchen. He listened attentively, allowing himself to look at Leila.

"It's as if the pianist goes back as if to replay, to redo the run of notes and the chords," he had tried to explain to Daphne over the olive-stone omelet. "I can see him go racing forward, leaning forward, coattails up, and then it's as if he sits back and knows he has to play it again, so he does and then he continues,

— 81 —

bending his head forward with a serious satisfaction." He wanted to know, he said, which concerto.

"Is it first or second or third movement?" she had asked, with the directness of a doctor requesting information about bowel habits. "Can you sing it?" was her next question. She paused as if waiting for him to sing the phrase. She knew a great deal about music. He knew that if he tried to sing, it would be quite unlike the real sound; it would make identification impossible.

"Is it something you've heard me play?" she asked. "I sometimes have a go at the piano parts of things. Have I played it?"

It could be but he couldn't remember, he'd said, trying to think about Daphne's piano playing. He seemed able to remember only her enthusiasm for the lute. Cecilia had once declared Daphne's true beauty was displayed when she played the lute.

Now, when he listened to the Mozart, to the piano and the orchestra, he thought of the composer holding the notes and the phrases in his head till they could be tried and written down. The piano notes in particular being held while the composer heard in his own head, at the same time, the other instruments in the orchestra—both groups of notes sometimes going in opposite directions but complementing and supporting and emphasizing each other.

Edwin from his side of the room looked across at Leila, who continued to write, in a round hand, not looking up once in his direction.

Affairs, Edwin thought during the stampede of piano and orchestra towards an abrupt finale, were not all simply a whipping off of dresses and a stepping out of underwear; they were hours of indecision, loneliness, partings and looking forward to future meetings. A whole life could be devoted to this way of living. It would be a great deal of trouble to arrange. Perhaps, at his age, he could not feel disposed towards taking trouble of this sort. All the same there was this eagerness, this wanting to meet, wanting to be with a person, excluding all others, wanting the excitement and pleasure of exchanging ideas, searching each other for wishes and thoughts, liking each other, loving, and not being able to stand being apart. The inevitable pain of parting would cloud every meeting and a time would come when it would be declared that it was not possible to continue. . . .

Accompanying the wish to be with one person was the terrifying wish and need to avoid, to not be with, the other person. Edwin, with a quick cringing movement, chose another piano concerto. There was no need for him to dwell on these things, because he was not having an affair. He thought he would make a note later of the profound realizations in his book of the intangible. It was not impossible—he glanced at Leila—that he might need to be reminded of these at some time in his life.

Leila's mother said that Leila had time to go out and post her letter. The potatoes, she said, needed a few minutes and she was not ready with the parsley sauce for the cauli yet. She had been held up, she said, by the agent.

"I'll come to the post with you, if I may." Edwin sprang up, eager to perhaps have the chance to speak to Leila by herself.

The agent, Leila's mother told him as they went through the kitchen, had just been and reported that the house next door was now free from all pests, but that the tenants were advised to occupy alternative accommodation till the effects of fumigation subsided. Since the agency felt responsible, they offered Leila and her mother a motel on the other side of town.

"Oh, please do consider staying on a day or two." Edwin's good manners and charm prevailed upon Leila's mother, who immediately said it was very good of him. Motel life, she said, did not appeal to Leila or to herself unless it was for the purpose of traveling and seeing the wonders of the world. The motel suggested happened to be in the less desirable part of town, not really very suitable for two ladies on their own. She was ever so grateful, she said, to Edwin, as both she and Leila felt really nicely at home in his house. A real homely place. They would be really sorry to leave when the house next door was pronounced ready for them. About dinner for tomorrow,

Leila's mother continued, did Dr. Page eat veal? She knew some as couldn't touch it, but if he liked it the butcher had told her he had some prime.

Edwin, who had misgivings about veal, declared it would be a nice change to have veal if Mrs. Bott would be kind enough to buy it and cook it. He put a handful of bank notes on the kitchen table, and with one of his little flourishes, he held open the back door for Leila to go through while Leila's mother gathered up the money quickly.

"Shall we walk through the pines?" Edwin asked as they stood side by side waiting to cross the road. He spoke in his most subdued and chastened voice in preparation for his sincere apology. Leila, clutching her letter, nodded. She seemed both younger and older away from her mother. He could not make her out. If Cecilia had been at home, the two of them, Cecilia and Edwin between them, would have made a little game, an act of bringing Leila out. They would have asked Leila's mother, Mrs. Bott, most solemnly, could they take Leila out? Yes, to dinner with friends. Really nice people. Yes, she would be home early; Edwin would bring her home—faithfully. Oh well, if you won't hear of Edwin leaving early we'll pop her in a taxi, all safe and sound home, like Cinderella, before midnight. Cecilia would take Leila under her wing and teach her to know what to wear and how to do her hair and what to put on her face and when. With Cecilia, Leila would blossom—for a time. But Cecilia was not at home and Edwin, at present, was not part of a broad-minded, fun-loving, pleasure-loving couple. He was by himself. He was going with Leila to post a letter. "Who have you been writing to, darling?" Cecilia would have asked, laughing and teasing. Kind teasing but teasing all the same, and she would have insisted that Leila tell her. Edwin did not ask. Good manners prevented him from more than scarcely glancing at the letter. It was addressed to a box number and he did not try to see the name above it.

Leila seemed different away from her mother's side, rather as she was not the same when, shyly, she slipped by him, unbuttoned, on her way from the bathroom to the spare room that first night. Edwin recalled something, as they crossed into the dark pines, about mother and daughter, the symbiotic relationship. For one of Cecilia's papers he had found a quotation about willow trees and how they needed to be planted in threes. A mother and two daughters. On reflection his quotation had not been applicable to the description of symbiosis. Perhaps Cecilia's audience had not noticed. . . .

He did not know how to explain things to this shy girl. He could not say that he did not want her and her mother to be in the house. How else could he explain what her mother had called a little fling? He still felt he did not want visitors in the house but, at the same time, it did not seem quite so awkward after all. When the house next door was ready he might even miss them. At least he would miss—he smiled to himself— Leila's mother's cooking. That he had hurt this shy girl was unforgivable. He knew from her look this morning that she had been hurt and that she did not understand why. Perhaps he should start by saying that he simply could not understand his own shameful behavior. Daphne was a thoroughly good sort; he would make a point of that. She had only meant to help. But help with what? To get Leila and her mother out of the house? He was back at the beginning of the impossible explanation. Gently he took her plump arm and guided her with his easy smooth way between the pines to the now hidden path. She seemed to soften beneath his touch. Physically he knew all the right ways to handle a woman. But how to explain to Leila? He had no idea what she was really like. She might behind her plump plain look be quite different.

"Aw! Get off the grass, willya. Just you watch it! Tough cookie, you'll end up with egg on your face!" What if she said this sort of thing in response to his quiet dignified protection of Daphne? She might be a tough cookie herself and scorn his ashamed apology. His charm, successful most of the time, might be wasted.

"Just you watch it!" He had heard the words often but never addressed to him, even in his imagination.

Because of the heavy cloud, the evening was dark early. Edwin, without meaning to, said he thought it was going to rain. They hastened their silent steps over the springing pine-needle path. They walked side by side, Edwin trying, in his nervousness, not to walk ahead of Leila.

"Mother will keep the dinner hot," Leila said. Edwin was wondering whether to say, "I must tell you I am deeply ashamed," or, "About last night, I must explain." Instead he said, "We turn out of the trees here; there's the post box. We might as well go back through the pines." He hoped that on the way back he would find the right thing to say.

"Hello! How absolutely jolly!" Daphne met them as they turned to walk back from the letter box. Prince came leaping and bounding towards them.

"He loves being one of the party," Daphne said, grabbing at handfuls of Prince's glossy coat. "I'm running rather late," she said. She had been to the vet, she told them, and Prince had been cooped up in the most, for him, evil of waiting rooms—mainly in the company of cats—so he had to have a walk before bed. He hated going to the vet.

"Not the lavender," Edwin said, trying to sound jovial.

"Sort of," Daphne said. She turned to Leila, explaining. "He ate a whole bush of French lavender this morning and then he was sick. The whole bush, Teddy"—she turned to Edwin—"he brought up the lot. It's practically complete; it might even grow. . . ."

"Oh, Daphne, don't, please." Edwin's pretended groans were wonderfully realistic. Leila gave a polite little smile.

"He's perfectly all right, the vet says." Daphne hurled a stick into the gathering darkness. "The vet says he's going to have puppies." They all watched as the dog approached from the gloom carrying the stick. "The condition," Daphne said, "seems to have given him a craving." They watched as Prince began to eat the stick.

"You'll have to call him Princess," Edwin said, and laughed too much at his own remark.

They were now at the edge of the pines, waiting to cross the road.

"I'll walk on a bit, I think," Daphne said. "Prince thinks his walk has been too short. Oh, by the way," she said, "I almost forgot—Cecilia phoned. She's been trying to get you, thinks your phone must be . . . She's perfectly all right; said would I tell you she's all right and would I report your phone. Nearly forgot!"

As he walked with Leila along the last part of the pavement Edwin remembered the pulled-out connection. Poor little Cecilia, trying and trying to phone. She always needed to tell him things. She might have needed to tell him something troublesome.

As they walked together Edwin's hand brushed against Leila's, or, he wondered, did her hand brush his? They were on the brick path leading up to the front door. Edwin, feeling that he had failed, suddenly felt Leila's hand take hold of his hand. He felt the smallness of her hand and a kind of soft dryness in the palm. He thought her hand was like a child's hand, but roughened with kitchen work, perhaps scrubbing floors and vegetables. Very lightly she squeezed his fingers, a tiny gentle squeeze, and then she stepped ahead of him through the half-open front door and vanished down the hall in the direction of the kitchen.

A feeling of relief and joy spread through his whole body. It was like the time of relief when a severe pain is no longer there after a time of its being unbearable. He went singing to wash before dinner. It was not like Daphne, he thought, to make a mistake like that about a dog. He was amazed at the mistake. Daphne and Cecilia, friends all their lives since their boarding school days, had followed different interests— Daphne medieval music and drama, and Cecilia the fleshiness of the human female and her functions—but Daphne was the one who knew about dogs and horses. As for himself, with his limitations, the Elizabethan and the Renaissance (and some desultory strayings), even with his narrowness he could tell at a glance a male dog from a female. He had never looked closely at Prince. He wondered how many puppies and whether Leila would like one for herself. Smiling, he went into the dining room and took his place at the head of his table. Surveying the steaming dishes and the devout heads of Leila's mother and Leila, he thought it would be nice for Leila to have a puppy.

Reaching out in darkness, Edwin answered the telephone. Cecilia's voice was remarkably close and clear. They, Vorwickl and Cecilia, were about to leave for London where she told him they were hoping to share an apartment within walking distance of the Diseases of Women. But she said we shan't be in London just yet. They had she said to do more of Canada first. Montreal next. She said she thought they had a bad line. He thought he said they were about to board the plane. He thought he heard the sounds of the airport. No she told him it was the canteen. She had escaped with Vorwickl from a lecture, a demonstration lecture on bonding. Blow-up dolls. He heard her laughing. They had to blow up the mother and child she told him, inflate them and then bond. He heard her laughing across continents. Exploding. He tried to wake up. She was dragging him from sleep he told her. You listening she asked. What time is it over there she wanted to know. Wait he told her while he looked at his watch. She said she knew it was luminous hadn't she given it to him at Christmas? Last Christmas or the one before. She chose it for him she said. I know he replied. It's 3 A.M. he told her. He was trying not to grudge her his sleep he said and the weight of an unbearable ensuing wakefulness. She was sorry to forget she said the twelve hours. We're having coffee she explained and Danish pastries. He told her he had a surprise for her. It's black he said with four legs and a tail. A parrot she said I'm only guessing. Right first time he said. She must be headfirst he said in an empty canister holding her legs nimbly together at the knees kicking frantic but only from the knees. Correct she said. He heard her laughing. Red shoes he said. He told her she had on her Italian red shoes. Boots she managed in the middle of her laugh. Vacuum-packed he said. Tinned she agreed. A parrot she said. She told him she had always wanted a parrot. She said she heard him groan and yawn. He said that was what she heard. He had his eyes shut he explained he hoped to be able to stay asleep. His neck ached he said with speaking into the phone lying down. Sit up she said. No he replied. Vorwickl she said wanted to speak to him. Go ahead Vorwickl he said. He told them he could hear them squeezed together in a telephone box. *Grüss Gott* he said he heard Vorwickl. *Guten Tag Gnädige Frau Doktor* he explained he was raising himself with an attempt at chivalry. Bravo! she said she could see his gold tooth the one at the back when he smiled. Good he said. Homage paid. Melancholy he said often follows courtesies. They were eating gooseberries Cecilia said it was her turn to speak again. Vorwickl bought a bag of gooseberries. Listen she said sharp teeth crunching fruit long distance.

◆ ◆ ◆

"How splendid to see pearl barley again." Daphne gazed into the large saucepan as Leila's mother stirred the contents.

"This soup," Leila's mother said, "takes three days."

"Good heavens!" Daphne fixed her thoughtful eyes on the wooden spoon as it rose and fell in the glistening liquid.

Both women sat down again to their teacups.

"Sometimes," Daphne said, "I look through my old school poetry book where I once wrote, just lightly in pencil, the names of the girls who read the poems aloud. And when I look at the names now I actually seem to hear their voices."

"That's nice," Leila's mother said. "That's very nice." She topped up her own cup, Daphne having indicated that she had had enough.

"I'm glad I kept my old schoolbooks and carried them across the world," Daphne continued. "One of the poems in particular that I like to look at is called 'Dedication.' *My new-cut ashlar takes the light . . .* Kipling."

"Isn't that nice now!" Leila's mother said, sipping her tea.

"Cecilia read that one," Daphne said. "Of course I keep forgetting that you don't know Cecilia. I do rather miss her," she sighed.

Leila's mother clicked her tongue. "The time soon goes," she said. "Before you know it, she'll be back."

"Yes," Daphne said. "Cecilia read in a very clear voice. I remember especially the lines:

> *The depth and dream of my desire,*
> *The bitter paths wherein I stray,*
> *Thou knowest who hast made the Fire,*
> *Thou knowest who hast made the clay.*

"I do worry about Edwin," Daphne said. "Cecilia thinks he can't look after himself."

"Most men can't," Leila's mother said comfortably.

"I suppose that's true," Daphne said. "Anyway Cecilia had a soprano voice, I'm contralto, we sang duets, you know, from *Orfeo* and *Fidelio*."

"That's nice," Leila's mother said. "Very nice."

"In the book were poems by Rossetti and Emily Brontë: *No coward soul is mine.* It was very fitting," Daphne said, "absolutely right that Cecilia should have been asked to read 'Dedication.' All her life, you know, she has been dedicated to her work and absolutely to Edwin."

"Isn't that just lovely!" Leila's mother said. "So you were at school in England?" she asked, changing the subject slightly.

"Mr. Bott was adamant about schooling. Leila went to an English school. We lived in London," she added.

"Yes," Daphne replied. "Father was in New Guinea for a good deal of the time and because of the climate he sent me to boarding school in England, and of course that's where I met Cecilia. Cecilia's mother's a dear," she added. "She's a widow now. She is a very clever woman. She contributed a great deal in her own field. She had two wasps named after her."

"Fancy that," Leila's mother said.

"Species, you understand," Daphne said. "We, Cecilia and I, have been friends for years. I do miss her!"

"Aw!" Leila's mother said. "It would be a shame if you didn't."

"That's true." Daphne seemed surprised. "Later I went to England several times to stay with Cecilia. After she married Edwin I only visited them once and then to my utter surprise they both, at the same time, got awfully good appointments over here—so here we all are."

"Well, if that isn't nice, very nice," Leila's mother said. "It's a small world when all's said and done."

"Father was a doctor too," Daphne said.

"Women's troubles?" Leila's mother was comfortable.

"Yes." Daphne began to collect up her bag and a few books.

"Well, we can't say they're not needed," Leila's mother sighed. It seemed to Daphne that a great weight of thighs, buttocks, abdomens and perhaps a few breasts were included in the sigh. She had never contemplated her father's work while he lived as she did now in the images conjured in this sigh from Leila's mother. Perhaps Miss Heller had managed to contemplate and to understand.

"Don't go," Leila's mother said, filling the kettle. "There's no need for you to hurry, is there? I expected them earlier; they should be back directly. Dr. Page took Leila to see his university. They'll be in for their afternoon teas."

"Oh, what fun!" Daphne said. "But I must go; I've been at school all day and Prince hasn't had his walk. I thought"—she paused—"that Edwin might have been in on his own. I thought that you would . . ."

"Dr. Page," Leila's mother said, "has asked us to stay on."

"Oh, I see," Daphne said.

Edwin knew that Leila, in an apron decorated with seafood, mainly a design of lobsters, was waiting with a new dustpan and brush to sweep the kitchen linoleum. He saw the shy shape of her waiting outside the back door. She was going to cook a dinner for him too. It was all arranged. Leila's mother had gone to visit her sister and would be very late, the journey being a tiresome one. He knew that Leila was looking forward to peeling the vegetables and to making everything nice for him. She had said so. She told him that she had enjoyed walking to the university and she liked his room there. It was a bit like his room at home, she said, but without the bed, of course. Both the rooms, she said, were like him.

"How d'you mean?" he asked, really wanting to know her opinion.

"I can't explain," she said, adding that both rooms smelled nice. The gardens at the university, she said, in her ordinary way, were very pretty. He said he had never thought of them as pretty; rather dull, in fact.

"I like neat clipped lawns," she said, "and flower beds with red roses."

When they were walking home she told him that she

wanted to be like Cecilia. "I admire Cecilia very much," she said.

Edwin, smiling down at her, said, "But you don't know Cecilia." Suddenly he wanted to show affection, to do something affectionate towards her, but could not in the street alongside the university, where an unseen colleague might pass in a car or, unnoticed by them, on a bicycle. Since the little walk to the letter box a few days earlier he had not been absolutely sure whether she had caressed his hand or not. He kept telling himself that he might have imagined the touch of forgiveness because he wanted it so much. He had been able to push aside the doubt as he listened to her voice. "I've seen her a few times," she said, "when she's been leaving the house and you wave to her."

"Ah yes, of course," Edwin said.

"And I've seen her nightdresses too," Leila said. "I've worn one, remember, the biggest one, the stretchy one. When I had it on, though I know I'm too fat, I pretended I was her."

"Oh?" He was amused. "And why did you do that?"

"Because—Oh! I can't tell you." Her face was turned away. He saw her ear, very pink, the tip of it showing below her short straight hair.

"Come on! Of course you can tell me." He enjoyed persuading her. "You surely aren't shy with me," he said.

"It's because of . . . in the nightgown . . . because she will have worn it next to you, so . . ."

"Yes? Go on." He liked teasing her. "Yes, and so?"

"So if I'm wearing it . . ." She looked up quickly, straight into his smile. For a moment he felt no one existed except himself and her. The sun caught the edge of her spectacles so that they shone.

Held by her smile, he said in his softest voice, "You are very sweet."

"Am I?" he thought he heard her reply.

"Yes, yes, you are. You must always be as you are," he said. "Never try to be like anyone else."

Now, in the kitchen, which was suddenly crowded with the Wellatons and the Honeywells—the Fairfaxes, Dippy and Ida, were unable to come, apparently, at the last minute—Edwin stood surprised as hot dishes were carried in from the cars and pushed into the oven. The visitors seemed bigger and noisier than usual and there was a clattering of heels across the veranda as more dishes were fetched. He stood wondering what to do about Leila.

"Darling! Teddy!" Paulette Honeywell screamed. "We've gone all Spanish." Edwin saw the flamboyant dresses, flamenco style. Paulette, in particular, was striking in a scarlet dress and a black mantilla. She had a red rose tucked behind one ear. "Soup matador!" she said, putting a large saucepan on the stove. "I'll be back in a minute," she cried, "with the pechuga valenciana."

"Paella—eggs and fish." Erica Wellaton pushed her dish forward. "Don't look so worried." She gave Edwin a kiss. "The pechuga is a sort of baked chicken, quite harmless. And"—she gave him another kiss—"how have you been getting on? All lonesome?" Edwin tried not to draw back from her third kiss.

"Sangria! Sangria! Open the fridge, old man!" Buffy Honeywell filled the door space. "It's naughty but nice and full of ice," he said. Edwin had to move some of Leila's mother's stored cooking to make room for the enormous pitcher, which he guessed was mainly vermouth, a drink he did not care for.

"Sangria!" Paulette screeched. "Don't look like that, Teddy—you'll simply love it! Buffy's been busy all day getting it dollied up. I always think," she added, "that vermouth's a medicinal drink. Cecilia's always said you like medicinal things. You do, don't you, darling?"

Edwin, dismayed, now remembered the dinner parties Cecilia had arranged for him during her absence. He had forgotten them completely when he suggested to Leila's mother that they might like to stay longer, perhaps even for a time to discontinue their rent next door. "Think about it," he'd said, surprised at his own words. The coming home to comfortable dinners and relaxed evenings outweighed the initial uneasiness of having other people in the house. Surprisingly the bathroom presented no problems. It seemed clean and empty at all times. He supposed that Leila's mother and Leila showered during the times when he was out. Leila's mother did seem to be very considerate.

There were to be twelve of these parties, a "happening" every month while Cecilia was away. This was the first. How could he have forgotten so easily? It was only a short time since her departure and here were the Wellatons and the Honeywells, friends, their set at the tennis club, come to look after him, to feed him and to cheer him up—Cecilia's words when she had suggested the idea a few weeks earlier. She had telephoned everyone. All the dates were arranged and written in Cecilia's firm up-and-down handwriting in a little red diary she had given him. The diary was on his desk, he remembered now; he had not looked in it. Somehow it had not been difficult to forget the diary.

There were several stories about Edwin's forgetfulness and his absentminded intellectual ways. Paulette and Erica had always been very understanding and forgiving.

He saw Leila's round brown head, like a seal, he thought, by the edge of the uncurtained window (Cecilia hated curtains in a kitchen). It was now quite dark. Only someone who knew Leila was out there would be able to see her. With another quick glance he saw her bending down, perhaps to fasten a shoe. She would not be in fact hiding, he knew, any more than she, feeling excluded, was hiding by being in the yard instead of the kitchen. Without knowing her very well, he was able to imagine that she would wait out there till these intruders had gone. He hoped she would not see things he preferred her not to know about.

The Honeywells and the Wellatons were, in their own words, awfully good sorts. He knew he should bring Leila in to them and explain that she was a visitor. The women, once they understood that Edwin unexpectedly had houseguests, would include her in their preparations. They would even put a red rose behind her ear in their generous endeavors. He, in his mind, saw the stalk of the rose refuse to stay in Leila's short straight hair. It was soft and fluffy today; she must have washed it. And the rose, a thoroughly awkward blossom, would lean and slip and need constant attention, little pattings and attempts to keep it in place, till it, in the end, would fall.

Paulette's rose was placed bewitchingly and would never slip. It gave an impression of being fastened by a long pin or a nail driven firmly into her fashionable skull. The rose seemed to make Paulette's eyes sparkle with mischief. Perhaps that was the intention. A rose might fill Leila's eyes with anxiety. Edwin, unable to move away, watched Paulette's thin capable fingers unwrap some special bread and various mysterious little jars containing sauces and, finally, some little biscuits which, she declared, were heavenly. He was unsure about Leila herself; he could not see how she would manage in the overbearing presences of Erica and Paulette. If Leila's mother had been there, he thought, she would in her large and heavy way have been thoroughly in command. Leila's mother, he had noticed in the short time of being acquainted with her, was a discerning woman. She perceived and acted immediately on her perception. He was not sure that he really liked this. There was something frightening, almost sinister, about the ease with which she adapted herself, fitted herself in. If Leila's mother had been there, Erica and Paulette would have been simply flattened into the position of being guests. But Leila's mother was a journey, two buses and a train, away. Her sister, Leila's mother said after dinner the previous day, had not been well and she was wondering, she said, if Dr. Page would mind if Leila stayed quietly at home. Her sister, she said, would be sure to want to talk about her illness, which was terminal—Leila's mother shook her head—and about her big operation. No, of course he did not mind. It would be a pleasure to have Leila stay behind, his charming smile reassured Leila's mother. He had then suggested that Leila should cook the meal for them both.

"It might just help to bring her out of that shyness," Leila's mother said.

"Yes, I think it might." Edwin smiled at Leila.

"And you need not be afraid being with Dr. Page," Leila's mother said to Leila. "It will be valuable experience."

"In familiar surroundings." Edwin smiled at them both. It was very useful to a young woman, Leila's mother declared, and it was a privilege, she was sure Leila would realize this, for Leila to be with a gentleman like Dr. Page for the evening.

Edwin felt as if he would choke. Moving nearer to the window, he found he could no longer see Leila. He could only see the reflection of all the color and the excited movements of preparation in the kitchen. The most awful part of the whole thing was that Leila had been looking forward tremendously—she had told him so—to the evening. She and her mother had been out to buy the apron and the dustpan and brush, there not being either anywhere in the house, specially for the evening. When the guests, with their fancy dress and exotic food, came clamoring through the house, Leila, with hardly a glance at Edwin, had slipped out through the back door and stayed outside.

The moment for introducing or even mentioning her had gone, he realized in the next few minutes, as he was bundled by Paulette and Erica into the cabbage-rose room, the lounge, they called it, where Buffy Honeywell and Tuppy Wellaton (all the men in their set had pet names which enabled them to get through certain aspects of married life) lifted the responsibility of host completely off his shoulders by pouring and offering him, in his own house, a double Scotch. They followed this with another as soon as he had drained the glass.

The Honeywells and the Wellatons and the Fairfaxes, Dippy and Ida, unfortunately unable to come, Paulette insisted on reminding them, knew just how much Edwin relied on dear little Cecilia. They had all promised her, practically weeping, that they would see to it that he did not get lonely and depressed.

"The Old Country!" Buffy said. They were still standing but would have risen if they had been sitting down.

"To Home. Here's to Home. Down the hatch! The Old Country!"

"The Queen!" Buffy was inspired. "God bless the Queen."

"I'll drink to that," Tuppy said. "God bless the Queen." Edwin, in silence, drank his share. With toasts it was impossible not to. In a minute, he thought, he would slip out and fetch Leila from the very awkward position she was in. A stranger in the yard, yet familiar. He looked at his guests. They were very good-looking and very good-hearted people. They would never knowingly hurt anyone, but Leila would be frightened of them. They were toasting their old regiments now. It seemed inconceivable that he belonged with these people. He never spoke or thought of England as the Old Country. He never thought about it as Home as they apparently, after many years, did. He believed this was described as a migration syndrome; he had heard the phrase. What was home anyway other than a place you lived in and came back to every night? These people could be said to be invading his home. Cecilia when she talked of home did not particularly mean England. She meant her mother's house, a place of Viyella nightgowns, of delphiniums and rosemary, of little vegetable plots with radishes and pale lettuces splashed with mud, and a neatly trimmed lawn in the front garden hidden from the road by evergreen bushes, rhododendrons. Home for Cecilia contained a mythology of coziness, of sharing chocolates or making buttered toast by a sitting room fire on a winter's afternoon. Years ago, because he was older, while she perched on his lap he had to explain more than once that home was where they were together. He had to persuade her to close her bedroom door at night instead of keeping it slightly open with a slipper, as all the doors in her mother's house were kept at night. He said, teaching her, that she must trust that the rest of the house would be safe while she slept. In any case the telephone disturbed him during the night when she was called out. If her door was closed he did not hear the phone so often. She developed the habit of putting a cushion on it and sometimes declared that it would be better for the emerging child to begin the battle unaided.

Edwin, burning his lips and tongue with the hot Spanish soup, thought he would rescue Leila between courses and smuggle her into the spare room with promises and explanations and something to eat, and after the guests were gone ... He groaned at the hours and the food ahead. The evening, in their pattern of doing things, was endless, hours of jokes and anecdotes, mostly with double meanings. They would eat and drink and talk too much in loud voices and play foolish games, probably sardines and photographers and—he glanced at their clothes—bullfights. Buffy was dressed as an eighteenth-century Spanish bandit and Tuppy resembled the doorman of the Edelweiss, an unexpected and expensive German restaurant in Madrid.

The evening would end with the ritual of keys in the ring since that was the way of broad-minded couples and they were all broad-minded and open, by declaration, in their marriages. The game, of course, because of their changing needs and interests and because of Buffy's prostate, was now something different. Always an act, it had become more so but with compensations, one of these being the chance to talk intimately, *even if under the influence* (Dippy's phrase), at times with someone else, the other half of a couple, *all aboveboard* (Dippy again), as it were.

"I give you Dippy Fairfax and Ida." Buffy tipped the great jug of sangria towards each glass.

"Dippy and Ida!"

"Down the hatch!"

"Absent friends. Love you, Dippy. Love love you, Ida."

"I give you Cecilia." Another pouring from the jug. Edwin felt himself swaying.

"Cecilia!"

"Darling Cecilia!"

"Here's to our one and only."

"I do believe Teddy's crying. Dry up and down the hatch!"

"Bottoms up! Don't howl, Teddy darling. If you do we'll all howl. I'm howling."

Suddenly he was remembering the golden sheen of a fine down in the small of her back. Cecilia's. Perhaps it was the vermouth. It was not his drink. Never had been. He'd had too much. Perhaps he was crying somewhere inside but it was not all for Cecilia. Why remember, of all things, the small of her back now? Damn Cecilia and the same to these people. Get out! he wanted to shout. Get out! He wanted to herd them all to the front door and out down the brick path. It seemed as if they would be in his house forever, and with that wretched game ahead, one of them would be. It was Leila he wanted. He wanted to be with her alone, to have her to himself. He did not want these people to know about her. He did not want Cecilia to know, not yet. They always did know about each other but this was something he wanted to keep for himself. He wanted to contemplate, alone, the small hollow of Leila's back.

"Pechuga valenciana, Teddy? Have some more?" He scarcely tasted anything with his soup-burnt tongue. He tried to eat and smile and nod his head. He drank too much as Buffy offered more of the adulterated vermouth, alternating it with whisky.

"Garlic bread, Teddy? Eat up!"

"Sangria? Drink up, Teddy!"

He wished Daphne would come. She was always invited and she sometimes came. When Paulette and Erica talked of her they called her "poor Daphne," referring to her being unmarried rather than her thin purse. Edwin knew that Miss Heller thrived in an expensive apartment, positively bulging with bank accounts, as Daphne herself would have described it if she ever permitted herself to descend into bitterness and the discussing of Miss Heller's money.

At last Edwin had a chance to slip out. The Honeywells and the Wellatons, suitably split up, were dancing, moving about the room very close to each other. It was what passed for dancing. Edwin said that while he made the coffee he would look for a special record Tuppy remembered. A tango he thought it was, very earthy music and erotic, powerfully erotic, just the thing. Tuppy was sure, he said, that Edwin had it. As he made for the back door Edwin was glad that Cecilia was far away. For once he was not wishing for her to come to the rescue with her laughter and her quick ways of dealing with whatever had to be done. He heard, in his head, the high-pitched laughing voice:

Well, folks! Let me present Leila, little Miss Bott, little Leila Bott, our little debutante, our little fresh flower of the evening, our little fresh apple, a new face of Eve herself, Leila! Cecilia, with graceful flourishes, would draw the reluctant Leila, freshly dressed in new clothes—absolutely the right clothes, in Cecilia's eyes, and absolutely the right hairdo—into the middle of the room. No elaborate hairstyle would suit Leila, not one; he frowned the images, with their green and coppery tints, out of his thoughts. He had seen Cecilia's efforts with some of the more clumsy daughters of their friends, everyone applauding the results. If Cecilia had only had a daughter of her own perhaps everything would have been different. Certainly there would not have been parties like this one. One of the latest ideas had been mock remarriages in fancy dress, in all sorts of odd places with useless extravagant and unusual presents. He rushed into the dark garden, calling Leila by name in a low urgent voice. He wrenched open the shed and he ran back to the garage. No voice answered his. Quickly in the overpowering smell of spiced food in the kitchen he hunted for a filter paper and put on the coffee. Taking some bread and butter, he went to the spare room. He switched on the light. Leila was not in the room. It was a curiously folded-up room, this Leila family nest. The guest room bedside books, Agatha Christie, Rupert Brooke and Kahlil Gibran, chosen by Cecilia, had been placed neatly along the top of the wardrobe. He was sure they had been put there with reverence. The counterpane, carefully folded, was up there too. The empty room, completely empty of Leila, gave the impression of everything being packed, the cases open but full of careful foldings, as if the owners were living in readiness to leave at a moment's notice. The room was airless, he thought, as if closed up. The window should be open. He was about to open it when he heard them calling.

"Teddy! Teddy!" they were calling. "Phone, Teddy."

"It's Cecilia! Quickly!" Paulette was in the long passage. He hurried back to them.

"I said a tango, old chap," Tuppy growled, "not a plate of bread and butter!" Erica, screaming with excitement, held the receiver towards him. Everyone crowded into the study. He heard Cecilia.

They Strudell Vorwickl and herself she told him were in Toronto still in the more French part. That's nice he said. Delicious cakes she said *charcuterie boucherie* and other tourist nonsense. *Blanquette de veau* he offered. Yes she said. *Pouilly fuissé* and perhaps an onion. *Flute baguette* he said. Yes she said. Tucked under one arm, Camembert and other cheesy delights *mon vieux*. They were exactly twelve hours behind still. Was he enjoying his party she wanted to know. He told her yes very much. Spanish he said. Olé Olé she said. He said yes. Was he being a good boy she wanted to know. Yes he told her he was and was she being a good girl. She told him yes. Yes he told the Honeywells and the Wellatons. She said she could hear them cheering. It was like being back home she said hearing them having a party. They had to swim in a heated pool she told him. Ridiculous he said they should break the ice. Remember Vorwickl she said. He said of course he could. Yes she told him he had said once that Vorwickl was the kind of woman . . . I remember he said. Listen she said. He heard her laughing. Vorwickl she said can sing solo eight bars behind the choir on Ascension Day. Who said he asked her. You said she said. She told him they were leaving for New York Strudell Vorwickl and herself and on to Montreal. Fertility failures she said and to find out . . . He heard her laughing.

"They're going to Montreal," he told the Wellatons and the Honeywells, "to find out where baby Eskimos come from."

She was on reverse charge she told him. That's right he said. She was homesick she said. He told her nonsense. She was loving it he said. He was the sad one he said he was missing her nibble nibble he said kiss kiss he told her. Here's Paulette he said.

"Darling Cecilia. Take care!"

"Hmp Cecilia. Buffycat here. Chin chin."

"Cecilia darling. Lovely lovely to hear you. Teddy's just fine, just fine. Love love darling. Erica."

"Goo'night m'dear." Tuppy beamed as if actually seeing her. "Not right time"; he tried again, making an effort: "Not right time eh? Goo'day then. Eh? What? Chow. You're a saint. Always remember that m'dear. . . ."

Edwin, listening on the edge of the little circle round the telephone, remembered reading somewhere about Saint Cecilia, that someone wanting to get rid of her tried to steam her to death in a bathroom. She did not die but endured and that was how she became a saint. Cecilia had the power of endurance. He knew that without putting her to any kind of test. In the haze of muddled excited voices talking to Cecilia in turn he returned to his earlier thought, one which he knew would persist especially after occasions like the present one. If he and Cecilia had had children, if they had a daughter, would their lives, life itself, be different? Would there be more meaning in the antics which were part of the daily performance of living? Or would it simply be a different set of antics, as meaningless as these present ones? He stumbled slightly as he took the receiver from Tuppy, and trying to steady himself, he accidentally dropped it. When he picked it up they, he and Cecilia, were cut off. Thousands of miles of land, mountains, plains and valleys, villages, towns and cities, oceans and rivers, all with their own sunrise and sunset, lay between them.

"Bad luck, old chap!" Tuppy consoled. "Bad luck!"

They forgot about the tango. It was time for the keys game. With a simulation of enthusiasm they gathered round in a crooked little group.

The two bunches of keys lay on the carpet. The women were smooth and sharp-featured, shadowed with fatigue, for though younger than their husbands, they were, neither of them, young. They stood close together as if holding out against some cruel fate. Edwin, because of the rules of the game, picked up one set of keys. He glanced at the waiting faces, and as if reluctant, with an air of regret, he paused and then handed the Honeywells' keys to Buffy.

"My time of the month," he sighed, with an exaggerated

grimace. He held one hand with its back to his forehead. "Not tonight, Josephine!" he said. Paulette turned on her sharp heel. Her face flushed dark over her cheekbones.

"He has a headache," Edwin said, adopting the third-person narrative. "H-h-he h-has a-a h-headache." He tried his trick of stammering, giving delicate little coughs and softening his voice into a lisp and the affectation of not being able to pronounce the letter *r*. "Wight now," he said, "he's an absolute weck." He smiled with an innocence created for the moment. "An absolute weck!" he said.

"Look here, Page, am I right in thinking that was a downright insult?" Buffy, flaring red in the face, stepped up close to Edwin.

"I'm sorry, Buffycat. It wasn't meant . . ."

"I'm not used to having my wife insulted. You took her keys." Buffy's voice rose, he began to squeak. "You swine, you barstard! You utter . . ." He began to swing his clenched fist.

"I say—I say." Tuppy thrust a fat arm between them. "I say, the old number one—the old enemy and all that," he muttered. "The sangria and all that. Keep your hair on, chaps. The sangria, my fault, don'tcher know, too much of the old ouzo. Not quite ourselves, eh? Eh, what?"

Edwin, in his present misery, thought of all the years of this terrible game. This swinging. This forcing himself to be gallant and charmingly chivalrous. Trying to be ardent when there was no ardor. He remembered, against his will, the times when he made himself learn the caresses which would lead quickly to the moments of required sensation. The combination of having too much to drink and a genuine lack of desire towards an unchosen partner were the ingredients for a certain kind of unhappiness. It seemed now, as he stood in front of Buffy's hurt fury, that the mistakes made long ago when he searched to be part of a new environment, to be part of a group, only became really clear when it was too late. The unbearable thing was the looking back to those evenings on board ship when, in meeting the couples, Buffy and Paulette, Erica and Tuppy, and the Fairfaxes, Dippy and Ida, he had with Cecilia, in an attempt to ensure friendship, closed in his own life.

The stupidity of it struck him. He put his hand on Buffy's arm and felt the elderly muscles trying to harden.

"Actually, Buffycat," he said, "I must ask you to take Paulette home tonight. I'm, er, not too well—perfectly okay really, but waiting for the results of a blood test. Actually I'm thinking of Paulette." He gave Buffy one of his famous little-boy-lost looks and began again to stammer and soften his *r* sounds.

"My dear chap." Buffy's pale eyes watered. "Of course—oh but of course. Paulette . . ." He drew her towards himself and whispered something out of the corner of his mouth.

"Try to get some sleep," Tuppy said, squeezing Edwin's shoulder. They all laughed; it was one of their quotations, one of the things they said to each other at moments when they needed a phrase.

"No hard feelings?" Edwin said.

"No hard feelings," Buffy said. It was another little phrase they had, something else to see them through.

♦ ♦ ♦

There were a great many dishes to be collected. Edwin stood in the kitchen while the remains of the evening were carried to the two cars. He had a great longing for them, his guests, to be gone. There was no hastening possible. He stood hardly daring to go on thinking of Leila. She must be somewhere quite near and he must find her. Trying to hurry the evening to an end was exhausting and not at all successful. The guests, intent on every little ritual, would not be hurried. They had no idea that Edwin suffered, other than his suffering because Cecilia was away. Even in his wearied state he knew he did not want Cecilia to know. He was grateful to Leila, he would when he found her take her in his arms, just in a kind way, and tell her he was grateful. If these people saw Leila now Cecilia would know very quickly. He had never deceived her before except with his own self-deception, which he now saw to be like a veneer painted glossily over them both.

During the exchange of cheek peckings and shoulder pattings Edwin felt deeply sorry for Paulette's hurt. He knew it was greater because once, when he had picked up her keys, they had with a certain amount of dignity taken off their shoes by the radiator in his study, and when thoroughly warm and comfortable, they had discussed earnestly, with some slurring of the more difficult words, what Paulette chose to call *the finer side of life*.

"Take books," she had said, "literature," she said, "books these days, the fuckin' books all got too much bloody filthy language in them and too much sex. What d'you think, Teddy? Can't stand lesbians. Teddy, what d'you think about 'em, eh? I mean for real."

After quite a long time Edwin had offered her a mug of cocoa which she had taken eagerly and gratefully, like a little girl, and then, quite gently and softly leaning against him, she had fallen asleep. He should have picked up Erica's keys. The refusal would not have hurt her so much.

He knew he should not have picked up any keys. He stood in the light of the open front door watching the cars reverse and turn out of his drive. All evening he had been aware that Paulette had been urging him with little signs to pick up her keys.

Conversations, dancing in whispers from years ago, came back to him. He thought of dinners where they sat with china plates, almost too hot to handle, sliding off their laps while the stems of the wineglasses froze in their fingers. The nervous jokes about homosexuals had given way to the more sinister references to disease. The muddled pattern of his life seemed to swim before him, in sequence, going back to his arrival and his first tentative game at the tennis club. There had been years of arranged things: arranged games at the squash courts, folk dancing on Thursdays—it still was on Thursdays and was sometimes changed to old-time dancing, with the nostalgia of music from the thirties. And more tennis, of course. There was swimming too; early mornings in summer, the whole set would meet on the beach. The older men, strutting, reached over their bellies for their toes, and the women, teeth bared, greeted each other in shrill voices.

"Oh, dahling, but your new cozzie, it's heaven. Truly!" There had been a time too of exotic bathing caps. Cecilia still had hers. It was made to look like a salad, a floating salad complete with a hard-boiled egg (plastic), halved, and a realistic-looking crayfish, its white flesh invitingly edible until proved otherwise by playful bites. And then there was the running and the jogging, very seriously taken up, but recently, because of Paulette's slipped disks (the unforeseen result of running) and subsequent weeks on traction and bedpans, having given way to aerobics. Arms and legs and sometimes bodies all moving in time to disco music. They were all into aerobics. It was possible, they knew, to sustain injuries even here, and they watched over their own and each other's tendons and ligaments lovingly.

During all the years of sports and games and building the body, right from preparatory school onwards, he really preferred to read. He liked to sit bent over his desk, reading and writing. But life and society, and the set, demanded physical beauty and prowess. Reading and writing, writing in particular, thickened the waist, made rolls of fat, and he must, he told himself, avoid these, especially now. He would, he thought, run—free of these people—in the pines at five in the morning. Every morning he would run and regain some of his youthfulness.

He watched the headlights with real pleasure as they dipped and turned. He felt the uneasiness still over Paulette. For some reason something else about her came into his mind. Once, when the floating salad was coming towards him in a calm warm sea after a wickedly hot day, he had dived, for fun, beneath the lazy waves and, for fun, had bitten Cecilia's thigh under water. Nosing up the inviting thigh he had bitten a second time, high up, almost where the thigh became another part of the body. In a flurry of churning water they grappled and suddenly he was face to face with Paulette, the salad pushed crazily to one side. She was wearing the crayfish and the hard-boiled egg to protect her new rinse. Cecilia, smoothing herself with oil on the beach, overcome with mirth, pointed and laughed till everyone was looking at him and laughing.

For some time at dinners and at dances the story was told with embellishment, and in the earlier tellings, Paulette enjoyed lifting her skirts and peeling down her panty hose to show Edwin's tooth marks and the subsequent love-bite bruising. She always took everything so well; Buffy too—he had enjoyed the story more than anyone. Edwin never wanted to hurt them.

The headlights picked out their way along the dark road and gradually he heard the cars gather speed alongside the black pines.

"Leila!" he called softly in the quiet house. He opened, one after the other, all the doors in the house. She was not in any of the rooms. Suddenly he knew he was afraid, he knew he had been afraid all evening. Fear was part of the nightmare. Something must have happened to Leila and yet what could happen? All she had done—he tried to be reasonable—all she had done was to hide successfully for the evening. In the kitchen he picked up a plate and put it down and took up another plate and put that one down somewhere else. Leila could have gone to the station to wait for her mother's return. That was probably what she had done. It was annoying, in one sense, that Leila and her mother had a very close bond. He made a face at the phrase. They had something that seemed to physically hold them together. In the presence of this he felt excluded, jealous even. He tried to laugh at himself, without success. They would be home soon, he told himself, the two of them, in a taxi from the station. Paulette and Erica had stacked the dishwasher, so the kitchen was not too bad. They, Leila and her mother, were probably sitting in a café somewhere near the station having coffee. Vienna coffee was what Leila's mother called it when she piled whipped cream on top of the hot sweet blackness. Leila would be sure to be telling her mother everything. They seemed to live their lives close, as if they were in a nest. Nothing seemed to upset or annoy Leila's mother, he thought, as he began to get undressed. It seemed as if she was prepared to put up with anything, even Daphne's hideous love song from the bathroom. He was sure now that she was, between sips of coffee, the cream fringing her upper lip richly, telling Leila that it did not matter that the evening went wrong. "Men forget their arrangements." He almost heard the comfortable voice as she must be speaking now to Leila. Life, she would be saying, had more evenings.

He thought he was beginning to feel unwell, threatened, insecure, lonely—all the things he knew he often felt during his life. He remembered a particularly tasteless white fish Cecilia cooked. She bought it because it had no bones. She couldn't stand, she said, eating with someone who was making a thing about bones. He remembered how hurt he'd felt at the time and how he thought about it every time they had fish.

The telephone rang as he was folding back his bed cover. "Leila?" He could not keep the eagerness out of his voice. "Ahh!" he said into the crackling sound. It was a very bad line. "Mrs. Bott—everything all right?"

Leila's mother was ever so sorry. She had missed her one and only train just by the skin of her teeth and had been obliged to go back to her sister's. She was ever so sorry, she said again, and she'd be home as soon as ever tomorrow, probably about noon, she thought, and not to wake Leila, she said. Leila would realize as she had not come home that she would be staying the night. He could tell Leila in the morning if he didn't mind. She was ever so sorry to ring so late. Her sister was all nerves and no body. He said he hoped Mrs. Bott's sister would feel better and yes he would tell Leila and Leila's mother said, "Thank you ever so much, Dr. Page." She said she was sorry it was such a bad line and he said it was not her fault.

♦ ♦ ♦

Edwin dressed quickly. All he could think of was Leila sitting and waiting at the station, seeing trains come in and not one of them bringing her mother.

As the headlamps of his car swung round, he thought he saw

something white in among the pines. He turned the car again in the middle of the deserted road and again thought he saw something. He left the car at the side of the road and walked into the trees. He had been there before during the night and knew that the trees seemed to move and sigh all the time. The bark and the needles were fragrant. He walked off the path, stumbling and knocking himself against the rough tree trunks.

"Leila," he called softly, "are you there?" It was cold and there was a continuous sighing in the treetops. Everything about himself seemed full of noise and clumsy movement. He thought he heard something ahead of him. His feet made too much noise and his own breathing deafened.

"Leila!" he called. "Leila!"

"I do always try and smile at the Hatchet," Daphne said, quickening her step, lifting her feet high over the tufts of wet grass. "Miss Hearnsted's a great but horrid little person," she said, "half my size, as you know. They do say, don't they, that short people either love madly someone tall or else they hate them." Daphne gave a snort; Edwin knew the sound. He did not interrupt her, partly because his mind was on other things. He had been justifying his recent actions by remembering the more negative side of his marriage. Cecilia saying in one of the more bitter moments that she felt trapped with him and that her work was her way out of the trap, so would he remember not to remark that she was always off to the Mary and Joseph. There had been other small bitternesses, but in complete honesty, Edwin knew that

—110—

he was trying to drag these to the surface and he knew he was having difficulty in suppressing the memory of the sweet, exceptionally sweet, way in which Cecilia had said she was sorry for saying something she hadn't really meant. He tried to listen to Daphne and to follow her remarks about the Hatchet. He knew Daphne tried, all the time, to appease this selfish and self-absorbed woman. He knew that she had been considered a great beauty in her time; he did not need to depend on Daphne's well-bred wailing. The headmistress was a disagreeable elderly woman made up to look young and failing. Her face, he had always agreed with Daphne, was like an ax head and did not in any way retain a prettiness she was supposed to have had. He could see in Daphne's serious eyes the hurt she experienced daily. He had always thought privately that her face, the Hatchet's face, was like a flint. "A faded but sharp flint," Daphne was saying, "made up with pinks and mauves and unwillingly wrinkled." Edwin agreed that Miss Hearnsted should not be Head of St. Monica's. She knew nothing and he felt, like Daphne, that she should not be in charge of innocent girls. He agreed on every point and said so, adding, "Yes, she keeps people back." All the time, though, he was thinking about Leila's wise and delightful decision to have a hot bath the night he found her shivering and crying, lost in the pines. He made an effort to keep up with Daphne's longer stride. She wanted to get Prince round the near edge of the plantation and home before going to a rehearsal at the school. Daphne's pelvis, he knew, was constructed in a way which gave her an advantage when walking.

"You are a dear!" she said. "Teddy, you are sweet. You've heard all this before about the Hatchet and yet you let me rave on and get it all off my chest. That woman has made so many difficulties. She wants the honor and glory of the theatrical performance—you know, parents' weekend—and all the way she creates problems. Small people do that, of course. My *bête noire*!" Prince lumbered off after a stick. Daphne, Edwin knew, searched for sticks for Prince often when she was trying to hide tears. "I'm sorry, Teddy," she said.

Edwin, remembering recent tender nights, smiled at Daphne. A whole renewal of love made him love her too. Leila was indescribably sweet. He sighed softly.

"She'll be just the same over the Wakefield plays, you'll see!" Daphne threw another stick but Prince did not bother to fetch it. "He's near his time," she said with a little laugh.

Edwin muttered some endearments. Daphne was rather red in the face and even more untidy than usual. Wherever she was she had to have a *bête noire*. He remembered an impossible librarian once; another time, her butcher fulfilled the requirements.

That Leila had recovered from her ordeal so quickly was a great relief to Edwin. At first she had run away from him in the pines. He realized at once that she thought someone was chasing her. He heard her sobbing as she stumbled between the trees. By calling her name, "Leila!" and louder, "Leila!" he managed to make her hear him and she sank down, crying aloud like a little child. He had crouched down beside her while she, drawing breath between sobs, explained that while the house lights were on she was able to know where she was. She had seen him, she said, up there in the doorway all lit up from behind while the cars were leaving, but then after the lights were off she had lost all her sense of direction. "I ran all over the place." The words were still in his mind as he went over again in his thoughts how, with his arm tightly round her thick shivering shoulders, he had guided her to the road and across the road. Even now he was unable to think of the right words for explanation and apology.

Once inside the house they had looked at her grazed and bleeding knees. Edwin, wondering wildly what he should do, even thought of calling Cecilia to ask her advice. Leila, who was still shivering, suddenly said in the most matter-of-fact way, "I think I'd better have a bath." The short *a* in "bath" made the suggestion even more sensible. Together they had gone to the bathroom and together they ran the hot water and then the cold; "mixing the bath," Leila called it. Again the short *a* impressed him, and at the same time it was amusing.

Now, as he walked half a stride behind Daphne, Edwin, knowing that the Hatchet, taking advantage of Daphne's many qualities, steadfastly refused to give her a position of permanence at the school, felt he ought to comfort her in some way. He tried to think of soothing remarks but instead kept allowing his thoughts to be filled with the memories of pleasure.

During that first night alone with Leila he had thought briefly of Cecilia while his arms and thighs were holding and caressing Leila's young body. He hoped Cecilia was not frightened over Montreal when the plane hovered in that sickening way before landing. Forgetting Cecilia, he offered Leila nothing more than warmth and sleep that night. He had continued his gentle caressing with a tenderness which held him in restraint. He found he enjoyed the sensation and the power which was in the restraint. Later he was obliged to lean over Leila's sleeping form to reach for some tissues. Not finding any, he had to move as lightly as he could from the bed and make his way with small, soft steps to the bathroom. Slipping back into the warmth beside Leila, he had been agreeably surprised at this guiltless return to a youthful action which was now followed by a feeling of well-being and contentedness without misgivings and without the customary bleak sense of being alone. He thought of Cecilia again, feeling he had enough tenderness to spare. His desire satisfied, he continued to hold Leila close while she slept.

Leila's young rounded pink body in the bath reminded him of Cecilia years ago, though really there were no similarities except those of the sameness of women. He had not expected any differences, but the difference was in the way he felt. Both he and Cecilia had found—they had discussed this often—that when they were away from each other for any length of time they each thought of the other as they had been years before. Cecilia, laughing, often said what a shock it was to come home to Edwin as he was now. Once she had nearly choked she laughed so much, because she had forgotten about his little corset.

Leila, liking the idea of a hot drink in bed, came quite naturally to his study. They had not spoken much because she was, after being so cold, wonderfully warm and could hardly keep awake. Edwin, fascinated, watched her drowsiness turn into a deep sleep. He undressed in the bathroom and was able to get into bed without waking her.

He wanted now to talk to Daphne about Leila. One of the things about Leila was this need he had to tell someone about her. He did not want to be clumsy. A recent and disturbingly pleasant conversation with Leila's mother was uppermost in his mind and he wanted to tell Daphne about that as well.

It was not easy to blurt out the words: "Daphne, I must tell you I have been holding Leila in my arms all night and every night for some nights now."

"She's jealous of you, Daph," he said instead, "the Hatchet. She's jealous because the girls all like you and your plays are a success. On Speech Day," he added with an extra generosity, "I could see her jealous bristling all round her when the parents were so eager to talk to you." He ached to talk about Leila.

"No," Daphne said, "it's simply because I'm tall, taller than average, and she's very short. She wants to be a goddess and everyone knows there's no such thing as a short-legged goddess. I'm not implying," Daphne added, "that I think of myself as a goddess, not at all, though I do happen to have rather long legs." She laughed, self-consciously, Edwin thought. "Though I must say," Daphne continued, "to attempt something, a production, utterly medieval in this day and age is ambitious to say the least. She's waiting to pick holes. . . ."

Edwin gave a little grunt in agreement. "Daphne," he said, "I want to tell you something. It's about Leila. She's going to have a baby."

"Good heavens!" Daphne said. "She's no more than a child, a very well-developed child. Of course," she added, "girls are nubile now at a much younger age. It's all the fast foods, the hamburger steaks, they eat. The meat—I've read about it somewhere—the meat's full of hormones. Quite little girls, only eight years old, start menstruating. Just imagine adding to all those years ahead!"

"Daphne, Leila's baby will be mine, my baby, mine," he insisted, "my baby."

"But, Teddy, I'm keeping an eye on you, remember?"

"Yes, I know, Daph. That's why I'm telling you. I want you to know." He heard himself pleading and was not sure why he should plead.

"You would qualify as Grandfather"—Daphne smiled at the idea—"for any child of Leila's."

"Yes, I know"—Edwin was meek—"but the child will be mine. I am the father of the child." At the word "father" a little shiver of pleasure went through him. "The baby will be mine and"—he paused—"and Cecilia's; that's part of the arrangement."

"Does Cecilia know?" Daphne stood still, facing him.

"Not yet," Edwin said. "It's to be a surprise. And we don't know yet, of course, if Leila has conceived. We're not absolutely certain."

"How old is Leila?" Daphne wanted to know. "How old did you say she was?" She did not seem at all shocked by Edwin's last remark or by the intimate possessive "we." If she was surprised she did not show it.

"You know how she looks," Edwin, feeling suddenly troubled, said. "She could be anything between sixteen and thirty-five."

"Well," Daphne said, "let's hope she's over sixteen or it could be carnal knowledge, or is it being done with a test tube?"

He knew she could be outspoken at times but he knew too that she would never intend to be cruel.

"It's all right, Daph," he said. "She's twenty-two."

"She seems so very young." Daphne seemed to be brooding. "I believe," she went on, "that conception is not at all difficult for human beings. It's camels who have difficulties. Did you know, Teddy," she said, "camels actually have to be helped to mate. I read it somewhere."

"You seem to be reading a great deal lately, Daph," Edwin said, with one of his special little smiles. Daphne ignored the smile. "All the same," she said, "Leila does give the impression of being young, very young, with a kind of innocence. My girls at school have far more *savoir faire*, are more sophisticated. I doubt if any of them would do anything like this."

They walked on in silence. "She does seem so very young," Daphne said again.

In literature and in real life, Edwin knew, mothers lied about their daughters' ages. Cecilia would have been a great help in this. She met, in the course of her work, all kinds of women. She would know things about them indicative of their ages. She would be familiar with the signs of previous childbirth or of certain diseases. She would be familiar too with women like Leila's mother and would know their ways of thinking and their motives and would be able to see straight away if a lie was being told.

"You can hardly," Daphne was saying, "visit the mother, Leila, in the Mary and Joseph. What on earth would they think?"

"Who? Mary and Joseph?" Edwin tried to make a joke. "They," he said, "are hardly in a position to be critical."

"Seriously, Teddy," Daphne said, "Leila couldn't go there. And what will you tell people?"

"Ultimately," Edwin said, "the truth, of course. There's a special name for it—the sugar mother." He gave a little laugh. "Leila's mother and Leila have agreed on a fee. We are arranging it privately between ourselves. At a certain stage I will hand over part of the fee; the rest is payable on delivery. Quite simple!"

"Sounds like a box of groceries," Daphne said. "But seriously, Teddy, and I am serious, what if this woman, Leila's mother, is pulling a fast one on you, pulling the wool over your eyes—about to cheat you out of several thousands of dollars? I presume it goes into thousands and I suppose they will go on living in your house with you?"

"Yes." Edwin nodded. "Yes," he said. Some nagging misgivings which kept coming at intervals returned now, as a pain might return. There was an uneasiness accompanying the whole transaction. It was like buying school shoes. It was like letting his mother pay for an expensive pair of shoes when he knew that they pinched and when there was still time to say that they did not fit properly. He smiled at Daphne in an attempt to reassure himself. One of the uncertainties, and there were others, was still the gentle brushing of Leila's hand against his hand. It seemed a long time since the evening when he had failed to explain and apologize for the stupidity which he, and most certainly Daphne, would never mention again. It was something he knew he would always feel ashamed of. He was, as now, often not sure, not at all sure, that Leila had actually touched his hand that evening.

Recently during the exchange of touching, a great deal of touching, far more than a tentative brushing of one hand against another, the moment for asking his question had passed. His smile for Daphne changed now to one of tender memory and it was a smile for himself. They, Leila and he, did not look back in every embrace but always forward to the next. He allowed himself one more thought of Leila and that was of her wearing the new apron bought especially for him. The apron suited her. He hurried to keep up with Daphne.

"Leila's mother is very good at the business side of it," he said. "She says it is usual to have a passing over of money when conception is confirmed; nothing is paid till then. She seems very understanding and open about it and feels, as I do, that a natural conception is more satisfactory than the more scientific method. And the final payment is only made when the child is actually handed over. She wants, she told me, to get back to England with Leila and her sister, who is ill. She needs the fares for the three of them to get back home, she says. Apparently a misunderstanding in Mr. Bott's life has brought them into financial difficulties. I gather Mr. Bott is not available at present. Of course I wouldn't dream of asking and she did not, at this stage, offer explanations. I understand that they have only been here a few months. Migrants"—Edwin, drawing breath, felt he was being his most pedantic—"migrants," he said, "either make it or they don't. I have not considered the problems of these people who are divided in their attitudes towards a change of country, but problems do exist, especially when—"

"Are you and Cecilia going to split up?" Daphne asked. She seemed upset, more so than necessary, he thought.

"Of course not, Daph." He turned his attention away from the unsuccessful migrant and the reasons for problems and discontent.

"I don't know at all what I would do"—Daphne choked—"if I didn't have you two. I need you both dreadfully. I know this sounds awful and selfish but I do need you. I haven't got anyone. I . . ."

"Yes. Yes, of course, Daph, and we need you," Edwin said in a low voice. "The whole idea is that we'll be more together. Cecilia will be at home more. We'll be more of a—well, more of a family, more together." He put an arm round her.

"Oh, Teddy. Sorry. Sorry to howl like this out here in the pines but I can't help it. And oh God—here's the road. We've reached the road and I shall have to fly. I'm frightfully late. One of the really awful things," she said, "about being friends with a couple is when they split up. Suddenly they're gone. But I must go, Teddy; it's late." She paused, standing still in front of him. "If a couple split, do you see," she said, "the person who is not part of a couple—and let's face it, we live in a world of couples—the person who is not part of a couple is alone. It's different," she went on, "with you and Cecilia. I never feel with you like that dreadful phrase, an awful phrase that people use: I never felt or feel, you know, like the fifth wheel. I know there's Miss Hearnsted and Miss Heller but I mean—well, you know what I mean. . . ."

"I'm sorry, Daphne." Edwin tried to think of words. "I'm sorry," he said again.

—118—

"I must look a perfect fright." Daphne blew her nose. "My nose is all red; it always is if I cry, and my eyes look awful. The girls will be waiting for the rehearsal. . . . They'll know I've been crying."

"I'm sorry," Edwin said again. "You look all right, Daph." He found he could not speak. He patted her arm.

"Prince! Prince! Here, boy!" Daphne's tremendous dog-calling voice hit the pines. Prince came lazily from between the dark trees. "Hurry up, Prince!" Daphne yelled. "I shall have to go, Teddy," she said. "Do put your thinking cap on." She paused. "And, Teddy, don't talk about it to other people: you know, *people*, our friends at the club; not yet anyway. Some people," she said, "don't have any standards or conscience, and gossip would reach Cecilia and hurt her dreadfully. It's one thing to hear gossip and not know whether to believe it and another to be told something straight out by the person concerned. Don't you see, Teddy, how awkward it's going to be? I'm not at all sure," she added, bending down to put an unnecessary lead on the slow-moving Prince, "about Cecilia. It seems to me that Cecilia would have had a baby herself, more than one, if she had wanted to. Do think carefully, Teddy."

◆ ◆ ◆

Edwin hurried home through the black pines. The rain was starting again. At this time of the evening the plantation seemed endless, like a wild place. Small wonder that poor little Leila lost her way in the dark. The idea of the plantation offering the possibilities of being lost and yet confined within two parallel but wide-apart suburban roads was quite pleasant. It was possible to walk for considerable fresh distances lost in the fragrance and the greenness and to know that ultimately it was possible to emerge, to come out, on safe roads any of which could be followed to find the way home. Because he was hungry he thought of Leila's mother. Surprisingly, he found it easy to talk to her and easy to think of the talking later.

"That is a great shame," Leila's mother had said about there being apparently no possibility of a baby son or daughter. "Leila," she had said, "Leila'll carry, if I put it to her, Leila'll carry for you. I'd have no trouble with Leila." To start with, he had not been able to understand.

"I'm saying," Leila's mother said, "Leila would oblige with carrying for you and Dr. Sissily. It's being done all over the place now. It's quite the thing these days."

He had managed to overcome self-conscious and awkward feelings.

"There's different ways," Leila's mother had said, "but I favor Nature's way myself. It's like home baking, as I always say; you know what's in it."

It was not hard to recall, as he walked alone, his thoughts and feelings about the idea, and contemplating Leila's fresh, youthful body in this way was not in the least disagreeable, especially since his restrained and tempting foretaste on the night she had been lost and found in the pines.

"Take it slowly," Leila's mother had said, "and never you worry, Dr. Page; just let Nature take her course. There's nothing to pay till conception and then we'll go from there. Make sure," she added, "make sure she turns and lies on her face. I'll tell her, but you remind her afterwards. Tell her to lie face down; that way she's sure to fall."

"Fall?" Edwin remembered now his perplexed question.

"Fall pregnant," Leila's mother had said. "It never fails." The idea made him smile.

He was hungry, pleasantly hungry. Leila's mother, he knew, was thinking of making a mutton casserole with rosemary and mint and peas and carrots and potatoes. Did Dr. Page like mutton? Edwin, not able at that moment to remember whether mutton was one of the things he never ate, said the casserole sounded delicious. "Lovely," he said, giving Leila's arm a tiny pinch. "Lovely!"

The plantation was a wonderful place, richly moist and soft and comfortably dark. Leila would be waiting for him. He ran.

The room where they sat was already full of people.

"The whatsaname, the coil, was in the side of the afterbirth. She'd had the mini pill—it's no use, I tode her, taking the mini pill the next day when you're s'posed to take it of a nighttime, s'posed to take it the night before, I tode her . . ."

Edwin had noticed before how Leila's mother attracted confidences from strangers. He had not been to many shops with Leila and her mother, but of the few, he could not recall one where they had managed to leave without Leila's mother being waylaid by someone with a story, usually something gruesome. Leila, he noticed, being used to this, always stood patiently by; often she slipped a few extra items into the supermarket cart as if to avoid wasting time.

They sat side by side on some shabby chairs. Leila sat in the middle, between her mother and Edwin. Leila's mother was leaning towards another mother and her daughter. A small child clung to the younger woman, who sat leaning back, with her hands across the tightly stretched material of her dress. It was impossible not to overhear the intimate narrative which was interrupted now and then with little moans of sympathy and curiosity as Leila's mother listened and nodded. Sometimes the child staggered two steps and, falling, had to be rescued unwillingly by his mother.

"Talk about trouble," his grandmother said proudly. "He's give us that much trouble, that one. Her and me we've not had two hours sleep of a night ever since he was born." The doctor's waiting room was crowded. Unused to such places, Edwin felt shy. He would have liked to talk to Leila but did not want the sound of his voice to bring about a silence among those waiting.

"After her fifth or was it her sixth"—both mothers looked at the shameless multipara—"blowed if they didn't have to remove the coil. Embedded it was. I mean it just wasn't stopping her. The doctor, you'll like her, ever so nice she is, the doctor said to her you're four months pregnant, she says, just you take that baby offer the breast at once but clever boots here said she was only one week pregnant. Shortest pregnancy I ever heard of, I said, now I arsk you . . ."

The doctor called in Leila's mother then. She was going to have her bandaged leg unbandaged and checked and rebandaged. A lengthy business, Edwin felt sure, especially as Leila's mother, on the way there, had expressed an enjoyment in a heart-to-heart with the doctor, who was, in her words, a lovely girl.

It was Leila's first antenatal appointment. She sat close to Edwin, who covered her hand with his hand. He wished they could be somewhere else. He knew from a careful study of Cecilia's textbooks the position Leila would have to adopt for the examination. She would lie on her left side with her left leg straight and the right leg flexed, with the knee almost on her chest. In the photographs of the position the patient had her face covered with a square of white cardboard. Like the woman in the photographs, Leila would lie still and when asked she would roll onto her back and allow the doctor's hands to press her soft belly and to gently squeeze, first one and then the other, her soft but somehow full breasts. Leila's breasts had been tender for a few weeks, he reflected. Gently he stroked her hand. She seemed docile and not at all nervous about being examined.

"Shall I come in with you?" he asked in a low voice.

"If you want to," she replied.

"I expect you'll be examined behind a screen," he said.

—— 122 ——

"I expect so," she said. It seemed to him that as on the night of the pines, when she was frightened and cold, she displayed an extraordinary calm, saying in her matter-of-fact way, "I think I better have a bath," she was wonderfully serene now. Accustomed to people who talked a great deal, he found this lack of speech refreshing and honest.

"All right?" he asked a few minutes later. He gave her hand a small gentle squeeze.

"Oh yes," she said. "I'm hungry, but . . ." she added.

"We'll go somewhere nice for lunch," he said.

"Yes," she said. "I love fish and chips with salt and vinegar; that's what I'll have."

There were several notices about fees pinned up on a notice board. Notices too about antenatal classes, postnatal clinics, breast feeding and child care centers. *How to Take Care of Your Episiotomy.* Edwin read the title of a forthcoming lecture. The world, he reflected, was full of mystery. He would look up "episiotomy" at home.

Leila's mother and Edwin accompanied Leila into the surgery when it was Leila's turn.

♦ ♦ ♦

Edwin sat in the car reading and making some fresh notes for his four-thirty lecture. Leila and her mother were choosing a green vegetable and some jars of pickles and honey in the market. They had asked to stop on the way home, Leila having declared a fancy for a particular kind of pickle. Normally, Leila's mother told Edwin, she made her own, but as Leila was bound to be a bit capricious during the next few months, pickles bought in single jars would be best. "She's as likely to go off them as soon as not," Leila's mother said, "and then what!" Leila's mother hated waste, she said.

On reflection it seemed to Edwin that the whole of life could be lifted up and pinned to a notice board. All feeling and thought and emotion could be reduced to little squares and oblongs of paper containing the passionless sensible care of the human body from conception onwards. The doctor's waiting room had not overlooked the elderly. A menopause support group, traveling dinners and a complete guide to funeral arrangements were included. He supposed it was a mixture of fortune and misfortune which made him one of those people who read every available notice. It sometimes took him several minutes to leave the corridors of his department because of the notice boards. Many of the notices there were completely out of date. Often he meant to mention this to someone. For example, Tranby could devote her energy to the complete reorganization of the boards and get her desired promotion. It was the sort of thing people did.

The things on the surgery notice board, many of them, were a part of Cecilia's work. She would be familiar with them. He did not want particularly to think of Cecilia, though everything about the appointment was ultimately to do with her. He wondered whether Leila craved a sweet mustard pickle or a more sophisticated chutney—spiced banana and raisin perhaps.

The booking of the bed, the suddenness of an actual date and an arranged bed at a maternity hospital, not the Mary and Joseph, brought the event very close and he found he had to make an effort to read. The doctor, not the one he always went to but a stranger, had seemed very efficient. He was too excited and too tender to think of anything other than Leila and her condition. He turned the page of his Renaissance text.

Vowing to perpetuate my name, I made a plan for this purpose as soon as I was able to orient myself. For I understood, without doubt, that life is twofold. . . .

Edwin made a little pencil mark beside this amazing similarity with his own life. The descriptions Cardano gave of his chosen meals were another source of satisfaction.

I consider nothing better than firm young veal, beaten tender with the back of a butcher knife and pot roasted without any liquors save its own. . . .

He had seen Leila's mother on her hands and knees slapping the meat on the kitchen tiles, something he was sure Cecilia did not know about. Leila's mother understood meat.

> . . . it has a way of drawing its own drippings . . . and thus the meat is far more juicy and much richer. . . .

There was his lecture to give before it would be dinnertime. He felt quite hungry. He was not accustomed to having a real appetite as he so often had now. He wondered if in some way he could open the four-thirty lecture with some of the mouth-watering details, the wings, the livers and the giblets of young fowls and pigeons. Forgetting that he avoided those parts of poultry, he tried to read on but wondered instead whether it was natural for a man of his age—he would be fifty-four soon—to be excited. Perhaps too much excitement would cause heart failure or a cerebral hemorrhage. He must be careful to protect himself from either of these. He made a note in the margin of his notes, a reminder to see his bank manager and his lawyer and to make arrangements to have his will put in order. Leila and her mother and the baby must all be provided for. Cecilia was no longer the "one and only"; three other people must have a share in whatever arrangements were made. This was an entirely new thought. There was an unusual pleasure in dwelling on his possessions and on what money he thought he might have to distribute. He wondered how Cecilia would feel being reduced to one of four beneficiaries. He made some rapid calculations and worked out an order of precedence to the grave.

Cecilia was fifteen years younger than he was. It had always seemed a startling difference in age. Buffy and Tuppy, both widowers, had much younger wives, younger that is than Buffy and Tuppy, smart and devoted and very hungry, and really, when you faced it, no longer young, elderly in comparison with Leila. Dippy Fairfax and Ida were the closest in age, he thought, suddenly seeing them all at Sunday tennis, good-natured and healthy, spinning their racquets and flexing their muscles. Leila was approximately eighteen years younger than Cecilia and about thirty-three (he had not been quite truthful, give or take a year, to Daphne) years younger than he was. He did not know Leila's mother's age. Cecilia would know at a glance if she was postmenopausal. In any case he felt sure he was older than she was. When the child was born he would be fifty-four years older than the child. It was quite clear that he would be the first to die, and it was his responsibility to see that all these people would be well provided for, especially the child.

The child, the thought of the child, filled him with a strange wonder and joy. He began to remember all sorts of things. When he was a boy there was a wooden train; till this moment he had forgotten it. There was a red-painted engine, some freight cars and a yellow caboose. The freight cars, as he thought about them loaded with sand and stones and coal and timber, became more vivid. He remembered scraping the earth with his hands to make tracks. He played, then, at the end of the garden in a part not used for vegetables. He had a trench hut there too, a hole dug in the ground with a roof of wood covered with turf. From the top it looked like a slight rise in the grassy place. There might be, he thought, a suitable spot in their garden where he and Cecilia could make such a hut. His own hut had a fireplace with a chimney. He hoped for his child to be a boy because of the idea of a hut.

One summer the dry roof of his hut caught fire. He had clear memories of his mother rushing with buckets of water, and of her tears when she found he was not in the hut but in an apple tree close by. He heard her crying again in the night. She wept without any deep voice consoling. She seemed to weep all night. Alone.

But about the wooden train. It was inherited, as was the trench hut, from the grown-up family in the household where his mother was employed. He remembered clearly now, with pleasure, how he played. He made a yard in the sandy soil. He banked up the earth into slopes and tunnels. He made platforms and sheds and a passenger station decorated with flowers. He had lights and signals and pens for animals. He made fences and planted bits of broken-off bushes to make trees. When it rained, realistic puddles lay in the hollows and he set about correcting drainage problems. He spent hours, he remembered, down at the wild end of the garden, day after day after day.

Outside the market, where he sat, was just such a place as his goods yard. His lecture notes slipped sideways off his lap as he looked out at the rough patch of gravel where recent rain had left patches of water, gleaming now in the sunshine. Some cars were parked as if a child had set them out in a game. One car had a horse trailer. Along the fence there were some trees, and immediately outside the entrance to the market were boards bearing chalked messages about the bargains to be found inside. He could have made this place in one of his games long ago. Perhaps every place made in childhood games persisted: yards for wooden trains, parking lots, shopping centers, police stations, law courts, schools, churches, hospitals, army barracks and houses. Perhaps every person walking along the street had been drawn, created, by some child somewhere. Perhaps that was why some individuals had no necks or were completely bald or devoid of teeth or, if they had teeth, seemed to have a mouthful of pickets. Some people had long legs and others had legs which did not match. And some, mainly women, had legs which came out of the edges of their skirts and could not, by any stretch of the imagination, fit at the tops of their thighs to their bodies. The legs, if you took a line upwards, would pass by each side of the body unrelated and useless. It was an idea of the ancient Greeks, he thought, that an idea, a vision, if written about, could be brought into existence. He wondered, as he saw them coming, who it was had created Leila's mother and Leila. They were laden with plastic shopping bags. Edwin, as fast as he could, picked his way across the wet gravel to help them. As he looked at Leila with a mixture of love and tender curiosity about her changed state, so closely and exquisitely linked to him, he did not pursue the question as to who was, at this moment perhaps, just drawing and decorating with paints or crayons their unborn baby.

"In the evening, overflowing with tenderness and a large quantity of one of his finer burgundies, a soft Pinot Noir, he wrote a letter to Cecilia. Not a long letter but one in which he stressed the importance of writing. He asked her to write to him; he said that phone calls were fine but he felt he was inarticulate and repetitive and then their relationship seemed brittle. In letters, he wrote, they could express their real feelings. He was pleased with the letter; it included spontaneously a line from Donne. As he sealed the envelope he realized that so far he had been able to take all phone calls privately in his study, out of earshot. Leila's mother never answered the phone. It was as if she had a small personal rule of never answering the phone in someone else's house. He felt she was the soul of discretion; he was sure that was how she would describe herself. He knew he had written the letter to try to avoid the possibility of Leila overhearing things, the "love love you" and the "kiss kiss" nibblings. He put the letter in his pocket and, with one gentle finger, stroked the soft neck which was near his knee. Leila was sitting on the floor. She had been playing with a sleepy puppy, the last and smallest of Prince's litter. She leaned her head against Edwin's knee. He wanted there and then to draw her up beside him as close as possible. He found, at such times, a real longing coming over him and he thought impatiently of the bed they had been sharing. His study seemed different, he reflected, as did the room in which they were now sitting. He glanced at the shabby roses on the wallpaper and seemed to be seeing them after a long absence. The doctor, a young, serious-looking woman, had offered with other words of congratulation and advice that continuing sexual relations were permissible, indeed desirable for good health and well-being. Leila was a healthy little primipara, she said, and she would see her again in four weeks time unless there were any problems and an earlier appointment was needed. As he fondled Leila's soft short hair he thought that this must be what real happiness was. He supposed people at his age began to consider whether they were happy or not. Once, during one of their nights, he had asked Leila, "Happy, darling?" and she had not replied. She lay with her head moving slightly, rising and falling with every breath he took because his chest was her pillow. She had not replied because she was asleep.

As if to heighten his contented feeling of happiness he had to recall that it was always his habit to ask "Happy, darling?" of Cecilia and she had always her little words of reply, always the same words, accompanied by the same little snuggle movement. He did not want particularly to think of this now; he was not sure that such thoughts enhanced happiness. He went on, in spite of this thought, to discuss in his mind the changes for the better for himself and Cecilia when the time came for them to be parents. They would never again, he thought, need an artificial life of parties to fill an emptiness. He tried not to think of Cecilia and of their lives. Thinking about her brought the keys game to his mind. Did Cecilia, he wondered, repeatedly sit on Buffy's knees and laugh and fondle with her icy little fingers his ears and, at the same time, laugh and twitter and pretend to be a bird to amuse him? In that repetitive game was that all she ever permitted anyone, himself included? Without wanting to, he remembered the constant high-pitched laughing, the laugh in a minor key, and the "Oh, exquisite, darling! You do love me, don't you." The words, not requiring any answer, were always the same. He found he was frowning and he looked down on the crown of

Leila's round head, at the place from which her hair seemed to spring. He thought of the silence during those solemn times when he, with reverence, took her soft youthful body in his arms and turned her towards himself. He smiled now as he recalled the way in which she moved closer to him, with the whole of her body and without laughing. Perhaps he was glad to think of the keys game and to dismiss it, to know that he need never play it again. Everything was going to change.

They sat together. The little puppy was asleep on his sheets of newspaper. Leila's mother, ever careful about other people's carpets, spread papers over all the places she thought the puppy would occupy.

Paulette, Erica, Ida and Cecilia talked too much during lovemaking. He understood this now. He understood too that his own elaborate preparations for being the perfect lover and the rituals employed to create an art called lovemaking were worthless. They—Paulette, Erica, Ida and Cecilia (there were others too)—told anecdotes, one after another, little stories with related conversations to hold off, as it were, the finale. Perhaps they talked in order to build up the climax like the suspending of drama in the writing of a good play or a novel. But so often the climax, the ultimate, the "all the way" as Erica called it, the "full out" (Cecilia), and the "over the top" (Paulette), was over without being anything and had lost the special afterfeelings of tenderness.

He bent forward and touched Leila's unpretentious clean hair with his lips. "How would you like to have your bath now," he said in a low voice, "and I'll come in a little while." She smiled up at him, her plain round face almost pretty with the pleasure of obedience. She scrambled to her feet and went away. He sat alone, staring at the sleeping baby dog. He could not bear the thought of Cecilia's homecoming. The inevitability of it was appalling. He must stop that arrangement for the Christmas visit to England; that much was certain. Other thoughts, as if someone had made an effigy of him and was sticking pins into it, came in a very unwelcome and sharp sequence. A sudden understanding of his position surprised him. Joy at the hoped-for certainty of conception was followed now by an ache which filled his whole body. In the settled arrangement it was time for the first payment. It was not that, not the paying of the agreed sum; it was the beginning of the farewell to Leila. She was pregnant now and he was not required to go on making her pregnant. He had not expected to feel as he did. To take advantage now would not be in keeping with the arrangement and not in keeping with the standards he wanted to adopt in his new life. He watched the little dog twitching in his sleep. He supposed life was simple for dogs. He tried to think of Cecilia, to turn some of his wishing in her direction. He tried to think of her as she was years ago but in his mind he heard her laughter and shrank from it. He must look forward to her return. It was unfair to her not to. He jumped up and made for the door. He turned back from the door. He must, he told himself, take his mind and his longing away from Leila. His desk, he said aloud, was a mess. He must get back to his work.

Leila's mother was in the kitchen, ironing and folding clothes. Edwin, as he entered, could hear the bathwater running. He could not help thinking of Leila's slippery body, partly submerged. Her body amused him. He smiled, thinking of the neat triangle of dark hair filled with tiny bubbles in the foam. For the full young breasts he felt a curious reverence. He took his checkbook and his narrow silver pen, a recent gift from Cecilia. "I think," he said to Leila's mother with his best smile, "that tonight I must make my first payment."

"If it's convenient," Leila's mother said. "There's no hurry, no particular hurry. Anytime this week or next."

"Cash, is it?" Edwin raised one handsome eyebrow.

"Thank you." Leila's mother moved a pile of clothes to one side. "I'll give you a receipt," she said, watching as Edwin wrote the check.

"Oh, that's not necessary," he said, immediately regretting his words; of course he might need a proof of payment at some stage. Leila's mother said thank you again and took the offered check, blowing on it to dry the ink.

"Leila's looking well," he said to cover any awkwardness and to dismiss the uneasiness he had caused for himself by grandly refusing the receipt. He wanted to say that he was sorry that his time with Leila was at an end. Unable to find the words for this, he continued to smile, saying, "I do hope that you and Leila will consider my suggestion that you continue to stay here till . . ."

"Thank you," Leila's mother said. "We're ever so pleased to stay. I hope you find everything to your satisfaction," she added.

"Oh yes, very," Edwin said.

"Perhaps I should mention," Leila's mother said, "Leila's had her little cry; just now she came in here to have her little weep."

"Why on earth?" Edwin was startled. "Is anything wrong? Would she prefer you to keep the other house?"

"Aw Gawd, no!" Leila's mother said. "It's not that at all. It's just that she likes spending her time with you but I've told her you've got your work to do. 'The doctor's got his writing and studying to do,' I told her. 'We've got to get busy and get things ready for the baby,' I said to her. 'The doctor's a busy man,' I said."

Edwin, knowing what she meant, wanted to ask her what she thought he should do. Even while he was thinking this, Leila's mother said, "A man knows what he should do and he knows what he wants to do, and if I know anything about men, they usually do what they want." With her mouth pursed and demure, she pressed the iron hard down on a heap of folded pillowcases.

"What d'you think I should do?" Edwin was helpless.

"If you're asking me," Leila's mother replied, "I think as head of your own house and you being a gentleman you should do as you think best." She jerked her head in the direction of the door. "I think," she said, "that's Leila now coming out of the bath"—she paused—"or is she just going in? I'm sure I can't tell from here."

As he left the kitchen Edwin felt like a young man, a boy

even, given permission, in a sense, but not knowing what to do with an apparent freedom. He had manners, knowledge and experience but none of these things fitted the occasion. He paused outside the bathroom door. He could hear Leila splashing the water—mixing the bath, she called it—and singing softly without tune. He waited smiling to himself and almost opened the door.

H e lived in Arcadia where he guarded flocks and matchless herds and beehives, took part in the revels of mountain nymphs and helped hunters . . .

Edwin tried to read during his sleeplessness. Muffled in the distance, the puppy was crying. Edwin heard the piteous yelpings. The puppy, lonely without his mother, had cried for several nights. He knew Leila's mother got up to it patiently, spending some time in the kitchen every night. The puppy lived a curious life, Edwin thought, with bursts of destructive energy alternating with sudden periods of unexpected sleep. A sleep with powerful qualities which restored the little animal quickly. He found himself longing for such a sleep. It was a night of wind and rain. He could hear the pines straining in the wind. The complications of his life, without the relaxation of the pleasures, seemed to rest heavily on him. He had never felt so alone. Without Leila his bed was incredibly empty. His life, even with looking forward to the child, was empty. The unborn child, the expectation of it, was not enough. In the unexpected realization of this he tried to console himself with the promise of Leila's company at breakfast. Without the secrecy of the night together the breakfast table would be barren.

Pregnancy: the doctor reduced the whole thing to forty weeks. Nine months. Thirteen weeks is three months. Thirty-nine weeks is nine months plus one week more. The twenty-eighth week would be Christmas. Swiftly she had worked out the approximate date of birth, March the fourteenth. Sitting upright in bed, Edwin, thinking about the weeks of his life which could be spent with Leila, added his own calculations. Leila's baby, the baby, would be about three months old when Cecilia came home. Eleven weeks old, to be exact. Cecilia would come home to be mother to an eleven-weeks-old child.

It was better, Leila's mother said, for the mother of the baby not to handle the child if she was to part with it. Edwin, agreeing at the time, wondered about a nursemaid. Now, during this long stormy night, no other woman seemed suitable for the care of his child. Cecilia herself would need a nursemaid. Edwin knew he could not hope for her to give up her work altogether; some of it perhaps, but not all. The thought of this settled heavily.

Cease to remember the delights of youth, travel-wearied aged man.

He sat huddled over his notebook of the intangible, unable to remember if the line was from Yeats or from *Oedipus at Colonus.* He was not sure if he had misquoted or put two different things together. It was not his way to be inaccurate though he was known to be forgetful. In some ways his forgetfulness now was because life suddenly had much to offer. He had neglected to go to the spring for water. The stained plastic containers were in a heap in a corner of the garage. He seemed to be in perfect health on Leila's mother's tea made with ordinary tap water. He understood that Leila's mother would never question tap water.

Knowing that he could not, he wrote in his book that he must go in to Leila even if it meant, as it did, invading the mother and daughter nest. He thought about the spare room and about the tidiness of Leila and her mother and how they folded everything into neat plastic envelopes. He was neat too. He always folded his pajamas every morning in a flat way to lie under his pillow. When he unfolded his pajamas in the evening and put them out on his folded-back bed cover, Cecilia laughed. At least she had laughed when they were in a room together. He did not think it was amusing to be tidy. Cecilia was untidy; she left her clothes everywhere: desperately untidy, he thought, forgiving her every time, knowing from films that surgeons stepped out of their white surgery boots, leaving them just where they stepped out of them. They threw off their gowns and ripped away their masks and rubber gloves before the nurse, trotting alongside, had a chance, with her pink nimble fingers, to remove them. Naturally Cecilia adopted their ways. She was one of them, and though the mess in her bedroom disturbed Edwin, he put up with it because it was the background to her work. There was no reason, he told himself, why he should have given up Leila. Tomorrow he would suggest that Leila come back. After all, Leila's mother said he should do what he thought best.

"What's an episiotomy?" he asked Cecilia as he picked up the telephone quickly. "Lord knows": he heard Daphne's voice. "Teddy, darling!" she said. "Most awfully sorry to call you at this unearthly hour. I know it's after midnight, almost one, to be exact, but it's Cecilia. Will you phone her, please. She's in a state because you haven't phoned and she says she hasn't heard a thing from you and wants to know if you're all right. I told her you'd ring straight back. She's waiting by her phone. I'm sorry," Daphne said, "I can't help with episiotomy, whatever it is. Is it anything to do with dogs? Nothing wrong with Blackie, is there? I've got an awfully good dog book. Teddy," Daphne said, "you'll have to tell Cecilia something. Apparently both of them, Cecilia and Vorwickl, are freaking out on Muesli. Vorwickl is enormous and is trying to reduce.

They've been measuring each other's waists and hips and thighs." Daphne, unsuccessfully, tried to stifle a yawn. "Teddy," she said, "you must phone at once. To put it plainly, it's getting awkward for me. Sorry to sound so selfish. She wants to know how the dinner parties are. You haven't canceled the Fairfaxes' evening, have you? How will you manage? I know Leila and her mother went to *Mary Poppins*—oh, sorry—*The Sound of Music,* the rerun, last time but what will you do about the next one? Oh, I see"—Daphne made little noises of understanding—"it's at the Fairfaxes' place. Yes, I'll try and be there, though you know, Teddy, it's awkward for me having to be careful what I say. It's pretty drastic, Teddy; I feel I'm losing you and Cecilia and I don't want to."

"I'll write to her," Edwin promised, "and I'll ring now," he said.

"Oh, you are a dear!" Daphne said and rang off. Edwin imagined he could hear her thumping her pillows to make them comfortable, as she might have done, with Cecilia in the next bed, at school.

Sometimes in the mornings the pines were green in the misty sunshine. The tufted grass from a distance looked smooth and soft, spreading carpet-like in little slopes and rises, making linings for hollows and hiding broken-off branches or stumps with a wonderful velvet quality. Close to, it was possible to see how the grass sparkled with moisture. In the early morning there was an ethereal quality in the light, and the sky, seen through the trees, was pale and clear. Later on, tall flowers, with pink bells on their stalks, would grow between the trees. These flowers always reminded Edwin of foxgloves as he had known them in England. They were not foxgloves. He always forgot about them from one year to the next. When he saw them he was pleased and, without any sadness, remembered real foxgloves. Somewhere, quite early in his book of the intangible, he had written about these flowers and his feelings of surprise at their faithfulness in being reborn in another country in a likeness which was familiar.

Leila's mother said during breakfast that it would be a good idea to start getting things ready for the baby. "Time flies," she said. Carefully she turned Leila's teacup round and round to see if the leaves gave any signs about a boy or a girl. "One thing's clear," she said, "you're carrying that baby in your face and your shoulders." She said she thought the little dressing room would be best for the nursery. She did not want to disagree with Dr. Page, she said, but there was no need to use Dr. Sissilly's own beautiful bedroom. Babies, she told Edwin, had only two things in their heads and these, being feeding and sleeping, could be done anywhere. The small room between Dr. Sissy's room and the study had a nice window and would be entirely suitable. Should it be painted? Edwin wanted to know. That was up to him, Leila's mother said. What did Leila think? Edwin asked, but Leila, unable to eat her breakfast, was leaving the table unable to speak.

"Go and lie down, Leila pet," Leila's mother called after her. "I'll fix you some juice and some nice bread and butter for later." She turned to Edwin. "No one ever lost a baby through the mouth," she said. "Being sick like she is, having the morning sickness as bad as she's got it, means she's keeping that baby. She'll not lose it. Throwing up like that, it's a sign." She poured herself another cup of tea. "Just don't you worry yourself, Dr. Page."

Edwin saw Leila's shoulders, rounded and thick with misery, and felt he was to blame. "Isn't there anything we can do?" he asked. Without expecting to, he felt helpless. "A doctor," he began, and thinking of Cecilia, he wondered if he should telephone her for a remedy for this awful thing.

"It's only the morning sickness," Leila's mother said. "She'll be over it directly and in a week or two she'll forget she ever had it. We'll go shopping," she said. "We'll get a few things, put a deposit on a pram and a crib and get the nappies; that'll take her mind off." Edwin took out his wallet and began counting notes. Leila's mother, with her eyes on the money, said, "She'll need three dozen Turkish toweling and a dozen of the muslin and three dozen disposable for taking in to the hospital. Babies' bottoms cost a fortune." She began to squeeze oranges.

Edwin heard, in the distance, Leila's distress. He wanted to rush to her to do the things people did for each other at such times. Without the experience of ever helping anyone, he suddenly felt he wanted to support her, hold her head, rinse her face flannel in fresh cold water and wipe away her tears. Long-forgotten times came back to him; he remembered his mother's hands and the incredible softness of her forearm. Perhaps it was during measles, he could not recall exactly, perhaps after overeating at a party.

They heard Leila calling for her mother.

"Just don't you worry, Dr. Page," Leila's mother said again. "Just you get on with your work and when Leila's better we'll be off out to the shops. She's looking forward to the shopping. She'll be as right as rain. She knows what she wants." She picked up the money. "I shan't need all this," Leila's mother said as she folded the notes into her purse.

"Leila might see something she needs." Edwin smiled.

"She might too," Leila's mother said.

Unable to read and unable to write, Edwin thought he should, after Daphne's telephone call, write to Cecilia. During the sleepless night he had dialed the long-distance call but clapped down the receiver as soon as he heard the telephone ringing. He then, as was his custom for a good deal of the time, disconnected the telephone. It was disturbing that he did not know what to say to Cecilia. He found, when he tried, that he could not write either. He stared at the sheets of paper on his desk and wrote Leila's name several times on one of them. He added words of consolation and endearment to her name. He sat thinking. He did not live in Arcadia but in a suburb desirable because of a pine plantation and an easy walk to the university. The Mary and Joseph was near and so was the tennis club. He had no flocks, beehives or matchless herds to guard, only the pine plantation, over which he did watch in an unprofessional way, noticing, with a comfortable vagueness, the removal of trees and the replantings, the burning off and the occasional stacks of trimmed trunks when the life span of certain groups of trees was declared by an authority to be over. In any case the pines were not his.

He must do something. Daphne's telephone call, which was really Cecilia's, could not be ignored. He would feel happier and more able to enjoy his newfound life if he straightened things out with Cecilia. With their attitudes towards freedom and individuality, the preservation of the individual within the accepted status of the couple (Cecilia's own words), why should this straightening present such difficulties? Christmas in England seemed pleasantly remote. He dismissed, as quickly as possible, Cecilia's mother and her sitting room lined with Christmas cards. Her festivity was manifest in the lighting of a fire in the cleaned grate in the front room, where the Christmas tree reappeared, year after year, in the same corner. Perhaps he should go and see Buffy. Some sort of strategic support was necessary, something conventional and military, with rules and acceptable ways of looking at the unacceptable. In simple terms all he had done was to father a child for adoption because Cecilia had not produced one. He had not expected his action to bring about the consequences he was experiencing.

Buffy had his own ways of dealing with the unconventional. Largely he would ignore it. He had phrases. They all had useful phrases but Buffy had the most. Perhaps if he called on Buffy it would be possible to reduce the problem. Discussion sometimes made things simple. And perhaps Buffy would know the best way to break the news; it would be called carrying dispatches to Cecilia. Buffy's language was useful in times of indecision.

Buffy's house was solid and double fronted, with a low veranda which had cement-covered brick pillars. Because of the deep veranda it was a cool house, freezing in winter; Paulette often shivered. Cane furniture, in hospitable arrangements, was plentiful in the shaded places.

The whole of the front garden was given over to grass, a wide smooth flat lawn, a replica on a small scale of the Anglo-Indian parade ground, the maidan. Buffy sat every afternoon with his sundowner, usually whisky with a dash of the tap, overlooking his lawn. Edwin often thought it was possible that in the smell of the freshly mown and watered grass, Buffy saw and heard the horses as he used to see and hear them. Perhaps, unseen by other eyes, there was, every day for Buffy, a series of remembered colorful parades followed every time by the thud and click as the horses thundered to and fro, their hooves throwing up fragments of soft earth and grass, bringing back to him the remembered sounds of the smacking of polo sticks against each other and on the ball. It was very possible that in the last glowing light from the sun, the maidan seemed wider and more inviting and the grass more fragrant, stirring memories from the days of the regiment. Often Edwin had wished for memories of this well-ordered kind. Retired early from duties in India because of the end of British rule, and a widower earlier than expected because India did things to your health, Buffy had clock golf on his maidan, a poor substitute, though he never said so, for the pleasure of riding the well-kept horses.

It was soon clear that Buffy and Paulette were not at home. Of course the car was not there; he should have seen that straight away instead of prowling to and fro on the dark varnished boards. He gave up trying to peer through the fly screens into the darkened rooms. It was tennis club day, he should have remembered; he should have been there: the numbers would be uneven. He had forgotten about tennis and about the club.

It was the Fairfax dinner party evening. He was supposed to go there. He told Leila's mother at breakfast he would not be in for dinner. They, of course, since he would be out, did not need to go to a long film or a play. The Fairfaxes owned several daughters, beautiful, graceful girls who knew exactly how to do their hair. They knew exactly how untidy it was possible to be to add to their beauty. They had mastered the wisps of the chignon and the maddening fringe to accompany the ponytail. They knew the colors which suited them and set them off deliciously against the subdued furnishings of the Fairfax lounge. The girls were charming and ornamental at the dinner table and afterwards, perched on the solid arms of the club-style chairs, they enchanted the guests with apparently naïve and innocent anecdotes. They handed coffee and chocolates and a particularly pleasant ginger sweet, which they made themselves, to every guest in turn. Naturally Dippy and Ida were very proud of them. One of the Fairfax girls was a student of Daphne's, she could never remember which one, she confessed to Edwin, who told her he did not think it mattered since they wore each other's dresses and were always changing their hair.

"But, Teddy, it does matter; she's writing about Cordelia's mother," Daphne said, pausing in the middle of the pines, "King Lear's wife," she said, "a feminist approach to the two endings of *King Lear*. You know, a conflation of texts." She sighed.

"I should have thought Lear's wife would have been well before the play," Edwin said, "not at the end. Surely she's hardly necessary for the plot."

"I know," Daphne said, "but it gets more and more difficult to find subjects. And I really must sort out which of those gels is actually doing the work. I suppose," she added thoughtfully, "Shakespeare, he has done this, the ending, as well as he can."

Edwin thought about the Fairfax girls. He would be proud too, so would Cecilia, of their child. He dismissed the dug-out garden hut and replaced it with a dolls' house. He would make a dolls' house with painted doors and windows and a trellis of paper roses. There were endless possibilities. A daughter like Leila would be sweet. Cecilia, he felt, would impose herself sufficiently on the child for people to declare they could see a likeness, but Edwin would cherish the Leila baby forever in his heart, for the child would be sweet like her sweet mother. It could never be like Cecilia. This much was certain. He wished, as he strolled across Buffy's maidan, that he did not have to think of Cecilia so often. When he was with Leila's mother it all seemed so simple. It was the other people in his life who made complications.

One of the rules, an unspoken rule in their set, which preserved friendship perhaps more than anything, was that they did not drop in on each other. They telephoned and they gave and accepted invitations. They lunched or dined by arrangement; even the summer Sunday mornings in the sea together were not casual. They took turns to invite—even to the beach. All the same Edwin had become afraid that someone, or all of them, would call at his house in an unexpected moment of affection to see how he was. When he thought about this during the night he tried to think of ways of explaining the presence of the little Leila family. Ms. Tranby, a recurring nightmare, might come at any time. She did not have the breeding to know about or keep to their rules. She might simply out of curiosity visit him and, horrors, Miss Bushby might accompany her. Perhaps he would be able to introduce Leila as his niece, but then Leila's mother would have to be his sister. Accustomed to being an only child, he was upset by the idea of a sister. Immediately there was a disgusting fleshy claim. He shuddered. And then if other details had to be released about what should be a perfectly natural idea, the birth of the child, then wouldn't that suggest, in lightly breathed words, incest? He had never used the word, never spoken it aloud, and now it was on his doorstep, in a sense, put there by himself. Buffy, in wise moments, often spoke about not bringing a catastrophe home. As a young man, he once explained, he, with his parents' unspoken approval, experimented with the housemaids with the understanding that a cradle would never be planted at his mother's feet.

Edwin wanted to go off to some remote place with Leila and, having her completely to himself, make love to her, not once or twice but all night long and the next day and the next night. It was not possible to be simply like an animal, a bull servicing a cow. He wanted to be with Leila to cherish her all day and every day. There was no such thing, he now discovered, as a once-for-all affair. Love was something hoped for and looked forward to and then hoped for again. And every time there was an indescribable renewal of reason and purpose, a restoring which was endlessly precious. Just thinking about Leila's plain round face—it was a little face—made him want her more. Her not knowing how to dress, how to make the most of her appearance, was endearing. He wondered, as he continued across the maidan, if he actually hated Cecilia. Hate was too strong a word. It was simply that if Cecilia were walking towards him now, across the grass, he would not want to meet her. He was glad that Paulette and Buffy were at tennis. Paulette would be sympathetic, he knew, but both of them, after listening to him, would secretly be upset and horrified at his disturbing the domestic calm.

He wanted to find Leila and her mother. He wondered which shops they would be visiting. He, suddenly wishing to be shopping with them, thought he might look for them. The idea did not seem impossible.

In the car he knew he must write to Cecilia. If he did not, there was every chance that she, thinking there was something wrong, might come home. Her work was important to her and so was her life with him. He thought he could write a letter now, something along the lines of the importance of work and life, lives, their lives. He remembered too Buffy once saying something when they, Tuppy and Dippy, Buffy himself, of course, and Edwin, were having an early sundowner waiting for the girls (Dippy), the womenfolk (Buffy), to come back from a hen party (Tuppy) somewhere. Buffy had spoken about the awful realization that someone might regard you with real distaste and irritation and that there was a deep gratitude in that however awful a marriage was, faults, quite bad faults, were often overlooked or at best tolerated. Speaking for himself, he had said he was grateful and they had all, with replenished glasses, agreed with him. He drove straight home.

He went round the back of his house to go in through the kitchen. Near the door there was an enormous tree whose branches creaked and strained even in the slightest wind. Edwin liked to pause there listening to the sounds, which reminded him of the straining timbers of a great ship crossing one immense ocean after another. Whenever he stood in his garden beneath the creaking branches he thought of the incredible progress a ship, her rail moving gently up and persistently down, makes. He had never forgotten standing on the deck of the ship one evening during the first voyage and being overwhelmed with admiration at the sight of the massive construction and the complication of ropes and pulleys which were only a part of the whole plan.

The ship, rolling sometimes and trembling with the pulsing

of hidden, well-cared-for engines, had seemed steady in the ring of blue water. Voices were snatched and swallowed in the wind, and the spray, on both sides, pitted the waves. Like the rhythmic creaking and straining in the branches of the tree, the straining of the ship's timbers did not change. The sustained strength and movement of the ship increased desire. He could not now ignore the memory.

Thinking of the voyage and of the passengers, he remembered the bluebell woods of his childhood. It was the eagerness of the other passengers about their chance to travel, to see other places in the world, to live in these places and to start afresh in another country, which made him think of those people, whole families sometimes, making for the bluebell woods in early summer to pick flowers. Many of these people, leaving the industrial towns, set off early in the morning on bicycles.

The people on the ship had been like these others, like the bluebell pickers who spent whole days bending down in the misty blue fragrance, industriously gathering. The flowers had to be pulled, he remembered, not snapped off. He remembered too the bundles of flowers, their blue heads darkened with dying, their long slippery stalks gleaming white in the dusk on the backs of bicycles as the pickers pedaled homewards after a day of unaccustomed fresh air and the delight of being in the middle of a mass of flowers. On those days the quiet woods resounded with the voices of the people. The woods did not change. From one year to the next particular hollows and groups of trees and little paths remained. Gone from the memory, they were recaptured, when revisited, with the sharp pleasure of recognition and an incredible realization that these places of the land did not move away.

The flowers, he knew now but did not think of then, were being taken back to places where there were no gardens, only streets of narrow houses where whitened front doorsteps were at street level, their doors opening straight onto the pavements. Behind the houses, which were all joined together, were only narrow yards and alleys paved with blue bricks.

Perhaps Leila's mother and her father had, when they were young, come home with their arms damp and laden with bluebells. Perhaps they, like others, had made the long journey by ship with all kinds of hopes. Disappointment, he knew, came in different forms. Who was to know what disappointment really was, since it was not possible to know, in the first place, the secret hopes which might never have been realized?

Not all people were the same. He had been amazed that Cecilia's mother, after making the long journey when she came to visit them, in spite of her contribution to a further understanding of the Wasp, was completely unchanged. It was as though she had crossed the world without any of its strangeness making any impact.

As Cecilia was, as usual, at the Mary and Joseph, Edwin had gone alone to the ship to meet his mother-in-law. Particular memories from his own journey came back to him vividly as he stood on the wharf watching the berthing. It seemed to him that the great ship was swollen with a mysterious knowledge and her movements, as she approached, were portly. He remembered from his own voyage the strange sensation of being in his cabin alone one evening and hearing faintly through the wall, from a radio, he supposed, some Arabian music. It was a thin monotonous wailing music, climbing at times to peaks of intense emotion. His imagination stirred then towards the lives of a remote people. Though he was in the cabin fetching something for Cecilia, he stayed listening to the music and trying to envisage a life as it would be if lived somewhere on the lower slopes of empty mountains in the squat little blocks of cement which he had seen and which, he presumed, were houses. What would it be like, he wondered then, to enter such a house through a doorless square hole and then to sit inside, with only a narrow shaft of light from the glassless slit which was the window to relieve the unchanging gloom within? Later he had watched an Arab's flexible thin fingers as he, with competence, counted bank notes. The man had gold-painted teeth and very fine eyes. The eyes, he thought, were expressive and yet revealed nothing for the curiosity of the traveler.

Cecilia's mother's main comment was disappointingly that because of the dried milk on board, she had not had a nice cup of tea since she left home. Edwin, somehow having wished for some additional, even if quite small, insight into the ways of the suddenly remembered Arabs, promised her tea, wondering whether he should make it with tap water or with the water he fetched daily, then, in an assortment of containers, from the spring. Neither, he knew, would taste right to start with.

On that first evening Cecilia's mother had asked him to lift Cecilia's sewing machine down from the top of the wardrobe. She began at once to make nightdresses for Cecilia from the Swiss cotton she had brought, folded in tissue paper, in her luggage. Cecilia, staying at home for the evening for once, agreed with her mother that ruffles at the neck and at the wrists would be pretty.

It was strange to be remembering the bluebell woods. Lilac and bluebells: he had forgotten about them till now. What was it that Cecilia's mother had invented—a garlic-scented table-cloth? Of course Cecilia was always making things up. She had said it was to boost the cottage industries in the suburbs of the English Midlands. But he did know that Cecilia's mother had had a species, some sort of beetle, named after her, and for this he respected her. Sitting that night in an easy chair, one of the ones covered in cabbage chintz, he contemplated his lecture notes, partly prepared. He paused then on the idea that quite trivial things in human life can be dramatic and that a person without conventional covering can be absolutely alone at moments of self-discovery. These moments, if accepted, could lead to escape. He wanted to relate this to ordinary situations in literature and to the ways in which prose took on the special distinction of poetry. He, instead of continuing with his notes, heard again the softness of the English voice, the voice of his mother-in-law, and this caused him to recall, in a whole series of images, the promise of a fine day in summer in the early morning mist and the endless calling of the cuckoo and the busy chirping of sparrows. He had forgotten about sparrows and he had forgotten the extraordinary excitement of not knowing how the day would develop. That sunshine mattered so much seemed hardly credible now. But he remembered clearly being aware of the intense disappointment evident in people on holiday when there were showers of rain. Irritable women snapped at apologetic men, who tried to hold umbrellas to shield them as they darted on angry heels across the cobbles.

In the sounds of the discussion on the suitable length for nightdresses Edwin remembered places and streets which had long been missing from his memory. He seemed to see again rows of distinguished terrace houses, the kind of houses he might have wished for once, even envying their owners at times. He saw too, vividly, the substantial house in which Cecilia had been reared. He realized then that though bored, he was comforted by the gentle conversation. Memory followed memory: the stillness of willow trees mourning along soft green riverbanks, the smell of river water and the smell of the deep grass of the water meadows where enormous cows, straying close to the field paths, waited to be herded for milking. He remembered a small shop in a private house where the front-room window had a display of dolls and dolls' house furniture.

"You don't want dolls at your age." He remembered the anxiety in his mother's voice. "Have some of Miss Benson's fudge instead."

Cecilia's mother's house was bunched and frilled with curtains, valances and eiderdown covers in material patterned with oak apples and acorns and unrecognizable small green leaves. The hawthorn perhaps. The little leaves they called bread and cheese and ate with pretended pleasure, pretending to be gypsies. All at once he was thinking of cow parsley, purple thistles, nettles and the dock leaves so close to the nettles, a remedy for stings. There were graves, grass covered with groundsel growing at the edges in a walled cemetery. It was curious how the sound of a voice could recall clearly these things which he had not seen or thought of for so long. Though the home-sewn fullness of her house, brought with her in the sound of her voice, made him feel as if he would choke at the time, he remembered, he almost felt fond, briefly, of his mother-in-law.

Perhaps Leila's mother, perhaps her presence, implied certain images, but because of what he was pursuing now with Leila, he had not noticed them in the same way. Cecilia's mother, he supposed, had wanted them to have a child. He remembered thinking then, that evening, that he had heard her, in a voice lowered for Cecilia alone, between hysterical bouts on the sewing machine, saying, "No little surprise on the way?" His own mother, if she had lived, of course, would have waited patiently for a little replica of himself. Women, he reflected that evening, as they got older wanted to be grandmothers.

♦ ♦ ♦

They had put a deposit on a pram and on a crib and on a baby bath. Edwin was shown the list with all the prices. The kitchen table was piled up with their shopping. "Three dozen nappies and these two soft white baby towels," Leila's mother said. She said she was going to sew the crib sheets herself and they had not bought a mattress for the crib because they wanted his opinion.

"Hair, flock or foam?" Leila's mother said. Edwin, close to Leila at last, did not have an opinion. "What do you think?" he asked Leila, looking as if he considered the question deeply. Leila had no special opinion either.

"Hair's best," Leila's mother said, "but a lot go for foam." She folded wrapping paper. "That's for the crib mattress, that's for later," she added. "You'll need a bassinet to start off with, of course."

"Oh yes, of course," Edwin said. He had drawn Leila's arm through his and was caressing her hand, feeling her skin with his as if he needed and could take nourishment from it.

"We haven't nearly finished the shopping yet," Leila's mother said as she filled the kettle. "There's other things to get and Leila's needing some clothes, she's getting big. She'll need"—Leila's mother lowered her voice—"she'll need some good nursing bras and I'll run up some little cottons for her."

"Oh yes, yes, of course." Edwin lowered his voice to match Leila's mother's. He was stroking the soft skin of Leila's forearm. He could not help stroking her. He was shameless and put his face close to her arm to breathe in as much of her as he could.

Leila's mother poured tea. "As I see it," she said, watching the golden steam from the teapot with approval, "there's a bit of a problem with the dressing room, using it as a nursery, I mean." She handed teacups across the table to Edwin and to Leila. "It's all cupboards," she said, "it's more like a walk-in 'robe. I don't know but it'll inconvenience Dr. Sissilly having Junior and all his caboodle in there." She stirred the teapot as she added more hot water. "I was having a little look-see, I wondered if some of the cupboards could be cleared, but they are packed! Dr. Sissilly"—Leila's mother drew breath—"Dr. Sissilly's got a hundred and fifty pair of shoes in there."

"Good Lord!" Edwin found it easier to sound like Daphne. He put on his little-boy-lost look. "Whatever shall we do?" he said. He had no wish to think of Cecilia's shoes just now. Unwillingly he considered her feet. "How many pairs?" Suddenly he was ashamed of his wife's feet.

"Not to worry," Leila's mother said. "We can move his lordship around to start off with; it's all one to a baby where he sleeps his first few weeks as long as he's near the pantry. The spare room," she added, "would make a lovely nursery, would be lovely for a kiddie, specially if you had a little bathroom, nothing fancy, built on."

"Oh yes, I suppose it would." Edwin put a quick little kiss, a perfect one, into the side of Leila's soft neck.

"And while you were about it," Leila's mother continued, "a bathroom for Dr. Sissilly's room would be very nice."

"It would indeed." Edwin put another quick little kiss on top of the first.

"Most go in for a convenient bathroom these days." Leila's mother seemed to disappear into a cupboard. She returned after the second kiss with a tin of biscuits. "Leila'd better have a nice lay-down," she said, "when she's had her tea. Drink up, Leila pet, there's a good girl. It's getting too tired as brings on the sickness."

"Oh yes, of course," Edwin said.

When Leila was on her way to the spare room to have her rest, Edwin waylaid her in the hall.

"Tell Mother," he said, catching her and holding her close to him, "that you are sleeping in the study tonight. I shall try and get away early. I'll not be late home."

"All right," Leila said.

Back in his study with the door closed, Edwin thought he would telephone Cecilia, to get the call out of the way, over and done with, disregarding, as she always did, the time difference. He hesitated; perhaps it would be easier to write after all. In the letter he would describe his need to be looked after, he would speak of Leila's mother as a housekeeper. He would send two letters, one about the housekeeper. Cecilia would be the first to understand his inability to keep house, and yet he had to admit they both knew he had done all this before quite adequately. The second letter would be about their changed lives, his hopes for their future happiness with a complete family. He drew the sheets of paper towards himself. His lecture notes with quotations . . . *I frequently put myself in the way of conditions likely to induce a certain distress* . . . fluttered off the desk and lay on the carpet.

The last time he had slept all night with Leila she had described a toy she had seen and was going to buy. Resting in his arms, she explained that it was an educational toy. It could be fastened on the side of the crib and consisted of a panel made of plastic. "That part's white," she said, "and there's all different things which make funny noises when the little red knobs and handles are pushed and turned." She said that was the first thing she was going to buy. There were pictures too, she said, on the panel and a colored ball that turned round and rattled, and there were little bells and chimes. "When the baby wakes up," she had gone on telling, "he can play with all the different things."

Edwin wrote last week's date at the top of the page and began to write. *My Darling Cecilia.* He put down his pen. He seemed to see already the nimble feet of his child pushing the red knobs on the white plastic panel as he kicked his sturdy little legs upwards to greet the morning while the household still slept. The child, he thought, would have thick little ankles. Leila's ankles and legs were thick, quite unlike Cecilia's, which were slender like the legs of an ornamental bird. He saw them as if fashioned of colored glass, dark red. He imagined how they would look snapped off. She would not, in those circumstances, need all those shoes.

He stared at the empty page. How could he, if only teasingly, ever have asked Cecilia, "How was it, Cecilia, with you and Vorwickl?" And teasingly, she, tossing her head, "Wouldn't you like to know!" Even the cliché amused him then as he watched her dressing and he would think of other, more daring ways of putting his question. "I mean, darling, *how* did Vorwickl? What did she *do*?"

My Darling Cecilia,

I must write to tell you we

It was suddenly clear to him that the impossible wish to have children was the reason for stories like *"Thumbelina," "Snow White"* and *"The Little Wax Girl."*

Once upon a time there lived a young wife who longed exceedingly to possess a little child of her own, so she went to an old witch woman and said to her, "I wish so very much to have a child, a little tiny child; won't you give me one, old mother?"

He seemed to hear his mother's voice, at dusk, reading aloud to him. Images, unchanged through the years, the tiny baby girl in a neat little shawl packaged in a cradle no bigger than a walnut shell, came back to him. It was as if the snowbound garden of his childhood were immediately outside the study window, and inside, his mother's gentle fingers turned the pages.

He heard the distant sound of the railway and was reminded of Cecilia saying once that everything was different now back home. The hedges, she said, had been uprooted (she must have been on one of her many study trips) and the fields in England, even in the home counties, were bigger and there were no longer elms in hedgerows.

Could he start his letter with that? Make it into some sort of metaphor? He filled his pen and then fussily filled his other pens; he had three, all good quality, side by side on the desk. All had been presents from Cecilia.

Leila's mother must have put some washing on the clothesline of the house next door. The white sheet pegged on the sagging line, with the dark green foliage above and at the sides of it, seemed to be the most beautiful creation. Gazing through his study window, he felt he was uplifted. It was the green and white, he knew this. He would make a note about the humble sheet on the line having the same effect as the stained glass of the Renaissance, perhaps the Adoration of the Magi in King's College; he could use the idea in his lectures "The Study of Man" and perhaps speak of it to Leila tonight. He would leave early to get back to Leila. The sweetest part of it—he allowed himself to slip into his dream of Leila—was the way he liked to hold her as if he were nursing her in his lap in bed, cupping her soft breasts in his hands.

He looked at his watch. It was time to take a bath and dress for the Fairfax evening. They were having an early start. Last time the Fairfaxes had made basket dinners for everyone. It was a good idea, having an early start; it gave people the chance to leave early.

"My earth-shattering news,"
Daphne said as Edwin, making his way through the Fairfax
party guests, reached her, "is that Miss Hearnsted's broken her
leg, her ankle." Daphne had stationed herself at the side of the
massive fireplace. "This dress," she said, "is so hideous I
thought it best to stand here where people will be attracted
to the log fire and notice its beauty. My immensity," she continued, "I hope is somewhat dwarfed by being close to this
enormous corner of the mantelpiece. Oh, Teddy, I am so glad
to see you, really glad."

"I'm sorry . . ." Edwin began the conventional phrases.
Daphne did seem to tower at least half a head above the other
guests. He wondered why she wore such high heels.

"Oh, there's no need for sorrow," Daphne said, "no need for
pity; the Hatchet's perfectly well and very comfortable. She
has her own telephone and receives adoration and cherishing
at all hours. Of course she's had a shock. We all have. It was
my beloved Fiorella, she of the love poems, an absolute deluge
I might add, she took the front-door steps, where the gels are
supposed never to be, in one bound just when the Hatchet in
a moment of uncertainty was tottering at the top. None of us
knew what she was uncertain about—because she had forgotten whether she was coming in or going out." Daphne sighed.
"Fiorella's dreadfully cut up. She's here somewhere. She is at
present a bosom friend of one of the daughters. There they all
are; aren't they charming!" Edwin followed Daphne's gaze
across the room to the pretty little group of Fairfax daughters

and friends. Beyond them he could make out Paulette and Buffy, Spaniards still, using up their costumes. Paulette waved and Edwin waved back.

"The daughters," Daphne was saying, "seem to manage to look like something out of Jane Austen. It's that white spotted muslin and those little shawls. Lovely! Everything else looks clumsy in comparison."

"Your dress is very nice, very becoming." Edwin, blowing a kiss to the distant Paulette, summoned his chivalry to praise the long emerald-green tube.

"It's completely out of date," Daphne said. "It used to be called a sheath. I feel like some sort of chrysalis. Can you imagine, Teddy darling, how difficult it is to do up the zip on a thing like this? The contortions were frightful. I still feel as if my spine and both arms are dislocated. One of the disadvantages of living alone." Daphne sighed. "The dinner"—she sighed again—"is a buffet; such a barbaric way to feed."

The Fairfax daughters and their friends carried plates and handed various dishes to those guests who did not straight away help themselves at the long tables. The amorous Fiorella plied Daphne and, more reluctantly, Edwin with dish after dish.

"Potato salad, Miss Hockley?" Fiorella almost stood on Daphne. "Garden salad, Miss Hockley? And there's a Stilton dressing, Miss Hockley. . . . Miss Hockley, the melon and pineapple—would you like the melon and pineapple salad, Miss Hockley? . . . Shall I fetch the garlic bread, Miss Hockley? . . . Miss Hockley, I'll bring the strawberry and avocado salad, shall I?"

They stood holding crumbed cutlets, partly wrapped in silver foil for convenience, and they gnawed delicately at bits of chicken and pheasant, their fingers curling round the foil-covered bones. The corner of the high mantelpiece became indispensable for all the glasses—for champagne, for chardonnay, for white burgundy and for a particularly pleasant, Edwin thought, verdelho. The conversations hurried on bent legs between the guests.

"I feel we are not mingling very well." Daphne ate with her fingers shamelessly. "However can we talk," she said with her mouth full, "manage knife and fork, hold plates and so on?— yes, Fiorella, you can remove these bones—but it's all part of it. In any case," she added, "I don't think I can sit down in this dress." Her sun-bronzed smooth shoulders were really fine. Edwin, soothed by the well-chosen wines, wondered if he should pay her the kind of false compliment which flew during the evening, along with the forced jokes about herpes and AIDS. He let his mind dwell on his homecoming. Leila would be curled up asleep in his bed and he would wake her. Since she slept during the day, it would not matter, disturbing her. He longed to kiss her, to wake her with kisses and kiss her back to sleep.

"Fiorella!" Daphne was saying. "I couldn't eat another thing; take that bomb Alaska somewhere and explode it privately. . . . I've promised her Rosalind," she explained to Edwin behind the girl's devoted back, "to more or less thank her, wordlessly you understand, for causing the Hatchet to be indisposed for an indefinite period. You can imagine my relief to have her out of the way. We're doing *As You Like It*," she explained, "for our next production. 'One of the Great Bard's lighter masterpieces,' as described in the Speech Day program. And I've allowed Fiorella, who is utterly unable to learn anything—let alone by heart—to be Rosalind. It's done now." Daphne sighed. "I'll have to prompt madly. Naturally Fiorella's mother is delighted and is embroidering a surprise for me as well as cutting out and sewing an enormous costume for Rosalind. As you know, Teddy," she continued, "no one is interested in who wrote the play; they are only concerned with who's in it. The Hatchet fainted twice last year, she was so annoyed when the juniors messed up their pageant. As for doing Shakespeare, we might as well put on *The Wizard of Oz* for all the parents care!" Daphne hiccupped. "Sorry, Teddy," she said. "I've nothing against *Wizard*, of course!" She hiccupped again.

Edwin grinned. The wine and the food and the lively fire

and the well-dressed guests and their lighthearted conversations, Daphne's contribution too, were a tremendous consolation. He felt soothed and rested. He glanced round the large room and laughed. Perhaps Cecilia understood him more clearly than he understood himself. Dear Cecilia, making so many thoughtful arrangements to ensure his comfort and well-being. She knew his needs.

The guests, still eating and carrying refreshments, were moving towards the studio, Dippy and Ida having built onto their already large house this additional spaciousness, a studio and a gallery, where culture (with encouragement) could flourish. This was their second event, a book launching. The art from the previous event still hung for inspection and possible purchase. Catalogues were handed prettily by the daughters. Fiorella gave Daphne two. Venetian glass and ceramics, waiting to be unwrapped, were on low display tables. A few guests poked at the straw and the sacking with simulated curiosity.

"Gallery One Two One," Daphne said, "like Father's paddock at his hobby farm. He had two gates and had a board on one gate, 'Paddock Number Fourteen'; it made us feel wonderfully wealthy!"

The book about to be launched was a local history. Edwin respected the value of such books and looked with admiration at the man who had written it. He noticed that the guests, invited to meet this man, largely ignored him. He was not one of their set. They continued their animated talking and laughing, keeping their eyes deliberately on one another, not allowing their attention to wander, as if for safety, to the paintings, the partly unwrapped exhibition and the well-set-out display of books beside which the historian stood. Edwin did not know the man. The Fairfaxes liked to take up, he knew, the unknown talent and nurture it. If the artists became well known they were no longer of interest.

The guests were being encouraged to examine the book. The daughters handed copies to everyone.

"Oh Lord!" Daphne groaned as Fiorella advanced with an

armful. Watching the girls, in particular the Fairfax girls, Edwin, thinking of Leila, could see how she could never fit in with them. She did not know the movements and the glances and the phrases these girls knew. She would be shy and awkward and unhappy in their company. Even though she was older than they were and experienced now, because of him— he lifted his shoulders a little and smiled to himself—with them she would be like a clumsy fourteen-year-old. Turning from the girls he watched one of the guests, glass in hand, gaze at the front cover of the book. She turned it over and gazed at the back cover, managing at the same time to continue her conversation without seeming to notice either the book or her surroundings. She had been, Edwin noticed, talking to her next-door neighbor as if the two of them had not seen each other for years.

The arrival of the great ships was an occasion . . . Edwin, opening the book, read a line and was immediately reminded of his own arrival at the port. He had looked then beyond the sheds, which were the customs sheds, to what seemed a flat land completely devoid of distinguishing features. Very few ships came now, he reflected, except the container ships, and who would throw streamers and sing to a container? There had been times, he remembered, when crowds flocked to the wharf to meet a ship. It was as if people went there hoping that someone they used to know in another part of the world would appear, as if by magic, waving with exultant recognition from the crowded rail.

The guests were beginning to move back to the other rooms. Edwin noticed the woman again picking up the book and staring at the front and at the back of it without any apparent comprehension, before replacing it. Edwin put down the copy he had been holding and followed Daphne. The historian remained standing, still in the same place. No one at all had spoken to him.

"You know, Teddy," Daphne said, turning back to Edwin and lowering her voice, "I just stopped Paulette and Erica from paying you a surprise visit, lunchtime last Thursday. They'd been having their hair done and the place where they usually have tea was crowded. They thought they'd drop in on you with a box of cakes. 'You know it'll only upset him,' I told them. 'He might be in the bathroom,' I said." She had to remind them, she went on telling Edwin, what an odd creature he was, so easily put out, disturbed—highly strung, "like a thoroughbred race horse," Daphne added as if to lighten the "odd creature" description.

"You managed to put them off then," Edwin said in a teasing tone.

"Yes, I did," Daphne said. "I had to invite them back for tea to ask their advice about this hideous dress. No advice, of course, could do anything to it but they made me put it on while they drank tea and ate all my bread, which I was obliged to toast. And another thing." Daphne paused and waited for his full attention. "The next dinner," she said, "is at your place, Teddy. What d'you intend to do? What will you do about Leila and her mother?" She was serious, quite red-faced with accusation. He felt like teasing her. While she was looking back at him, waiting for his reply, he leaned across to where Paulette was standing close by and gave her a long and exaggerated kiss.

"Long time no see!" Paulette said, hanging on to him and pressing herself close.

"*À bientôt.*" Edwin released himself and caught up with Daphne.

"They've seen *Murder on the Nile* twice now," he said, "and a rerun of *Mary Poppins,* but *Hamlet*'s back and Leila's mother says she has always admired Shakespeare. And it is a very long film. She seems," he added, "to be, in her own way, quite an educated woman. Everything is arranged—"

"It certainly is," Daphne interrupted. "*He is a haven where I shall find safe mooring*. . . . Leila's mother is onto a good thing. Perhaps I shouldn't say this, Teddy, please don't be annoyed, but you've got to open your eyes! It's Medea and

Aegeus. You've given Leila's mother a kind of insurance policy. She'll get from you all she'll ever need for future sanctuary. Look it up if you don't remember it."

"That's a bit steep, Daph." Edwin laughed. He began to feel a return of his earlier uneasiness. He drank quickly and helped himself to another glass as a waiter went by. He did not want to think he was being used, being lived on, was parting with considerable amounts of money and letting his work and his writing fall into the background. Certainly Leila acquiesced readily as if made by her mother to do certain things, but that could not really be how it was. He helped himself to another drink as the waiter came by from the other direction. Leila, in bed, seemed to want him very much and he was sure that he pleased her. She had no sophisticated ways but it was unendurably pleasant to teach her. He could not mention this to Daphne.

"Bottoms up!" he said, draining his glass. His voice, he thought, showed his lack of confidence. When he had, earlier this evening, asked Leila to come to the study she had simply said, "All right." That was all. He wondered now if that was enough.

"Leila's mother wouldn't have a clue about the *Medea*," he said to Daphne, "and she won't know Aegeus. You've been around teaching that stuff for too long."

"That's not the point," Daphne, unlike her usual self, seemed to snap. "It's ludicrous, Teddy." She sounded as if she was going to cry. "This whole silly business," she said, "has come between Cecilia and me. This—this thing you are doing. I can't write to her, really write to her, to Cecilia, don't you see? I can't be myself when she phones. And I put off phoning her and that hurts her. She hasn't heard anything from you for simply ages and I tell her you're busy. I know your life is your own affair but, Teddy, without wanting to be I'm in it too. I can't deceive Cecilia, I really can't. She's my friend." She turned away from Edwin and seemed to stumble through the guests, many of whom were dancing, not exactly with each other but up against each other. They danced facing each other and, turning, they went on dancing, facing someone else. For a moment Edwin watched the dancing and then he tried to follow Daphne. How could he have said what he had just said to her? He had sounded just like that Tranby woman. The dancers were pressing on all sides. He could see Daphne, her cheeks scarlet, making for the door awkwardly. He must go after her and tell her he never meant to say what he had said. Something had brought him down to Tranby level. Once after the impertinent remark about the colors of the Elizabethan court, when the Tranby woman was still only a newcomer on the staff, she had said the same words to him:

"You've been around teaching that stuff for too long!"

"Excuse! Please!" He tried to elbow his way between the moving bodies. "Excuse!"

"Hey! Male menopause!" Paulette was dancing, two steps forward and one back. "What's wrong? Dance, man! Dance!"

Edwin gave her the tiniest wave. Because the Tranby woman knew how to sigh and flutter her green eyelids and because she had then a head of red curls she could toss, she, in her own words, got away with murder. He'd heard her, years ago, telling how she'd been able to raise her marks. An A for a lay, that sort of thing. Vulgar. The kind of cliché people in departments everywhere repeated. Eff or Eff. Fuck or Fail. Without wanting to he muttered the phrase now, disgusted with himself.

"Hey!" Paulette, breathless with exertion, was too brightly animated. "Dance, man! Dance!" Edwin shook his head. She took his arm and hung on to it, still laughing. "Help! I can't breathe!" She kept on laughing. "Oh! This music!"

"Move along," someone behind them said. "Move! Rattle yer dags! Move, there!" The dancers surged forward and then back. "Move! Move!" Dippy Fairfax this time had musicians, a group.

"Look at the little dark one with the guitar," Paulette said, "the way he's right in there! Wow! Teddy," she said, "let's go to your place. We could go. I'll tell Buffy you're taking me home. He's over there." She jerked her head. "He's playing cards—they've made some tables. Let's go to your place, now." She pressed herself close. "Now," she said. "I've been waiting for you all night." They moved together. Edwin, in his practiced way, steered her through one of the doors to the terrace and on towards the end, where there were no lights. Somewhere there, he remembered, there was a chaise longue.

"I've been waiting for you," Paulette said again. Her hands soothed and her lips were cool and competent. "Not possible," he said, his lips in her hair, "not possible . . ." But Paulette did not hear. She drew his face down to hers once more. He tightened his arms about her, knowing her need.

They would not come out at home. There would be no throwing off of bedclothes and Leila's mother would not come, fastening her dressing gown, down the hall to meet them. If he took Paulette into Cecilia's room, into the blue and gold, into the clean prettiness, Leila would not spring from his bed and rush in upon them. All would be quiet and discreet, he was sure of this. Paulette's quick eye might pick up some small detail of other people's lives in his house, but at one o'clock in the morning, and with other things on her mind, she might not. It surprised him that during the embrace he was calculating the possibilities. He returned Paulette's kisses, surprising himself again, wondering if he had had too much wine and knowing that he had.

"I've had too much to drink," he confessed. "I might disappoint you. Most certainly I might."

"Oh heavens, Teddy, darling! Do stop being so *intellectual*." Paulette raised her scented arms above her head and clasped the back of his neck so that her breasts were offered. "Come on, Teddy!"

He allowed a certain helplessness to take over and he felt her warmth through the thin material of her dress.

They heard the guests calling his name and hurriedly straightened their clothes. Dippy Fairfax was making his way slowly along the dark terrace. Repeatedly he called "Edwin" into the dark garden. It was Cecilia, on the phone, reverse charge, from London.

Edwin took the call in Dippy's study. It was more an office really, stacked from floor to ceiling with files and boxes. The small space was crowded with people, all wanting to talk to Cecilia. They made way for Edwin and gathered close to hear the one-sided conversation.

How was the party she wanted to know. Why hadn't he telephoned? She would have been insane with worry if Daphne, except that Daphne . . . Was he okay she wanted to know. He told her yes he was all right. He told her he was sorry. Time flies he told her. Did he still love her she wanted to know. He told her yes yes kiss kiss nibble nibble yes yes he loved her. Love you love you he told her. She said she could hear the party people cheering. He must sure be having a great time. Yes a great time he told her. Did he miss her she wanted to know. Very much he told her. Vorwickl she told him lost several pounds. No not money she told him *avoirdupois*. He told her Good. Vorwickl she told him ate a cocoon in the muesli. No he said. Yes she said. She said it was delicious even when she knew it was a cocoon. Good old Vorwickl he said. He supposed Vorwickl had gray hair now. Not quite she said. Flecked. He supposed her hands inspired confidence. She told him yes and her hair reached below the backs of her knees. Good old Vorwickl he said. In a bun she told him with hairpins. Neat he said. They were she told him Vorwickl and herself within walking distance of Artificial Insemination and Abortions. Ectopics he asked. No she told him that was Canada. London she said they went shopping. Good he said. Lovely fur cape. Heavenly she told him. See through? he asked. Of course she said it cost the earth. He didn't mind did he she wanted to know. He had said to buy something. Of course he said kiss kiss love you love you. She said she didn't know she had it on. Light he said. And warm. He told her he was pleased. She told him she had a little fur hat. Round and snug she said. Russian? he asked. Omsk Tomsk and Vladivostok she said. How was the surprise she wanted to know. Growing he said a lovely golden melon he said. Oh lovely she said. Here's Daphne he told her passing the receiver to Daphne

—— 163 ——

who tried not to take it. He dived through the guests and made for the door.

◆ ◆ ◆

Leila had left the desk lamp on in his study. The little dog was asleep at the foot of the bed. As Edwin gazed at the sleeping dog and the sleeping Leila he swayed slightly.

O a cherubim, he said in a thick low voice, *Thou wast that did preserve me. Thou didst smile, Infused with a fortitude from heaven . . .*

He knew he had had too much to drink. He was not home early as promised. It was almost three o'clock. He made a small movement towards the bed, disturbed by the suddenly remembered lines. He was not Prospero. Not tonight, never; it would amount to . . . He sought for the word, not finding it on purpose. He steadied himself, ashamed, at the side of his desk. Leila must have tried to keep herself awake for his return. There was a book under her cheek and he supposed she had brought in the puppy to play with for the same reason. She looked very young and soft and desirable. He knew he should explain to her that she must go to her own room and that she must look forward to her own life. He had been very selfish, he must tell her; his own life must continue for the short time it had left. She would forget him; he must explain this. The thought was too terrible. He leaned down to her soft warmth, unable to stop himself.

Leila woke as his lips caressed her hair and her cheek. She sat up, pink where the book had creased her cheek.

"Oh," she said, "I'm hungry." She smiled at Edwin. "I'd like some bread and butter," she told him, "and a hard-boiled egg."

They went quietly down the hall together because Leila needed, she said, the bathroom. Edwin, with the comfortable feeling of being the provider, went on to the kitchen to boil eggs, Leila having decided on the way that she might need two.

Edwin called Leila dumpling and listened for the sound of her soft footfall in the passage outside his door. They took little walks together in the pines, breathing in the warm fragrance. The pines seemed lighter and the bleached grass gave way to patches of sand. Leila had to stop to empty first one shoe and then the other. Edwin, as usual, was surprised how he could forget, from one season to the other, these gifts from the pines, the gentle sighing of the wind in the tops of the trees and the warmth and the sustaining quality of the air. While Leila emptied her shoes he supported her tenderly.

The yellow flowers on a spiked bush outside his study window leaned towards the panes. The whole tall hedge leaned and pressed the woody centers of the bushes towards the house. From his desk he could look up into the thickness of the dividing hedge and through it to glimpses of a faraway blue sky. The scent of the yellow flowers and of the Chinese privet filled his study, especially at night. Further down, out of sight of his window, the loquat tree blossomed and fruited and they heard the birds every morning noisily in the branches. He told Leila it was too much trouble to eat loquats, they were best left for the birds. Leila's mother said loquats might be acid for the baby. She watched Leila's diet carefully.

At the back and at the front of the house everything seemed to be coming into flower: cape lilacs, honeysuckle and the olive trees. But especially there was the bush outside the study, with the brilliant splashes of yellow against the clear blue sky.

There was a piling up of color and sweetness, a burgeoning of life in the outside world as the season made changes towards summer. And inside the house Leila blossomed. Her skin glowed and her hair shone. Her eyes seemed larger and her expression softer. She carried the enormous bulge in her short plump body, Edwin thought, bravely. He told her she was brave and she asked him why. He put his hand where he thought the baby's head was.

"He's the wrong way up," she told him. "He'll turn later and point down," she said. The doctor had explained everything very clearly; that's how she knew. Sometimes it seemed to Edwin that the head or the feet were at Leila's side, in her side. He expressed concern.

"I suppose he turns around," Leila said. Her fullness made her seem shorter and more solid and she was very calm. Edwin thought she seemed happy and confident. He thought he had never before seen real happiness like this. Quietly the house was being made ready for the new occupant.

"Here's a man as has shed two thirds of his body weight." Leila's mother read the paper during a late breakfast. "And the Duchess of Windsor, poor woman, they should have given her a bit of peace and happiness. Fabulous emeralds go a long way but alone they aren't enough for happiness." Leila's mother consulted her knitting pattern, drank up her tea, concentrated on a stitch, scratched her head delicately with a knitting needle and turned the page of the newspaper. "And here," she said, "here's someone I've never heard of about to reveal some incidents he could never tell anyone. The things they put in the papers these days! Give me your cup, Leila pet, and I'll read the leaves." Every morning breakfast was late and comfortable.

Edwin in his study, searching for and finding references and quotations suitable for the writing of the lectures for the following year, felt safe. It was as if he was being carried along in the progress of Leila's pregnancy. There was a hitherto unknown serenity in the monthly visits to the clinic, in Leila's increasing size and weight, and in the recent acquisitions which seemed to be in all parts of the house. Leila's pleasure in the new things gave him pleasure.

"Where are you, little sugar mother?" he called as soon as he stepped indoors. Leila, as if she spent her time listening for his key in the lock, was in the hall before he needed to call a second time.

One evening they spread out all the new little clothes. Some had been made by Leila's mother and by Leila and others were bought, chosen carefully to suit any child so that a baby boy need not lie in his cradle distressed and fretful because he was wearing colors and clothes intended for a girl.

"There wasn't any old things to cut up"—Leila's mother allowed herself a complaint—"nothing to cut up for little sheets and pillowcases," she said. "Dr. Sissilly has everything all new!"

"Are these enough?" Edwin, used to a plentiful wardrobe, surveyed the little collection of tiny singlets and jackets. He picked up some small white knitted things. "Oh," he said, "they're socks."

"Bootees," Leila corrected him.

"They grow that fast," Leila's mother said. She unwrapped another plastic bag. "There's some bigger sets in here," she said, "and once the birth is announced and all your friends know, Dr. Sissilly will get no end of presents: clothes, toys, books—you name them, they'll come." She sighed. "She'll not know where to put them."

"I see." Edwin could not help a small frown as he saw the procession—Paulette, Erica, Ida, Ida's daughters and others—bending over the cradle. Where would Leila be by then? Somewhere in England, out of reach, in a small suburban house, probably something mean, semidetached. He wanted to say "Don't go" to Leila, there and then, to make a big change in his life. One night in bed recently, Leila had said she didn't want to leave and he had comforted her, kissing away her words, saying that he was old and she would soon forget him and that she would be very happy with someone else. And to comfort himself he had caressed her possessively, making love to her to find forgetfulness. Looking at the baby clothes now he felt worried and deeply ashamed.

"And these"—Leila's mother was unwrapping a large fold of white tissue paper—"are the christening gown and the shawl." A froth of the softest cotton and lace and the finest cashmere wool lay like snow on the table.

"They are a surprise," Leila said. "Mother made them at times when we were out. We never saw her making them." Edwin *was* surprised. He was suddenly overwhelmed with the idea of so much love and devotion being stitched into clothing for his child. He looked at Leila's mother as if he had never seen her before. She, bending down smoothing the gown, did not notice. He thought the clothes were beautiful and said so. They made him feel humble but he did not know how to say this to these two women. He wanted to ask what had to be done about a christening. How was it arranged? In his lectures (first year) he often discussed the various rites of passage, the ceremonies which changed the status of the individual, one of them being the naming of the child and the acceptance by the church of the offered child. The statements in his lecture were about to become a part of his own life, except that he and Cecilia never went to church. It was always the tennis club on Sundays. He wondered if it was possible to simply choose a church and ask to have a baby christened.

Promises would have to be made and kept. He supposed in their new life they might prefer church to tennis. Happiness, he reflected as he watched Leila's mother fold away the fine white soft things, was often marred by an unexpected uneasiness. The shawl—he allowed himself the pleasure of the thought—must be symbolic of the garment which has no seams. He supposed Leila's mother did not know this but was simply carrying out a ritual of preparation. He felt he wanted to thank her and did so, his voice deeper than usual because of the overwhelming feelings of gratitude. Leila's mother smiled.

"I've enjoyed it," she said, "enjoyed every minute of it all, the sewing and everything." It was a pleasure, she added, to keep house for a gentleman like Dr. Page. "It's not often," she said, "that you get paid to enjoy yourself."

"I like those little yellowy shawls babies have," Leila said, "little stiff yellowy shawls; we haven't got one of them. I like them best."

"Just you wait," Leila's mother said. "Those little yellowy shawls as you call them is what a shawl like this one gets like after all the washings. Oh!" she cried suddenly. "Whatever am I saying!" And she burst into tears.

Edwin, packing winter clothes unwillingly, paused to look, without wanting to, at Cecilia's letter to see which of her things she was asking him to bring. He had found the gloves she wanted. She had changed her mind about a certain dress she had asked for earlier, as she was all on for raging in a couple of little bargains, in sultry patterned satin, picked up when shopping in London with Vorwickl. She now had two pantsuits; he would rave over the camisoles, she said. That's what they call them now, camisoles. Revealing. She had two as Vorwickl, who had chosen the hot pink, couldn't squeeze into the below-the-knee pants. Her own choice had been the purple and silver, the sequins absolutely irresistible.

Edwin shook the mothballs out of his woolen (Jaeger) underwear and pushed too many pairs into his case. Cecilia was longing, she said in her letter, for Edwin to come. Vorwickl, she wrote, had already upset Mumsie during a previous visit, just a weekend, with her ideas on the alternative life-style and she, Cecilia, needed Edwin to be there at Christmas as he was always so soothing for Mumsie. She was sure he would calm her down about Vorwickl's habits. Cecilia loved Christmas in England with all the remembered pleasures of childhood. She had never been able to enter into what she called "the spirit of Christmas" in the hot climate.

Cecilia went to church on Christmas Day. They all did. Buffy intended, every Christmas, to go to church more often, but he never did.

Edwin pushed an enormous long-sleeved pullover with a crazy Fair Isle pattern into the case. Apart from his hating the sweater (made by Cecilia's mother), it took an effort of will to even consider these warm clothes. Like the preparations for living in an unknown country, he reflected, it was similarly impossible to plan a whole year ahead, especially if the plans were made for another person, as Cecilia's plans were. He tried to think of her with affection and so hated the pullover even more. For one thing, it took up far too much space. He tried to make himself think of endearing qualities. An intellectual approach had often saved him when the physical failed. He would be seeing her, he told himself, in some of her more lovable moments, eating boiled fowl with greedy enthusiasm, dipping pieces of crusty bread in the golden broth while her mother looked on, smiling. Cecilia's mother's soups were always clear, glistening with beads of melted butter and often delicately speckled with fine green herbs. Her cooking was one continuous boiling fowl. He found it too rich and always ate as sparingly as he could.

The dinner parties so thoughtfully arranged by Cecilia had fallen through quite quickly, through no fault of Edwin's or anyone else's. As Daphne said, "*A throw of chance—and there goes Death*— Sorry, Teddy, for the thoroughly unsuitable quotation; you will know what I mean."

First Paulette was back on traction and bedpans because of her disks and Buffy sat by her devotedly.

"My head's going bald with lying here." Her voice was squeaky with indignation.

"Only at the back, m'dear," Buffy reassured her. "It's only a small patch; it will grow again. Look at old Baldypate here." He bent his white-fringed rosy head playfully towards her. At the time, Edwin, seeing Buffy do this, felt ashamed of his own lack of faithfulness and fondness. Leila, for a long time now, had been feeling the movements, thumpings she called them, of the baby, and Edwin's heart and mind were occupied with thoughts of the most tender kind, but not for Cecilia.

Buffy himself, when Paulette was better, had decided to face the knife and have his prostate removed, and Paulette sat by him. They all visited and sat and admired the clean scar which Buffy, himself amazed, was proud to show them. Leila needed new and more powerful bras and Leila's mother said she was sorry they were so expensive but to save money she had run up some little cottons to accommodate Leila's greater width instead of buying maternity dresses which, she said, cost the earth. Edwin said he thought the little cottons were charming, especially the ones with the round white collars. "Yes," Leila's mother said, "the little Peter Pans are very sweet." Edwin did not understand the reference and noted it in his book of the intangible, meaning to explore it more fully later.

Paulette and Erica, first one and then the other, had to have their veins done. Quite a prolonged business, as Buffy, laden with roses, said to Tuppy, who had chosen carnations, when they met on the steps of the hospital. Later, back at home, taking turns to be at each other's houses, Paulette and Erica had their bright banana lounges side by side. Edwin dutifully visited with fruit and flowers and read aloud to them from Edward Lear and Gerard Manley Hopkins, Paulette wanting to be amused and Erica needing to be submerged in images.

Everything in life was unpredictable, Edwin knew, except the changing of the seasons and the progress of Leila's pregnancy. Though that had to be carefully watched so that the rest of Daphne's unsuitable quotation could not come into use.

Leila's mother's sister died before the fulfilling of her last wish, which was to get back to a certain street of a London suburb. "It was for the best," Leila's mother said in her practical way. "I doubt if the house she was thinking about is still there," she said. Myra would never have stood the journey. Traveling without an invalid would be much simpler and Dr. Page was not to give it another thought. Edwin could see that Leila's mother's eyes were red and swollen. On his way home from the university he bought an armful of flowers.

Leila did not want Edwin to go away for Christmas. All along she said nothing, so that it was a surprise one night when she begged him not to go. She cried so much that Edwin was afraid some harm might come to the child. In the end he was obliged to fetch her mother, who made tea for them all.

They sat together like characters in a Russian novel, Edwin thought, who never slept but prowled about all night creating problems and facing terrible truths in their nightclothes. Only the little dog, who had grown very quickly, slept on in his basket, twitching and uttering little growls from his dreams.

"It's normal to have a good cry," Leila's mother said. "Crying won't hurt Junior," she said. "If crying was bad for a unborn baby everybody would be born ill or deformed," she said. Women were meant to weep while they were carrying. It was all part of nature.

Edwin thought about the ritual washings in literature discussed so often in his lectures and promised Leila he would be back very soon. As quickly as he could. When they went back to bed the long fingers of the first light pushing across the sky outside gave him a great longing to make love to her. He felt it might be an action which would be out of place and even harmful. Cecilia, though he did not want to think about her, would have known what was all right in the circumstances and what was not. Leila was calm and sleepy. He was grateful that she was not crying. Their bed seemed even more comfortable than usual and safe, as did his study and the whole house. Leila's mother, it seemed to him as he half-slept, kept watch. She kept his house in order.

Edwin was at the airport early, well before his flight departure time. The others, the Honeywells, the Wellatons and the Fairfaxes, were all going to Bali for Christmas, to a hotel which promised, among other things, a Christmas dinner in traditional English style with English Christmas cards, a yule log and a visit from Santa. Santa, they were assured, spoke beautiful English. He was not quite white but he liked older people and was especially fond of English folk and English children.

Edwin, with his out-of-date overcoat over one arm, waited to see them off and to hand over small but expensive packages, gift-wrapped in shops, from himself and Cecilia. Cecilia had chosen them all before she left. He, in turn, would be burdened with fond phrases, messages for Cecilia, and similar little tinseled parcels would be pressed into his hands during the affectionate embracings at the exit gate for the flight to Bali.

Bali offered a great deal to visitors: faith healing, temple dancing, erotic carvings, duty-free shopping and "I've been to Bali" T-shirts.

◆ ◆ ◆

In the silence—for it did seem very quiet even in all the crowds at the airport—after they had gone Edwin moved towards the place where he was supposed to push his luggage onto the weighing machine and ask for a nonsmoking seat. He did not feel his usual nervousness about flying. He did not even think of it. He scarcely noticed the weight of his heavy coat, which was full-length instead of the fashionable short coat which most men, if they had coats, wore. It hung over his arm, causing some people to turn and look at the elegant and conspicuous fur collar.

He walked up and down among the people. He put down his case, picked it up and walked some more. He went out to the street and let someone open a taxi door for him.

"Missed the plane": he would send a cable to Cecilia as soon as he could. He would get a refund, a partial one at least, on his ticket. Sitting back in the comfortable taxi, allowing himself to rest luxuriously, he worded his cable: "Missed the plane. Dreadfully disappointed. Letter following. E." It seemed simple.

"I think I have found your Mozart piano concerto," Daphne said to Edwin during the wonderful peacefulness while the baby slept. "The concerto you asked me about, remember? It was some months ago," she continued, "the one in which you thought the pianist seems to start and then makes a mistake, he pauses and goes back and then forward as if to put right the mistake."

Edwin said he remembered.

"It's number eight," Daphne said, "number eight in C major, *C Dur*, the third movement, but it's not as you said. It's not the coming to the mistake and going back and playing over again to correct the mistake. It's not a putting right, not a fresh start—only something going on in the way it has been going. It is the actual music; in the actual music, I should say; it is the way it was written—it's even more inevitable that way." She went, as quietly as her heavy feet allowed, across to the bassinet. "He's still asleep," she said in what was, for her, an attempt at a whisper.

"Ought we to pick him up?" Edwin crossed the room as if on a tightrope. "He's sleeping long after he should have been fed." They stood at the side of the cradle watching the sleeping child.

"Leila's mother," Edwin said, "always said if you looked at a sleeping baby it would wake up."

"Doesn't seem to work," Daphne said.

"She also said," Edwin continued, "that he should have only little sleeps during the day to give him the idea of the long sleep during the night."

"Good idea," Daphne said in a low voice.

"Leila, you know"—he felt a tightening in his throat and cleared it noisily—"Leila," he said, "used to pick him up and play with him. She's left all these instructions." He sifted through a little sheaf of pink and blue pages which were covered with the familiar round handwriting. At the sight of the sprawling words he felt his eyes fill with tears. "I'm going to sneeze." He fumbled for his handkerchief and was able to bury his face in it for a few moments.

"It's awfully good of you, Daph," he managed to say, "to come and give a hand like this."

"What else could I do?" Daphne said. "Simply a baby needs more than one person, except when he's asleep. And you can't leave him alone in the house while you go out, and you do have to meet the plane. You can't let Cecilia arrive without any sort of preparation. I don't want to keep on about this, Teddy, but heaven knows how you are going to manage to tell Cecilia . . ."

Cecilia, he knew, would begin to talk, to chatter, as soon as they met. It would be impossible for him to tell her anything. He imagined himself putting a hand, a gloved hand would be best, over her pretty little mouth. "I must tell you, darling, we've got a baby." He looked at Daphne.

"I don't know," he said. "I really don't know."

It was not only the baby, the little boy, his child; it was Leila and her mother too. It was the sugar mother family. During the year, because of that impossible thing of having to tell someone something and being unable to, he had been living in two separate worlds, which now had to come together. He did not want to give up his new life, not at all. Plans made by people, from their ideas, often neglected, he supposed, their feelings. There was no planning possible for feelings, for the emotions, as they would be called in a tutorial discussion. It was never, or hardly ever, possible to anticipate how someone might feel. He had never imagined his present feelings as being a possibility.

"Everything looks wonderfully clean and neat." Daphne glanced quickly round the room. "I suppose the whole house is absolutely in apple-pie order." She seemed to be trying to save him from his thoughts, perhaps preventing him from pouring them out to her. Telling her that he no longer loved Cecilia, that he did not want Cecilia, would be unthinkable. He supposed she must know really and even understand. In spite of her lack of tact she had good manners and these would prevent questions.

"Yes, yes," he said, "all in order." He had been round the rooms himself and had seen everything restored to the proper places. Even Cecilia's spare room choice of bedside books had been lifted down from the top of the wardrobe and replaced on the bedside table. He reflected how neatly Leila's mother lived, and Leila too, out of their suitcases, everything (they did not have a great deal) folded in plastic bags. The only big things they had were their fur coats and these were, he discovered, quite expensive. They would need them once they were in London. He could hardly bear the thought. He understood again that Leila's mother, though he suspected that he was older than she was, made him feel young and safe. He thought now about her constant approval of him and how she was able to make him feel that what he thought and did was all for the best. He knew that he loved Leila. He knew that he had encouraged her in her first feelings of love for him knowing that he should not. The whole delightful adventure of discovery was shadowed by guilt. It surprised him that at the age he was he had not been wiser and more thoughtful.

"All in order," he said again. He was used to phrases, to using phrases, which disguised. "Leila and her mother," he forced himself, "were up very early, all packed, sheets washed, beds made, everything cleared away except for . . ." He found he could not look towards his child.

"Except for . . ."—Daphne nodded in the direction of the cradle—"and his things."

"Exactly," Edwin said, unable to forget Leila's small, plump but capable hands folding the white diapers into the correct shape, nimbly slipping a liner into each one, so that they were ready to use. Because his little son kicked and wriggled it was almost impossible to put any clothing on him. Daphne would have to hold him still.

"The kitchen's perfect," Daphne said, returning from a brief tour of inspection. "We must keep it that way for the next few hours."

The next few hours. Edwin groaned somewhere inside. Cecilia would be stiff and aching; the last five hours of the long flight were always the worst. Compared with the sea voyage, air travel was barbaric; they had often agreed about this in comfortable moments of dinnertime conversation with Buffy and the others. He wished that Buffy and Paulette and the others had agreed not to come out to the airport. Though they all found the broken night troublesome, they insisted. Cecilia would expect them. She would expect them and would expect the party to go on till breakfast and later. She would want to unfasten the straps on her luggage and bring out her gifts, everything chosen especially for each person. It was as if he could hear in advance her exclamations and her laughter. He wished he could feel enthusiasm for her return. The great test for two people was whether they wanted to meet and, having met, whether they wanted—needed—to be together for the rest of their lives. The final part of the test was: could they exist without each other, did they want a life each without the other?

Daphne, coming back once more into the room after more restless wanderings in the rest of the house, said she had never seen the bathroom so clean. "I hardly dared go to the loo," she said.

At school, Cecilia once told Edwin, they all had, on a certain day, usually a Sunday before church, to clean the school. "Every one of us had to do something," she said. "We had to notice," she explained, "something during the week which was not clean and then go for that thing, either to clean or to tidy or to weed, you know, getting plantains out of the tennis courts or sorting out bookshelves and gramophone records in the common rooms, whatever it was we had noticed." It, the untidy or the dirty thing, had to be written down on a piece of paper, Edwin remembered, and then the mistress on duty, either the gym mistress or the sewing teacher, went round the whole place examining and ticking off on her list all the things as she inspected them.

"Of course," Cecilia said, "we all thought the lavatories were awful, quite disgusting sometimes." But it was Daphne, she went on to say, who, with a great brush and a mop and a bucket, cleaned them. It was like Cecilia, Edwin thought now, wondering why all this was crowding his mind so painfully, to clean something which already looked nice. She had always, she told him, polished one of the urns or one of the sports trophies in the front hall of the school. He easily imagined her standing, a pretty schoolgirl, beside her chosen polished silver. Because she was fair and dainty she always looked clean. Standing in the middle of the room, hesitating before waking his sleeping child, he faced an awful truth. Perhaps it was too awful to write in his neglected books of the body (the intangible, though it could be the external and the internal as well). He could hardly bear to acknowledge it but he was comparing the sweet freshness of the whole of Leila's young and well-washed body with something which had, over the years, only the appearance of being fresh. Such things were never discussed, were in fact unmentionable, and he was ashamed of his thought.

He stood uncertain still, at the side of the cradle where the baby slept. The child's face, rounded now and flushed slightly, was completely serene and at rest. The mouth was closed as if resolutely. Leila's mother had been pleased that he slept with his mouth closed. "He's breathing through his little nose as he should." Ever to find the fond remark, she kept thinking of favorable things to say, one of them being how like his daddy the little boy was. An exact likeness. But Edwin searched the little features, either animated when crying, or in repose, for Leila's face. "His hair is dark like yours," he said to Leila once when the eager tiny head was pressing into her full breast. "Babies never keep their first hair," Leila's mother said then. "He'll most likely be fair; see how fair-skinned he is, like yourself."

The child had not been fed since Leila and her mother left. They had got him used (Leila's mother's words) to the bottle. Leila would have to endure her breasts for a time. She was all bandaged, poulticed with cabbage leaves. Everything would come right but meanwhile she would have to endure. Thinking about her pain, Edwin felt he could not bear it. He felt angry with Cecilia for being on her way home earlier than she was meant to be. He knew too that it would be as impossible if she had kept to her original plan. He knew he was to blame if anyone could be blamed. Leila's mother had said repeatedly, "Not to worry, Dr. Page. Just don't you worry, Dr. Page." He was frantic with worry over Leila. He walked to and fro on the thin carpet. They would be at the airport, Leila and her mother, the little sugar mother family, robbed of one whole part of themselves. Their plane would be leaving some time before the arrival of Cecilia's. He hated the airport in advance. He would have to be there among all the vacuous faces, the selfish faces of travelers and their selfish friends and relatives, all coming and going, insensitive to his suffering. He would walk where only a short time earlier Leila, overdressed, and her mother, also overdressed, would have walked. About to be reunited with Cecilia, he would be thinking that he would never see Leila again. And even worse, as he looked at the child, however much he and Cecilia wanted him and cared for him, the baby was not going to have his own sweet mother. He was not at all sure how much Cecilia would want him in any case. He could not help wondering what Cecilia would find to laugh about as she went through the rooms of her house. She often laughed at quite surprising things, things which he did not find amusing.

Cecilia had said in one telephone conversation, the one just before Christmas, when she had described the long walk she had in the snow, with the white soft snow to the tops of her boots in places, that Vorwickl might be coming back with her and could Edwin see that the spare room was vacuumed and the bed made.

Yes, he had said. Yes, he would do that.

At breakfast Leila's mother reading the tea leaves could see no sign of an accident, nothing, plane, train or bus. Nothing tragic near home or far away.

"What about a private car?" Edwin asked.

"Nor a car neither." Leila's mother put down the last of the cups. It seemed an auspicious day entirely for traveling. Leila, holding the baby, complained that he had wetted her, right through.

"It's good luck, Leila pet," Leila's mother said. "Slip your dress off and I'll rinse it; it'll be dry before lunch. Sign of good luck!"

"Would the tea leaves need to be read a bit later on?" Edwin felt he ought to feel foolish asking his question.

"Nearer the time?" Leila's mother shook her head. "Not really, but I'll have another read midday to be on the safe side." She was studying for their own safety, for the takeoff, Edwin knew, but he, deeply ashamed, hoped for some sort of deliverance from the arrival. He, knowing that it was not right to wish for death, either for oneself or for someone else, was wishing that Cecilia's plane might never arrive, that it might hover somewhere high up above the clouds, lose power quickly and break up into a million fragments, all of it, passengers included, all hurled immediately into a painless oblivion, all kept above the cloud level forever by a curious phenomenon, a new reversal of gravity. A suitable subject perhaps for an honors thesis: not his department, of course, but it would be possible to pass on the idea. . . .

His reverie was interrupted by a wailing noise in another part of the house. He stopped his restless pacing and listened. Blackie never made any such noises and, as far as he knew, Prince was outside the kitchen door. He wondered where Daphne was; she kept leaving the room and then returning, only to disappear again. The scraping wailing continued.

"What on earth's that noise?" he asked Daphne as she came in with the baby's milk.

"Oh, Teddy," she said, "I hope you won't mind. It's Fiorella. Remember Fiorella? The enormous Rosalind? She's in the bathroom, practicing. The violin. It's Bach, J. S.," she added as if hopeful for approval. "It's the school orchestra," she explained. "No, they're not all here; of course not. Only Fiorella. She's simply got to practice and I thought if she was where I could hear her I could call out to her now and again, some sort of correction and encouragement. Mostly correction, I'm afraid. It's so that the violin concerto for two violins, etc.— Fiorella's one of them, isn't it terrible?—won't be too awful. Also . . ." Daphne paused to make a sort of clucking over the cradle. "Oh, Teddy, he's awake! What a darling little nose and face. Also," she continued, "I must confess I did feel a bit nervous about being here while you went to meet the plane and Fiorella, d'you see, is the eldest of eight and is awfully experienced."

They heard the violin start again laboriously.

"I've got the doors open a bit," Daphne explained, "so that I can teach from here." She leaned into the passage and sang the notes for Fiorella to imitate. "Sing!" she called. "Sing, Fiorella, with the violin and make the violin sing!"

The baby in the cradle stretched and yawned and twisted

his face and sneezed and made the grunting creaking noises Edwin had become accustomed to recently. He still had his account of the childbirth to write up and, daily, had extra notes to make. He sometimes wondered if he would ever be able to find adequate words for the description of the amniotic membrane and fluid.

◆ ◆ ◆

"Teddy, he doesn't seem to be getting any of this milk." Daphne held up the bottle. "He's been sucking valiantly at this but it hasn't gone down at all. It's as full as it was." Edwin, taking the bottle, shook it.

"Must be blocked," he said. "I'll get another." Daphne made more of her noises at the baby, who looked at her with solemn eyes.

"I wish he would smile at me," she said.

"He will later," Edwin said.

The child lay undressed between them, his little thick pink legs stuck upwards, like the legs of a stuffed toy, and his tiny arms waved, flailing, from side to side.

"I think he's cold," Daphne said. "Look, his chin's quivering. I'm sorry I'm so slow and awkward."

"You're doing fine," Edwin said, welcoming his own nervous anxiety.

"I can manage Prince," Daphne said, "but he doesn't have to be dressed."

It was not the first time Edwin had changed his son, but Leila had always been there at the other times. It was not the first time that he had had doubts about Cecilia's reception of the surprise. But it was quite some time since his other doubts, the uneasiness about Leila herself. Leila, at the end, did not seem to find it hard to leave him.

There had been nothing amiss with the arrangements. Leila and her mother had carried out their share of the deal faithfully. The birth being sooner than expected, Edwin's arrangements for a nursemaid were not completed so Leila and her mother stayed on. On Cecilia's apparently sudden decision to come home earlier, Leila's mother made herself and Leila ready to leave with efficient haste. Edwin paid all that he owed. He paid off the two fur coats too, as Leila's mother confessed that Mr. Bott still owed on them. Edwin said he was pleased to complete this purchase for them because of all the extra things Leila's mother and Leila had done for him.

That Leila had seemed not to mind going was like a constant pain. He felt ashamed that she did not seem to mind and ashamed because he cared so much in what was after all, in the first place, meant to be a business arrangement. Of course her painful breasts, and they must be unbearably painful, he knew, were enough to stop her showing any feelings. She must have been, and he could understand this, completely wrapped up in her pain. If only he did not love her and want her so much. There was no one to whom he could talk in a purely selfish way about Leila. He wanted to tell someone that he had experienced something so unexpected and immense it must last forever. He wanted, now that it was too late, to tell Leila.

Daphne was concerned because the baby was still not sucking properly.

"He prefers his mother, I suppose," she said. "We'll just have to keep on trying. Wrong note!" she bellowed through the partly open door. Fiorella started again at the beginning. "Sing!" Daphne bawled. "Sing with the violin."

During the last few days, Leila's mother, after binding up Leila, sent her to sit with Edwin in the room with the cabbage-rose wallpaper. It was better for them to keep away, she told them, because the sound of the crying would only make the milk come more. Without the child in her arms Leila did not have much to say to Edwin, and in the face of her silence, he had not known what to talk about with her. During these times he checked an indescribable longing to take her in his arms and bury his face in the soft creaminess of her neck.

Leila never talked a great deal, Edwin consoled himself now, and therefore was not lavish with the words of farewell. He always did most of the talking. During the last afternoon she simply sat nursing the contented child and then put him in the cradle, with the little teddy bear, which he always ignored, beside him. The special toy was fixed to the side of the big crib, "in readiness for when he is older," she had explained. The panel, once described during a night when they were sweetly pressed close together, was shaped like an elephant and was white. It was made from some sort of washable plastic and had several knobs from which it was possible to produce various rattlings and whistlings and ringings. Leila had demonstrated them all to him. She said she thought red was a good color for the knobs. When Edwin passed the prepared crib, now he could hardly bear to look at it. The toy on the crib seemed to collide with another thought, something so terrible that he refused, at the times when it came to him, to allow it to persist. It was that the child was not his, that Leila and her mother, finding themselves in difficulties, had simply picked out a suitable person to pull them out of their troubles. Daphne hinted, at the beginning, at something of this sort but neither of them, in their conversations, alluded to it again. Edwin knew that such a thought, if fed, could assume enormous proportions. One only had to read, and he did read, widely.

He took the child from Daphne, who stood holding a shawl in an awkward and useless way. "Oh Lord!" she said. "He'll never feed while he's crying like this. Walk up and down with him." She put the shawl over Edwin's shoulder. "I'll put on the cassette," she said. "Fiorella needs to listen to the Bach. She hasn't the faintest feeling for the tempo and babies are supposed to respond to music. Fiorella!" she shouted into the passage. "Rest!"

Prince howled at the kitchen door and Blackie whimpered in reply and the Concentus Musicus Wien, with conscientious precision, began to play Johann Sebastian Bach. Somewhere in between, Fiorella, inspired, went on with her own interpretation of the music. She was up to a later passage. And above all this Leila's baby, whose voice was powerful, cried.

"Shall I feed the dogs?" Daphne's voice came from a distant place. Edwin walked up and down patting the baby, holding him upright in case he had some sort of pain.

"At least it's not a pin"—Daphne was back at his side once more with a crazy pile of roughly made sandwiches—"since we haven't been able to put a pin on him."

"I don't think the music's having any effect," Edwin said. Daphne turned it off and they heard Fiorella's violin scraping. The notes climbed slowly higher and then, with a screeching sound, slid down the scale to the lowest notes, and after an agony of confused noise, the climbing began once more. Daphne ate a sandwich and nodded with momentary unexpected approval. "Not bad," she said. "Not bad!" she shouted into the hall. "Eat something," she said to Edwin in her sensible way. "We must keep our strength up." She munched a second sandwich. "Here," she said, "let me hold him while you eat—you must eat, Teddy."

There was a smell of burning in the room. It was the dust in the electric heater. It was strangely cold for March. There were two fans placed so that Leila was able to have the coolest spot during the height of the heat. Now Edwin had to put on the radiator. He was afraid that the child might have been chilled during their lengthy undressing and dressing. Leila's mother, with her way of approving of everything Edwin did, disapproved of air-conditioning. The Pages did not have it and Leila's mother often consoled them at breakfast, while they were struggling, after a sleepless hot night, with chops and eggs, saying that there were some terrible diseases straight out of air-conditioners. Take Legionnaires' for a start. It stuffed up people's systems, causing more deaths than you'd like to think about. She wouldn't be at all surprised, she said, if most of the world's troubles came from air-conditioning. She'd rather be hot, she said, than poisoned.

For a few days before the departure of Leila and her mother and the arrival of Cecilia (possibly with Vorwickl) the sky was laden with clouds. In a poetic moment Edwin thought the sky seemed quiet. The ridges of cloud seemed filled with silence. Daphne would have said, if he had spoken of it to her, that the sky was always quiet. There was a feeling of autumn in the new coolness and it was possible to imagine that the summer was over. But in spite of the delicate mist, which softened the outlines of the pines, the summer was not over and the sun, with burning heat, would make the fans indispensable again. The pines could be quite motionless and dark beneath the low cloud, they could groan and labor in the wind when it came and, almost at once, be motionless once more with the uncanny stillness and the fragrance familiar in the great heat. The hot fragrant air was as refreshing at times as the cold wind.

It was almost impossible to think of snow when walking over the sun-dried grass and the hot sand between the pines. Cecilia, crossing the world, was coming from the snow. The winter in England, especially in London, had been long and intensely cold. Reminding him what it was like to wake up in the morning to the curious silence of a snowbound world and the strange light it spread on the bedroom ceiling, she said the slush, when it came, was awful. Black wet slush; she said it froze overnight, did he remember? It was hard to walk. Vorwickl clung to the railings alongside the pavement when there were railings. They clung to each other and, one day, had fallen. A terrible shock because Vorwickl, who was big, had not been able to get up for some time. The taxis all had chains on.

Better to go by underground, Edwin had said during the particular telephone call when she said she would never again complain about the heat. For some time after that call he sat remembering her flushed and happy during their first winter. *That winter*, Cecilia always called it, when they had chased each other round her mother's own special garden disregarding the hidden flower beds and the pruned-back rosebushes. Then, throwing snowballs, they had spattered the leaded panes of the dining room windows. Because they were laughing so much they could not throw properly.

There was the toboggan too; Cecilia's father seemed pleased to unearth it from a refined sort of potting shed where he kept, among other things, ornamental frames for crumbling nudes and other antique art. After rushing down the hill together on the sledge, Cecilia wanted to make love in the park in the snow, but Edwin, with a natural prudence, reminded her that too many windows overlooked the snowbound gardens and the park. Even if they buried themselves in a snowdrift someone would be sure to see them; after all, it was a suburb.

He knew his last-minute avoidance of the Christmas visit upset Cecilia but, as usual, she talked and laughed herself into an acceptance of what was simply bad luck. She had been ill over Christmas and lost her voice. He noticed the huskiness which still persisted. A dreadful flu, she had said. A lot of it around, he replied, hoping the telephone call would be brief. The worst part was, she said, that the house was all stocked up with food. Mumsie was dreadfully upset about all the food which she could not eat, and Vorwickl was only eating lentils and bran and perhaps a small handful of nuts. He understood the loss of voice following the infection would have been largely due to what he called nerves. Several pages of the notebooks of the internal and the intangible were devoted to manifestations of this sort. In the rather touching husky voice she had asked him to send the *Battersea Polytechnic Cookery Book*; it was the one they had used at school; Daphne would know it, the one with the yellow American cloth covers which stuck to the other recipe books in the cupboard. Vorwickl, she said, had expressed an interest in the idea of an even more sparse diet and the suggestions for meals during the Depression (at the back of the book) might prove to be what she wanted. "Cold Cabinet Pudding." She had started to laugh and cough. "Take four slices of stale bread, half an apple and four raisins . . ."

Edwin glanced at the clock. All that burdened him was on the way home. How quick thoughts were and how easily thoughts could be crowded with painful and impossible things. The child in his arms was quieter now but was still crying in what seemed an almost grown-up way, as an older child might cry. He had only heard his angry or hungry baby cry before. It suddenly seemed as if this was the crying of the heartbroken, as if all the cares of living suddenly were pressing on this tiny skull, as if he knew already that he had come into all the difficult and intolerable things which had to be faced every day. Edwin felt the tears coming into his own eyes when he saw tears on the baby's face.

"I didn't know they cried tears," Daphne said. Edwin was touched and appalled to see her eyes fill and spill over so that she had to find a tissue.

"Don't, Daph," he said gently. "It's all right," he said, "don't cry."

"I'm sorry, Teddy," Daphne said. "I'll fetch us some coffee; Fiorella's brewing some."

As he moved the child from one arm into the other, the soft hair and skin brushed against his cheek, filling him with an incredible tenderness. He moved his lips secretly across the top of the little head, feeling once more the softness of the wispy hair.

Leila and her mother, he reflected, would need the fur coats as soon as they stepped off the plane in London. The money apparently owing on them was considerable. He, to his surprise, found himself wondering whether the coats really were still to be paid for—"paid off," Leila's mother had said—or whether someone, Mr. Bott or an accomplice, perhaps a respectable buxom thief, had stolen them. Daphne, if he mentioned it to her, would be sure to say that it was more than likely that the extra money he had handed over was not needed as a contribution to the coats at all. It was unpleasant, awful—to use one of Daphne's words—to have thoughts like these. There was nothing he could do about the money except stop his check first thing in the morning. But the thought that Leila might suffer in some way because of this action made even thinking of such an action impossible.

After a short rest the child was crying again. Crying and crying. Edwin, rocking the baby in his arms, began again to pace to and fro. The crying seemed to contain more despair than ever.

He heard, through the crying, the front doorbell. Cecilia. It could not be Cecilia. She could not possibly have arrived sooner than expected. He heard the bell again. It was probably Buffy and Paulette coming to fill in the hours of waiting. He heard, still through the child's crying, the small commotion in the hall and a moment later Leila came into the room. Leila's mother, carrying the fur coats, followed and Daphne came in last.

Leila, without a word or even a look, dropped her ugly handbag and took the crying child from Edwin. She sat down on the sofa and, unbuttoning her blouse, held the child close, her arms folded round him as if to keep everything and every person away. She bent her head so that her lips rested in the softness of the down-like hair. She was, Edwin could see, completely absorbed in her son, in comforting him and in protecting him and in feeding him. In spite of all the arrangements and all the money he was, without question, her son. She rocked to and fro on the cushions. There was no sound in the room except the little gulping murmurs of swallowing which the child made. Leila, rocking, began to sing, a low crooning song. Edwin, having heard this song before, was very moved. He stood in the middle of the room gazing at Leila and her child.

"She's cried and cried, cried herself silly, cried till she threw up all over the place." Leila's mother, letting her armful of coats slide to the floor, sank into an armchair. Edwin nodded. It was like the night when he had come straight back from the airport just before Christmas.

"She's cried and cried, cried herself sick," Leila's mother, meeting him in the hall, had said then. He had dropped his luggage and his coat and gone straight in to Leila and taken her in his arms, feeling the solid shape of the child between them as he held her gently and steadily closer.

Daphne had come in that night, he remembered, not expecting to see him, and was immediately worried about Cecilia, saying, in as soft a voice as she could manage, "Teddy darling! But you will have to let Cecilia know at once; she'll be waiting, expecting . . ."

"Yes, yes," he'd said. "Of course, Daph, of course I'll tell Cecilia. I'll cable. I'm not able to get away after all."

It had been clear that Daphne, not particularly liking Leila or her mother, had visited, as she thought during Edwin's absence, out of kindness. He had realized then how deep was her sense of friendship and affection for him. Leila and her mother were isolated in the life they had with him. Daphne, aware of this isolation, had regarded them as being ordinary, to be visited in an ordinary way. He remembered now how this had touched him at the time, and he had always meant to say some words of thanks but never did.

Daphne did not go away at Christmas though the others often tried to persuade her to go with them to Singapore or Bali. Once they had been to New Zealand. It was not so much that they liked to travel but they enjoyed the idea of traveling. They liked to have traveled. At Christmas Daphne, on Christmas Day, always took Miss Heller to church and then for a little ride in the car and a picnic, which Miss Heller ate greedily in the car, not looking at the sea or the river or the hills. Daphne packed things which Miss Heller could eat with little plastic spoons from neat little plastic containers because that was what Miss Heller liked. Edwin knew all this about Daphne. He knew too that some, perhaps two or three, girls, boarders at St. Monica's, did not go home for holidays and, spending their holiday in school, were offered music and drawing and some watercolor painting. Daphne, for very little extra money, was supposed to go in every day to provide these. She always included in her holiday program an outing either to the museum or, for sketching, to the zoo.

The school Christmas dinner, to which Daphne was invited and at which she was expected to be present, was on Christmas Eve. Miss Hearnsted, carving a chicken, even two sometimes, served rather mean helpings for herself, Daphne and the girls. As the school kitchen and boardinghouse staff, on board wages, had Christmas Day off, the girls made toast and cocoa for themselves in the school sick bay. One year, Daphne told Edwin during one of their walks in the pines, the girls had telephoned for a taxi to bring a pizza to the front door of the school. They had been obliged to hide it immediately, as Miss Hearnsted, taking a sudden walk, had appeared on the front-door steps (which were absolutely out of bounds for the girls), suggesting that she would play dominoes with them. The pizza, hidden under a nearby bush, was stone cold, of course, when they were able, after twenty-three games, which they lost, to eat it.

Edwin, because he did not know what to do, continued to stand, uncertain and half-smiling, in the middle of the room. Leila's mother leaned back in her chair. "There was nothing I could do," she said. "She's cried and cried. She would have all of them cabbage leaves off in the toilets at the airport, ripped them off. I kid you not, that girl, Leila, wasn't going anyplace leaving her baby behind. No way!"

"Oh, dear!" Daphne said. Her remark, which was clearly inadequate, was ignored.

"There was nothing anyone could do," Leila's mother said. She looked exhausted. "There was nothing I could do," she said.

"No, no, of course not," Edwin said gently. Daphne, he noticed, was slipping through the door; not slipping exactly, but more as if backing out like a large expensive car with a quiet engine and only just enough space on either side. He watched in amazement as she who was usually so clumsy achieved this. Everything seemed changed. There was the sudden silence, for one thing, broken only by the regular small noises of sucking. This did change everything; even the braid on the cushions where Leila sat seemed bright and fresh in spite of being old and worn as it really was. He was unable to stop looking at Leila and the child. Suddenly he was an outsider, not the child's father at all and not at all sure that Leila's mother was entirely truthful. Leila's supposed "crying and crying" now and at the earlier time when he had come home instead of going to Cecilia for Christmas: was Leila's mother making this up? Leila was certainly composed, very calm now, and that time earlier, when he had folded her in his arms, it was more his feeling that he remembered. His feeling of joy at returning and not hers at having him return.

Daphne was at the door, edging in sideways, carrying a tray. Edwin, roused from his tender worship, remembered his customary chivalry and took the laden tray, making little noises of thanks and appreciation. Daphne had used the large teapot, the one they never used because it was too big, and the wrong cups.

"I've sent Fiorella home," she said in a low voice. "I've told her, 'not a word to a soul,' or else no violin in the orchestra."

♦ ♦ ♦

"It's a bit like Shakespeare," Daphne said, taking a large bite of the cake Leila's mother had made and left in a tin "against Dr. Sissilly's homecoming."

"The ending," Daphne continued, surveying with approval the place where she had bitten the cake. "Shakespeare," she said, "has done this, the endings of some of his plays, *Lear*, for example, as well as he can."

Edwin said yes to Daphne. He was thinking, as he continued to look at Leila, of the Madonna. Dürer, he thought, "Madonna mit dem Kind." Benvenuto di Giovanni, "Madonna and Child Enthroned Between Two Angels." Leila sat with her mother on one side of her and Daphne on the other. He remembered the elaborate dressing up of the Christ child and watched Leila as she replaced her baby's little embroidered jacket with a fresh one which had, not a herringbone stitch in gold thread, but tiny blue forget-me-nots all round the neck, the loving work of Leila's mother some weeks earlier. The child, contented now, lay across his mother's lap and it seemed to Edwin that the little fat limbs, dimpled in places, hardly fitted the strangely wise face.

"My son," Edwin wanted to say, "my dear son." He felt his eyes fill with tears. The baby's face was like the experienced face of an elderly man.

At Christmas, during that unexpected and intensely happy time together, they had listened to carols and looked at

Edwin's books of paintings and reproductions of illuminated manuscripts. He saw again in Leila, as she sat resting, the Madonna-like quality, the tenderness in the tilt of the head and the possibilities of silence, patience and endurance. The gray-haired Joseph, he recalled, had a wan starved look which he felt he could match immediately with his own reflection in the bathroom mirror. Like Joseph, perhaps he was not the father of this child. Perhaps there was, in the theft of the fur coats (if they were in fact stolen), a young, spotty-faced male accomplice who regularly received the letters Leila wrote in her large handwriting on decorated notepaper. Perhaps the thief, if there was one, was not after all a fleshy woman. For an unknown reason, Edwin reflected, the stealing of fur coats should rightfully be the work of females. He supposed they simply put them on and then walked cozily out of the shop. Then, hugged in the warmth, they joined a bus queue or, if feeling it more appropriate, hailed a taxi.

Turning away from doubts about his claim on the child, he tried to think in a more hopeful way. He now understood in these quiet moments how every person is, at some time in his life, the subject of adoration and love and that this, from necessity, gets forgotten. Modeling himself as usual on Cardano, he thought he would turn his meditation upon the blessed Virgin Mary; he tried to think of the exact words for a quotation. These were almost correct. It was the material from which writing could spring. He thought he would write something, a parable. A suburban parable for an entirely new bible. But to make sure that this bible would be purchased and, more important, read, it would have to be written with a strong story line and to a pattern, a formula already familiar, based on real life and contemporary issues, with real characters with whom hoped-for readers could become involved. He remembered reading somewhere that characters in stories and novels must be created from the imagination and not merely remembered as relatives or friends were remembered. Suggestion could come from real people and from real experience but something more should be offered from which the reader could make his own connections. And, like the Greeks, they should be able to predict the events so that the drama could move from the surface of human life to the depths. To write something he would have to create from the original, and he was aware of the difficulties. He might find such writing impossible. And why, at his age, should he confront something which was so hard to do? And why should he put himself in the way of a possibly spiteful reviewer, someone who might have achieved even less than he had himself. Such a person might exist. It was possible.

All this was, he knew, a method of not thinking the thought he had just previously banished. He knew himself well enough to know he was doing what he always did. He was taking a false way, a falsely intellectual way out. It was his habit to think of something else other than the immediate when the immediate, that he might not be the father of this baby, was too unpleasant.

He felt as if his chest would burst. He longed for fresh air. He wanted to escape into the pines and walk there. He wished, in a hopeless way, that he and Leila could be walking in the pines, in the dark, that they could be lost there together all night and he would protect her as he had the night she was lost. He wished he could walk endlessly in the pines knowing that they could be together forever.

Leila's mother gratefully stretched out her bandaged leg to allow Edwin to slip the footstool under it. And then she leaned forward while he placed the cushion, with the peacock design, in the small of her back. He thought he had never seen her looking so worn and tired, and though she blossomed as she became more comfortable, it was clear to him that she had suffered during the last few hours. There was an air about her as if she was depending on him, as if everything now depended on him, on his decision.

Daphne ate two pieces of the cake. "It seems to me," she said as if with a new strength, "that a decision must be made. We must decide and act quickly. Cecilia's return is imminent!"

Edwin glanced at the clock and at Leila. With the now

contented child, seeming to be almost a part of her, she was falling asleep. He remembered all too clearly her wonderful childlike quality, the gift of sleep. It was enviable, this gift.

Leila's mother, looking lovingly across at Leila and the baby, said, "He's a beautiful child." She sighed and studied the tea leaves first in her own cup and then in the others. "Not a thing," she said, "in any of these." Edwin wished for something. Anything. An assassin, without any conscience and without relatives, in the bottom of his cup. Someone who would hijack Cecilia's plane, insisting on Cuba or, better still, the North Pole.

"Perhaps you could"—Daphne spoke gently, as if she were patting a horse—"rent the house next door?" She glanced at Edwin. "It's empty again, I think."

"Yes," Leila's mother said, "it's been empty awhile; we've noticed it was empty—about three weeks, isn't it, Leila pet?" But Leila and her baby were asleep.

"Well," Daphne said in her practical way, "if you rented the house and if the"—she paused—"if the Leila family all moved in there, you could decide when Cecilia's here, and when she's rested after the flight and everything, which house, Teddy, you'll live in, either here with Cecilia or next door with the Leila family."

There was no anger or sarcasm in Daphne's tone. Edwin could see she was trying to help. She was offering him a choice. She was not trying in any way to dictate to him or to put forward moral standards, which he felt sure she had. "It's awfully late," he began. "It's after midnight," he said.

"We can't break in," Leila's mother said. "It's burglar-proof—we know! We'll never get in there. Remember?"

"Perhaps an hotel," Edwin began once more. "If I took you all to—"

"It's never too late for people like agents," Daphne interrupted, "and since they're packed it should not take long to move. Everything," she said, "absolutely everything should be moved out of this house now. While you are moving," she said, "I'll go orf to the airport. It takes oodles of time with customs

and everything. I'll meet Cecilia, the others will all be there.
. . . You, Teddy, you must get it all in order here. You'll need
to move the surprises," she added, "both of them."

Edwin, who did not handle dogs, moved Blackie a bit to one
side with the toe of his shoe.

"You'd better phone the agent," Daphne said.

"Wait on!" Leila's mother was rummaging in her large
handbag. "I've got his after-hours somewhere in here. Yes,"
she said, "here's his card." Edwin stood up and, taking the card
from her, reached for the phone.

"Wait on!" Leila's mother pulled a little bunch of keys from
the depths of her bag. "My!" she said. "Is my face red! Here's
the spares. Remember the night we locked ourselves out?
Well, I never ever thought to give this set back. Here . . ."

"You've actually had the keys, then. All this time, then!"
Daphne did not hide her annoyance.

The study phone was ringing.

"I'll get it," Daphne said. "It's probably Paulette or Erica."

Leila's mother leaned back in her chair and closed her eyes.
Edwin began to put the cups together on the tray. Daphne
reappeared almost at once. "It's Cecilia," she said. "She's in
Cairo—with Vorwickl. The plane had to be diverted—some
sort of trouble, I didn't quite . . . You'd better speak, Teddy.
They'll be held up there for some time. Cairo of all places!
How absolutely ghastly! It's miles away! They'll be done up!
Completely and utterly done up."

Edwin went to his study. The phone was lying on his bed.
Daphne had left it as if sprawled on the red blanket. He went
towards it, taking a long time, going right round the end of the
bed. He did not want to pick it up. He had not realized till this
moment how much he hated the telephone, this one in particular.

I know your surprise, Cecilia told him. Miss Hearnsted saw
you walking with *her* along by the university holding hands.
Miss Hearnsted told me she was passing in a taxi. She hardly
ever takes a taxi and that day she did and she saw you. You
were holding hands. A mere schoolgirl, Miss Hearnsted said,

and not at all the quality of the girls at St. Monica's. Miss Hearnsted said that you would say you were not holding hands but the whole thing is, she says, even if you said you were not holding hands you would have been wanting to hold hands—which is the same thing, isn't it. Of course that's the annoying part of it and I daresay it's also annoying that you didn't know that the others knew. It would have saved you all the trouble of keeping secret and you would have been able to enjoy yourself without all that worry. Everything would have been so much easier if Miss Hearnsted had told you about her seeing you. Miss Heller saw you too, once when Daphne was driving her to the bank. She, Miss Heller, said the girl was obviously pregnant. What did she get? I should say, I suppose, what did you get? Also they never answered the door. Once when Paulette and Erica called—even though you told them you didn't want visitors they called. And they knew someone was in because the TV was on, they heard it quite plain, and because they know you never watch TV in the afternoons they peeked in and when they peeked in—I know peek isn't a word I usually use but it suits here—when they peeked in the dining room window they could see them as plain as anything. They'd got themselves squeezed in under the dining room table hiding, the two of them, hiding. Yes, I said hiding and what's more the table had a cloth on it, a fringed cloth, and you know how I hate tablecloths, especially ones with fringes. And another thing—Evelyn Tranby saw you getting flowers, whole armfuls of them, from the university flower shop. You spent the earth, she said; she saw you choose an armful, positively every flower they had, and then you bolted straight out of the door. Put them on the account, Evelyn heard you say that. Since when have you had an account there? Romeo? Who has accounts at flower shops! I don't suppose you saw Evelyn but she saw you all right, you and your flowers. I suppose they were for *her* or *her mother.* And then there's Mr. Taylor at the bank. What's all this about inheritance and making arrangements to have your will put in order? Just who are these people who must be provided for? I'm to get used, am I, to the idea of not being the one and only. That's rich. Me being reduced to being one of four beneficiaries. Mr. Taylor, the bank manager, I'd like to remind you, is *our* bank manager. You seem to forget that we're double income and always have been, and without being vulgar, you seem to forget, with regard to your apparent wealth and possessions, the pronoun is plural. Evelyn Tranby says you're hardly ever in the department these days. You still perving around the children's playground? Everyone in the department, they all know that you leave early and hang around the park. Perv . . . perv . . .

Cecilia had never used that word, would never use it, and in any case it wasn't true and it was not anything that Cecilia would think about him. *A world of disorderly notions . . .* He staggered, trying to ignore his own imagination. He must ignore the tirade which was all of his own making. He almost tripped as he leaned across the bed to pick up the receiver. He was—what was the word?—hallucinating, that was it. He must remember to write it down. It was not an illness but a manifestation of something more intangible. Guilt was too simple. It was something more than that. He held the receiver to his burning ear.

"Hullo," he said, "hullo! Edwin here." He repeated the greeting without enthusiasm. "Cecilia?" he said, wishing that he were not saying it. "Cecilia, is that you? Are you there? Cecilia?" He listened to the crackling sound and thought that, through it, he could hear a tinny complaining voice, like a wasp caught in an empty jam tin. Cecilia's? He thought he heard another voice. Vorwickl? "Vorwickl?" He strained to listen. It seemed to him that he heard a child crying in a distant place. The crackling was louder, deafening; he held the receiver away from his ear. His head, it seemed, was full of the sound of a baby crying. It was the kind of noise which stayed in the head. He had not known until this evening that children, babies, could cry for so long.

"Vorwickl?" he asked in a self-conscious voice, but now there was nothing to hear, not even the crackling. He stood bending forward slightly, his back aching as it often did; he held the receiver close to his ear now and waited. He recalled Vorwickl's large white arm. The first time he met her she had asked him to help her.

"I haf, as you say, wounded mein selluf." She pronounced "wounded" as if for winding a clock, "wound." He, restraining himself from a correction, took the small bottle of iodine and the tiny brush she offered. Rolling up her sleeve, she presented him with her large elbow, on which was the painful-looking graze. "Pleess to paint," she urged. At the time, Edwin, unable to stand the smallest sight of blood, flinched at her pain, noticing that she made not the slightest movement of wincing. Later he said to Cecilia that Vorwickl had just the muscles for delivering babies and Cecilia, laughing, had said that the doctors did not need muscles because the mothers had them.

"They do all that side of it," she said then. That evening they spent the time soothing Cecilia's mother, who was distressed because of all the simply awful things spilling from Vorwickl's enormous cabin trunk: a human skull, some huge forceps, a thing which Vorwickl said was a Body Brush, a tennis racquet—Cecilia's mother was particularly upset by the racquet.

"Feel the weight of it," she moaned. "It could be a man's!" Still trying to hear either Cecilia or Vorwickl, Edwin thought of the female smell of Vorwickl. He thought he could smell it now, and afraid that he was really ill, he put down the receiver. He began to shiver and to wonder where he had put the thermometer.

"Cut off." Still shivering, he sat down in the other room, grateful for once for the cabbage roses. He could feel the sweat gathering on his forehead. He leaned forward to put his head down, pretending to retie a shoelace. The made-up pictures, wrestled from him by Leila's mother, crowded in on him. Cecilia, somewhere in the mountains in a white room with thin white billowing curtains, weeping after her abortion, sorry, miscarriage, her thin hands clutching at him for comfort, it being all for the best really, the whole thing bundled, a small uneven bundle in a piece of white sheet, in the gnarled hands of a knowing nun . . . He knew really that Leila's mother had not made him tell these things, make them up and tell them. Something inside him felt the need to provide Leila's mother with what she was, or might be, wanting. He had during the last months provided a great deal, if providing was what was being considered. Vorwickl, when she was young, enjoyed being provided for. It was as if she had to eat and eat to replenish the years which were lean with convent life. He supposed she still enjoyed eating. Like Cecilia, Vorwickl had loved food. He remembered clearly the way in which she, Vorwickl, attacked a plate of spinach and eggs. She held her knife and fork firmly but with a certain restraint as if they were surgical instruments. She held them pointing downwards and took the food in a delicate way from the tip of the fork as soup is taken, in Europe, from the tip of the long oval-shaped spoon. She never sat at meals with her hands in her lap, but always had, as if in readiness, both fists on the table.

"All right now, Teddy?" He heard, as if from a distance, the anxiety in Daphne's voice. She was leaning over him, her large face close to his face. He looked straight into her worried brown eyes.

"Perfectly, thank you," he said. "Must have got up too quickly—that sort of thing, you know." He heard his voice, low and muttering, offering explanations. He stood up.

Leila's mother was still lying back in her chair with her eyes closed. Edwin sat down again because he needed to.

"Blithering idiot!" Using one of Buffy's ways of reprimanding himself, he tried to grin at Daphne.

"We'd better move everything into the other house," she said in her most matter-of-fact way. It was possible, Edwin knew, to know exactly how Daphne would behave in the middle of a collapsed tent during an all-night gale.

"Oh Lord!" He could hear her voice and he could imagine her heaving her great strength and height against the sodden canvas. "Grab the pole!" He knew how she would tell the others what to do. She was always expected to accompany the girls from St. Monica's when they were at a school camp, banished with very plain food to remote and wildly beautiful places for literature and drama. It was thought, Daphne had explained once, that she enjoyed these camps so much that she was not paid for being there.

Here she was now, taking control. "And then," she said, "we'd better try to get some sleep. We can't know exactly when they will arrive; it's clear it'll be hours."

"Yes, yes, of course." Edwin got up quickly. He steadied himself against the arm of the chair. "Watch it, Gran'pa"—he seemed to hear Tranby's voice—"the old ticker, Gran'pa."

"What would you like me to do first?" he asked.

♦ ♦ ♦

They walked in single file down the little path to the front door of the house next door. Daphne led the way with the two suitcases. Leila's mother, carrying the two fur coats, followed. Leila, with her baby son asleep in her arms, followed her mother. Edwin came last with the folded-up crib and the special toy for the side of it. He would have to go back for the cradle and the baby bath and the little cupboard of clothes. Daphne would fetch Blackie, she said, and any other things they needed.

"I hope there are no rats." Leila's mother gave an exaggerated shudder. Daphne unlocked the front door and switched on the light.

"Electricity's on," she said, with a triumphant note in her voice.

"*Ecce puer*," Edwin said half to himself as the hall light shone across the child's head. He said he hoped the house was not dirty. Daphne was opening cupboards and examining the beds. Edwin without wanting to recalled a day when, with Cecilia on their own front veranda, he had seen some tenants moving into the house. This was before Leila and her mother had moved in.

"There's only a single bed going in there," Cecilia had said, looking up from her book, "and a double mattress."

"That might be awkward." Edwin remembered his reply. It had seemed to him then that having a double mattress hanging over the sides of a single bed would damage it, the mattress, dreadfully.

"They'll be sleeping on the floor, silly!" Cecilia had giggled so much she had rushed indoors so that the new neighbors would not be embarrassed. Since that time the owner had furnished the house and asked a higher rent . . . well, he supposed a higher rent.

"Teddy darling," Daphne said, "do hurry and run back and get the other things. Leila and her mother do need to get to bed. Bring some tea bags and the milk, put them in the cradle—you know, just a few essentials."

"Oh yes. Yes, of course," Edwin said.

"I'll come with you," Leila's mother said. "Gentlemen often forget things."

"Oh yes," Edwin said. "Thank you, that is most kind." With his usual chivalry he helped her up onto the old veranda boards of his house. A few minutes later, laden with provisions, he helped her down from the corner of the veranda and escorted her gently back to the house next door.

"I could just see—well, imagine," Daphne said to Edwin when they were back in Edwin's study. "I can just imagine," she said, "how Vorwickl's eyes must have been shining. Are you listening to me, Teddy?" she asked. Edwin, trying to peer into the darkness across to the house next door, was only able to see the reflection in the uncurtained window of his own book-lined study and himself and Daphne in seclusion there. The house next door had seemed clean. It was just a bit airless; Daphne had thrown open some windows. She had closed them after helping to arrange the luggage in the bedroom, as Leila's mother was afraid of burglars. "You can contact the agent tomorrow." Daphne spoke then in her kindest voice.

Later Edwin listened while Daphne telephoned the Honeywells, the Wellatons and the Fairfaxes to tell them about the delay. Now she was stretching her long body in one of the comfortable study chairs.

"What can you imagine?" Edwin, still peering, thought he should ask.

"I'll tell you in a minute," Daphne said. "We'll have a drink and then I'll tell you."

Daphne had been having quite a long talk with Buffy. Edwin, listening, was sure that Buffy was telling her something trivial but, at the same time, important to him. It was something about people; he had gathered some of the meaning from what he heard in Daphne's replies. They had been out to dinner, Buffy and Paulette and Tuppy and Erica, filling in the time before going to meet Cecilia. Buffy's indignant conversation was apparently because he could not understand how people professing to be knowledgeable about food, gourmet people of all things, could fail to chill their white wine and then, on top of that, serve tasteless, partly cooked food. Edwin, half-listening to Daphne's sympathetic noises, longed for a life of small worries and irritations about food instead of all that weighed on him. He could not stop thinking of Leila and the child, the precious child, now far away in the house next door. His own house was terribly quiet. He could not think who could have served the badly prepared meal. He wondered, for a moment, which house they had been to to eat. Perhaps he was hungry himself. He tried to think about food. He was hungry but not for food. In fairness to Buffy, he reminded himself, Buffy had had his share of worry and sadness. Tuppy too. Both had ornamental framed portraits of the handsome

Mountbatten in their dining rooms. Both had left India with Mountbatten in the rather rushed exodus, as Buffy described it once. And both, just before that time, when they were quite young men, were suddenly widowed. The young wives were ill, after the same party, with an infection. The sort of thing, Buffy explained from time to time, that you picked up in India. Perfectly all right first thing, a bit seedy at eleven, decidedly orf at luncheon and dead before sundowners. Each retelling was accompanied by a small shining of tears and an unmistakable huskiness in the voice. In their houses they had left-over cane chairs, tabletops of brass, and various basins and jugs of bronzed metals reminding of endless polishings. They had silk-covered screens and wall hangings embroidered with tigers (rampant) and elephants (in repose). They talked still of tiffin and said *doodle ally tap* when someone uttered something which they did not fully understand. They were now in their middle sixties, Edwin thought, and, with the added energy of their second wives (both younger and certainly still youthfully adventurous), had several years of what is called life expectancy. It would be pleasant now to talk to Buffy—he could have a soothing effect with his expected phrases—but Daphne, after a series of telephone gruntings, had replaced the receiver. It was Buffy who often made enlightening remarks, divulging once the secret of married happiness. It was the ability, he said that time, to know when and how to slink away. The women had not been present on that occasion and there had been a certain pleasure, Edwin remembered, imagining the secret slinkings Buffy must have managed. Edwin leaned forward now, holding his head with both hands, and began again to torment himself with the thought that the child was not his and that Leila and her mother had made use of him because he was soft and rich and they were in a predicament which needed a kind man and a man who had enough money. Furthermore—and this thought shocked him with its depths, not the depths of the thought itself but the implications it carried—they needed a man who was lonely. The implications were deep. Hurriedly he began to think of Leila differently.

That she wanted her baby was absolutely clear. She had been unable to leave him; perhaps now that she was back with the child she would realize there was someone else she needed too. He groaned into his cupped hands. He could not give up Leila and the child. He had never expected to feel like this. Never mind who the father was. If *he* was not, he loved Leila enough to have fathered several children in the time they had had together. He would have to check the possibility of this in one of Cecilia's books. Oh God! Cecilia! He groaned aloud. It was unbearable. In the end, what did all that forty weeks reckoning mean? Leila and her baby had ignored the reckoned time. The baby had arrived sooner than expected and Cecilia was on her way home earlier than arranged in her original plan. But the baby? His baby? His and Leila's? Or whose? He must keep his mind off these thoughts. Then there was the birth certificate. He had never seen it to know if his name was on it. There was no one to whom he could speak about this. How could he have not remembered during the recent swift changing of arrangements to ask Leila for it? Perhaps she had put it safely with all the other baby things. Perhaps it was in the little pile of pink and blue instructions. He supposed, if it was there, it would be a narrow beige-colored folded piece of paper. Without wanting to, he remembered his own guilty search for his birth certificate, which his mother thought was so carefully hidden. That one, in an elegant but cramped copperplate handwriting, simply had her maiden name on it and the words "male child" beneath a date. For his mother's occupation was the single word "domestic." The signature of the registrar was equally elegant but, unlike the other details, illegible.

"Just don't you worry, Dr. Page." The familiar words of Leila's mother consoled him at all times. She was dressed for going out with Leila. The baby, closely wrapped, was in Leila's competent arms. "Leila'll register," Leila's mother said, "she'll see to all the necessary, won't you, Leila pet?" And Edwin at his desk, "The Study of Man" spreading to the edges, had smiled across to where they stood at the door of his room. He remembered now his smile and his vague words. It was the same when he refused his first receipt. He was never offered another. It was his own fault.

But the birth certificate. Where was it? And what was on it? How could he have been so stupid? Not much use to fret over it now. His thoughts were too painful. Perhaps the birth certificate was a way of slipping clear of the even more painful. He almost spoke to Daphne. She would applaud anything, he knew, which would keep him and Cecilia together. She wanted them to remain as a couple and any doubt about the baby's father would strengthen any argument she might have. She might even applaud the help, what looked like help, as she saw it, that he had given Leila and her mother—seeing them through a difficult time, through Leila's pregnancy, which might have been an unwanted one. The father having shot through—he had heard the phrase—it carried echoes of Tranby and Bushby, or was it Burton, gossip. Daphne might see what he had done as one of the things people did, at times, for one another. His own beginnings, though he had long ceased to consider them, were similar.

He remembered the sloping ceilings of the attic bedrooms and the neat sitting room at the side of the kitchen from which his mother could be summoned at all hours of the day. His mother, he remembered, liked being there and later when he was at boarding school that was the place he longed for.

Would Leila's baby have a birth certificate with "domestic" carefully written beside his mother's name? His bookshelves, his desk and his layers of carefully written pages seemed now to belong to an insignificance. Trying not to allow the tears to spill from his eyes, he looked up and saw Daphne opposite. She was looking at him.

"I wanted . . ." he began.

"Teddy. Darling." Her large face was tired and lined with concern. He almost told her then that the morning sickness came on very early, that Leila's breasts were full and tender almost as soon as . . . but he could not speak to her, to Daphne, of these things. The radishes, a long time ago, after their first breakfast, Leila in the garden next door eating radishes hungrily as if there was something in them she needed. "Craved" was the word Leila's mother used when she spoke of it, telling him that Leila had not been able to keep them down. He supposed he could read now, in one of Cecilia's books, the actual time of the onset, the expected onset of morning sickness. In the textbook it might have a more professional name. Morning sickness suggested folklore, an old wives' tale. There was another private and very intimate question about Leila, something which he could not mention to anyone.

It was easy, he knew from literature, to see onself as a victim. He tried to grin at Daphne.

"I'm sorry, Daph." He felt his eyes about to overflow once more. "What was it you were going to say? You started saying you could imagine. What was it you could imagine?"

"Did I?" Daphne said. "It seems like years ago. It was because of the telephone call. Didn't you hear anything? Really? Teddy?"

"Not a thing," Edwin said. "It was a bad line, all cracklings and hummings, and my head, in any case, was full of the sound of the baby crying. You probably heard it too; felt it perhaps is a better way of saying it." He paused. "I keep expecting to hear him cry again." He wanted to tell Daphne about his son, about his little legs and feet. Had she noticed how sweet they looked? Yes, "sweet" was the word, when they hung below an arm, Leila's arm, when she held him sitting on her arm, upright against her breast. Children's bodies were sweet. He had always known this.

"I think," Daphne was saying, "that I was going to say that I could imagine Vorwickl's eyes shining; she always seemed to speak with her eyes. It belongs with German. I have noticed that people, when they are speaking German, do seem to be very expressive with their hands and their eyes—mostly their eyes." Daphne stood up and stretched. "Vorwickl," she said, "seemed quite excited about being on the banks of the Nile. It didn't seem to put her out at all, the plane being diverted; the engine trouble or whatever it is seemed to amuse her. Her

English is quaint and I suppose there is something exotic about a hotel bedroom in Cairo. One does not go there often. My head, like yours," she added, "is full of the noise of a baby crying." Daphne sat down again. "You see, Teddy," she said, "I actually began to have a foolish little fantasy about a baby, a little princess, starting her life on the edge of the Nile. You know, the Nile, *great father of waters, thou that rollest thy floods through eighty nations . . .*" She sighed and continued. "I know there is no child there but I thought, I imagined, what it would be like to cherish and nurture a child who has played on the grass and the sands along the banks of that great river."

"And knows not one house," Edwin said, *"that is not haunted by some fury that destroys its quiet."*

"Oh, I'm sorry, Teddy, for being clumsy," Daphne said. "We ought to draw the curtains and have a drink. Let's have a drink, Teddy. I can't possibly sleep just now. We can phone the airline later and see what's happening."

Edwin, knowing that he was incompetent, fetched two glasses and tried to decide what to offer Daphne and what to have himself.

"Come on, Teddy!" Daphne said. "You're going to have to make some decisions; you'd better start now."

Edwin thought he heard a rustling and a tap-tapping at the window, as if someone low down on the path outside was trying to reach above the sill to knock on the glass. He stood still to listen.

"D'you hear anything?" he asked.

"Yes," she said. "It's that old woody hibiscus and broom you've got out there; they're scraping against the house and your window. You need to do some judicious pruning, otherwise there won't be any way through. The path's almost disappeared."

"There it is again." Edwin hesitated by his desk.

"Yes," Daphne said, "it's all those branches; a lot of dead wood to be cut out." She thumped the cushions of the chair, rearranging them and settling herself against them. "Champers!" she said. "We've got at least one bottle left. Lucky! Let's share that." Obediently Edwin fetched the champagne.

"Just perfect!" Daphne said, draining her glass and holding it out to be refilled. "What d'you bet," she said, "that they"— she nodded her head towards the house next door—"that they won't be there in the morning. It makes me mad"—she gulped, apparently without noticing, the rest of her drink—"it makes me mad to think of all the money they've saved on rent."

Edwin, thinking of the purgative qualities of champagne, shivered as he remembered the sheer suffering ahead of him.

"About the Wakefield plays . . ." He made a great effort to change the subject. "If a rewriting is under consideration . . ." But Daphne, tired out, was falling asleep. He wished he could ask her to stay awake. He hoped she would wake refreshed after a short sleep. He was afraid that the sugar mother family might indeed slip away sometime during the night. He was afraid that the phone might ring. He was afraid that someone would come in at the back door; it was not locked. He was afraid that the sugar mother family might still be next door in the morning.

"Wake up, Daphne, please," he wanted to say. But Daphne needed to rest. He got up quietly and pulled the red blanket, the one Leila liked, off his bed and put it over her. He poured the rest of the champagne, reflecting on the impossibility of the little princess, a spirit child like a little cloud, on the Nile. The enormity of his foolish belief earlier that Cecilia would ever give up even a part of her work to carry out the duties of a mother overwhelmed him completely. Telling another person something that needs telling had proved impossible too. It seemed such a small detail and yet was immense.

Sugar mother. Every day he had called Sugar Mother, as he opened the front door of his house. He could not help thinking about these homecomings, which became every day more and more precious. He put his foot out as if to step into the hall. Sugar Mother, he called to Leila; he always called her as soon as he stepped into the hall and she always came at once to meet him.

Alongside the university, for part of the way, was a high gray wall of stone. Once when walking there with Leila, when they had been to see his rooms, he had longed to show her some affection. Every day when he walked home he remembered how they had walked there. He knew he would never forget the afternoon when they had seemed to be the only two people in existence. Always on the way home he watched the children running and playing in their little playground in the pines. It was the thin nimble legs which attracted. At the backs of the childish knees the endlessly strong and tireless ligaments were clearly visible beneath the skin. Quite tiny children climbed the rope ladders with fearless happiness. He felt restored and rested as he walked on through the pines, walking faster as he drew nearer to his house. . . .

A war would solve everything: World War Three. He held up his sparkling glass towards the light. "World War Three," he said aloud, putting aside his pacifism, which he had never declared in any case. How could he have ever made such declarations when Buffy and Tuppy were always toasting their old regiments?

If a war broke out now Cecilia would be holed up (Buffy's words) in Cairo indefinitely. She would have Vorwickl for company and since babies were born everywhere and all the time, there would be no difficulty about employment. Perhaps a boardinghouse, a pension, rather than an hotel, for a longer stay . . .

He knew really that wars, though appearing to occur suddenly over some trivial incident, were really in preparation over a number of years. He tilted the champagne bottle but it was empty. In order to have a war, tremendous mass production, and full employment, should already have been in operation. Mass production of weapons, boots, uniforms, tents, blankets, ration books, posters—all kinds of things to be in readiness to accompany the battle cries and the prayers for victory.

He tilted his glass; it was empty. Putting the pages of the "Study of Man" lectures within reach, he drew the notebook of the intangible towards himself and waited for the expected stomach cramps.

FOR THE BEST IN PAPERBACKS, LOOK FOR THE

In every corner of the world, on every subject under the sun, Penguin represents quality and variety – the very best in publishing today.

For complete information about books available from Penguin – including Puffins, Penguin Classics and Arkana – and how to order them, write to us at the appropriate address below. Please note that for copyright reasons the selection of books varies from country to country.

In the United Kingdom: Please write to *Dept E.P., Penguin Books Ltd, Harmondsworth, Middlesex, UB7 0DA.*

If you have any difficulty in obtaining a title, please send your order with the correct money, plus ten per cent for postage and packaging, to *PO Box No 11, West Drayton, Middlesex*

In the United States: Please write to *Dept BA, Penguin, 299 Murray Hill Parkway, East Rutherford, New Jersey 07073*

In Canada: Please write to *Penguin Books Canada Ltd, 2801 John Street, Markham, Ontario L3R 1B4*

In Australia: Please write to the *Marketing Department, Penguin Books Australia Ltd, P.O. Box 257, Ringwood, Victoria 3134*

In New Zealand: Please write to the *Marketing Department, Penguin Books (NZ) Ltd, Private Bag, Takapuna, Auckland 9*

In India: Please write to *Penguin Overseas Ltd, 706 Eros Apartments, 56 Nehru Place, New Delhi, 110019*

In the Netherlands: Please write to *Penguin Books Nederland B.V., Postbus 195, NL–1380AD Weesp*

In West Germany: Please write to *Penguin Books Ltd, Friedrichstrasse 10–12, D–6000 Frankfurt/Main 1*

In Spain: Please write to *Longman Penguin España, Calle San Nicolas 15, E–28013 Madrid*

In Italy: Please write to *Penguin Italia s.r.l., Via Como 4, I-20096 Pioltello (Milano)*

In France: Please write to *Penguin Books Ltd, 39 Rue de Montmorency, F-75003 Paris*

In Japan: Please write to *Longman Penguin Japan Co Ltd, Yamaguchi Building, 2–12–9 Kanda Jimbocho, Chiyoda-Ku, Tokyo 101*